Temptation

THE HUNTED SERIES – BOOK 1

IVY SMOAK

This book is a work of fiction. Names, characters, places, and
incidents are fictitious. Any resemblance to actual persons,
living or dead, events, or locales is purely coincidental.

To my fiancé.
Without your encouragement, The Hunted series would not exist.

PART 1

CHAPTER 1

Tuesday

I pulled my phone out of my backpack and scrolled through my messages. There were still no new ones. I dropped it back into my bag and stared into my coffee cup. He had told me he missed me, so I had come up to campus early to surprise him, but he hadn't returned my two calls. *I shouldn't have made that second call.* Now I was sitting in his favorite coffee shop hoping to casually run into him.

Luckily my roommate, Melissa, had showed up yesterday so I wouldn't have to be alone in our dorm room. We had walked up to Main Street, despite the rain, to buy our books, then spent the whole rest of the day catching up from summer break. Mostly we complained about our minimum wage retail jobs. It had been her idea for me to grab an early coffee here in hopes of running into him. She had even helped me with my hair and makeup this morning. He wasn't here though, and now I felt rather like a stalker.

My phone buzzed and I grabbed it eagerly. I slid my finger across the screen and looked down at the message icon. But it was just my alarm, reminding me that it was almost time for my first class. I had to get across campus. I hastily tugged the zipper of my backpack closed and lifted the strap over my shoulder.

The coffee shop was abuzz that morning. None of the other students were used to waking up this early either. Caffeine was a necessity. I grabbed my umbrella in one hand and my coffee cup in the other and squeezed my way past the other patrons.

The floor was slick near the exit from everyone tramping in and out into the rain. Despite Melissa's protests, I had worn my rain boots, and I was glad I had when my feet slid slightly on the linoleum. As I regained my balance, someone came bursting into the coffee shop. The door swung in and collided with my cup. Coffee splashed onto my shirt as my cup fell to the ground. As I began to slip again, I suddenly felt two strong hands on me, holding me steady.

"I'm so sorry. Are you alright?" said a deep voice.

"I'm fine." I kept my eyes on the ground. "It wasn't hot anymore." I left off the fact that it was cold because I had been sitting in the coffee shop for half an hour acting like a crazy stalker.

His hands slowly fell off my waist. "I'm afraid I've ruined your shirt."

I looked at the brown coffee stains that showed clearly on my blue tank top. "Oh, crap, I have an 8 a.m. I don't have time to change." I wished I had worn a coat to protect myself from the cool rain instead of bringing an umbrella.

"Here," he said. He put down his satchel and lifted off his gray sweater. The white dress shirt he was wearing underneath lifted slightly as he pulled off the sweater, and

I caught a glimpse of his abs. I let my eyes wander to his face. It looked like he had stepped out of the pages of a magazine. He looked older, possibly a grad student. His hair was dark brown and wet from the rain. The way it was sticking up made it look like he had just run his hands through it. His jawbone was sharp and there were dimples in his cheeks. His eyes were a deep brown like his hair and they were staring at me intently. My heart began to beat fast. He handed me his sweater.

"That's okay. I can't take that," I laughed uneasily. "I'll be fine." I moved to the side so he could pass by me. I felt my cheeks begin to blush.

"I insist." He had a slight smile on his face. "First day of classes," he shrugged. "You'll want to make a good first impression."

I took the sweater from him. "Thank you," I said quietly. I pulled the sweater over my head. It was huge but comfortable. The scent of sweet cologne drifted off of it. It made me feel slightly dizzy. I could feel myself staring at him. "I'm sorry, I have to go, I'm going to be late." He was so handsome that I was acting even more awkward than usual.

His lips parted like he was about to say something, but then they closed again. I smiled gratefully and walked out of the coffee shop. As I made my way to my class I knew I must look ridiculous. A baggy sweater, leggings, and bright red rain boots. I must look like a child. But I was grateful. Coffee stains down the front of me would have been worse than a baggy sweater. Melissa was going to love this story.

CHAPTER 2

Wednesday

I looked down at my schedule to double check the room number before entering. After yesterday's embarrassment at the coffee shop I didn't want to make myself look like a fool today too. I was one of the first ones there, so I made my way to the back of the classroom. At most professors' annoyance, I was more of a spectator than a participator in class. This class was going to be my worst nightmare. Most people put it off until senior year, but I wanted to get it out of the way early. Now I was regretting my decision.

I sat down at one of the wooden desks all the way in the corner, pulled out a new notebook and pen, and stared out the window next to me. "Forget about Austin," Melissa had said last night after hearing my story. "I like the sound of this new guy. Plus he smells like a million bucks." I didn't disagree with her. I had folded the sweater and left it on my desk chair, but its smell wafted into the room. My dreams had been filled with coffee shop encounters with the stranger all night. Dreams where I didn't run away in his sweater and forget to ask his name.

"Welcome to Comm 212 - Oral Communication in Business. I am Professor Hunter." The professor paused in his introduction and I turned from the window to look at him. He was staring directly at me. I took a deep breath. It was the stranger from the coffee shop. He cleared his throat and looked away from me.

"I know that most of you are seniors and have waited until the last minute to take this class. I haven't met a student yet who was excited about Comm. Heck, I don't even like teaching it."

Light laughter broke out amongst the students. I just stared at him in horror.

"Seriously, we have to teach this class on a rotating basis. I'm not even sure I'm qualified. I promise it won't be as painful as the rumors have made it out to be, though. I tend to grade rather easily so there's no need to be nervous when you're giving speeches. But I like to jump right into things. I'm going to take attendance. When I call your name, please stand and tell me one interesting fact about yourself. Then I'll stop torturing you and you can all leave class early. Not so bad, right? Okay, Raymond Asher."

A boy in the middle of the classroom stood up from his desk. "Hi, I'm Ray. Hmmm, one interesting thing about myself? Well, I'm pretty good with the ladies."

"Yeah right, Ray," the girl beside him teased.

He tried to kiss the girl on the cheek when he sat back down, but she pulled away.

"Well I can tell we'll all be enjoying your speeches. Ellie Doyle?"

A girl stood up in the front of the room and began talking, but I tuned her out. My heart was racing fast. I barely liked saying "here" when a professor called my name. I stared at Professor Hunter as he listened to the answers his students were giving. Every now and then a smile would break over his face. He was so handsome.

"Tyler Stevens?" Professor Hunter called.

He was getting close to my name. I looked down at the blank paper in front of me and tried to focus.

"Penny Taylor?"

My throat went dry.

"Penny Taylor?" the professor repeated.

I slowly stood up. "Hi everyone, I'm Penny." I could feel my face turning red. "Unfortunately, you'll need another of me for my thoughts."

I sat back down. *What did I just say?*

"Weird," some girl scoffed near the front of the class. A few other people around her snickered.

A smile spread across Professor Hunter's face. "A penny for your thoughts. Well I guess I'll have to bring my piggy bank with me on Friday. Mia Thompson?"

I exhaled slowly and tuned out Mia's answer as I attempted to slow down my accelerated heart beat. A penny clanged on top of my desk. I looked over to my right at the boy sitting next to me. He had shaggy blonde hair and scruff on his face. His eyes were a bright blue.

"I'd pay for your thoughts any day," he said with a smile.

I had been too busy freaking out to have noticed what he said in his introduction. Instead of saying anything, I tucked my hair behind my ear.

"Sigma Pi is having a party Thursday night. You should come, Penny." He handed me a flyer.

"What's your name?"

"Tyler. You know, the guitarist."

I nodded at him politely, knowing that I should have already known his name and his interesting fact.

"You should pay better attention. And since there's no homework for this class, I know you aren't too busy, so I'll see you Thursday," he said with a wink. He picked up his backpack and slung it over one shoulder.

The room was clearing out. I put my notebook into my backpack. Professor Hunter looked at Tyler as he left the room, and then his eyes fell on me. I felt my face flush again. I gave Professor Hunter a small smile and then looked down as I passed by his desk. His chair squeaked and then I felt his fingers as they grazed my forearm. I shivered slightly at his touch.

"Miss Taylor, I'm sorry again about your shirt."

I folded my arms across my chest, suddenly cold. "Oh, no, I'm sorry."

He was quiet for a moment as he looked at me. "Why are you sorry? I was the one that hit you with the door."

I didn't know what I meant. I had a habit of apologizing for everything. "I just meant, about taking your sweater. I'll bring it back."

"No rush. I have quite a few," he gestured to the one he was wearing. It was identical to the one he had given me, except it was a grayish green.

A wave of his sweet scent suddenly hit me. I looked up into his eyes. My fantasies from the previous night wanted to escape. I had a strong desire to be bold, but boldness was only for my dreams. "I didn't realize you were a professor," I blurted out.

He smiled. "It's more fun when students think of me as their peer. I believe it fosters better learning."

That wasn't what I had meant. I meant that he looked really young. *How old is he?* I realized I was staring at him and silently cursed to myself. "Well I should probably go. I'll see you Friday, Professor Hunter."

He lowered his eyebrows slightly when I said his name, as if he was offended. He nodded to me and said, "Miss Taylor."

CHAPTER 3

Thursday

"Come on, it's Thursday night!" Melissa said as she looked through my closet.

"Yeah, which means I have classes tomorrow." I had a sinking feeling in my stomach when I thought about what I'd have to do in Professor Hunter's class the next morning. I wasn't sure if I could handle standing up and talking every class. Especially in front of Professor Hunter. Why did he have to be a professor? Melissa had talked me out of going to my advisor and dropping the class. And she was right, I would regret it if I put it off. Melissa didn't know that I was having dreams about Professor Hunter though. He was just so sexy.

"You were invited to the party. Which means you need to go so that I can get in."

"Just take the flyer," I protested. "They'll let you in. It's a frat and you're a girl. That's all you need."

"Stop moping around, Penny. Yes, Austin was a jerk. Yes, mystery coffee shop man is your professor and therefore un-datable. But you're forgetting about the third guy. It sounds like Tyler is cute and funny. A funny guy is always charming."

"I don't know, frat parties are always so sleazy."

"Penny, there is nothing you can say that will get you out of going to this party. Now put this on," she tossed some clothes at me.

I rolled my eyes. "Fine. You win. As always." I went to the other side of the room and slowly undressed. I pulled the sparkly blue miniskirt on and put on my best pushup bra and a low-cut, white tank top. I was just finishing my mascara when Melissa walked back into the room.

"Penny, you look amazing."

"I look like a hooker. Melissa, it's going to be cold out tonight. Shouldn't I wear a little, well, more?"

"These are the last few days of summer. You have to rock that outfit while you can. These shoes," she said and handed me a pair of shimmery heels. The heels had to be at least five inches tall. Melissa was dressed similar to me, except her skirt didn't sparkle, and if possible, it was slightly shorter than mine.

"I can't wait for autumn," I said, and strapped on the shoes. I glanced at Professor Hunter's sweater that was still folded up on my chair. All I wanted was to put it on, curl up in my bed, and watch T.V. all night. Instead, Melissa grabbed my arm and pulled me out of our dorm room.

When we exited our dorm building, we walked arm in arm along the sidewalk toward Main Street. Boys whistled as they walked by us and cars honked.

"Do you think it's going to rain?" I asked her.

"Stop worrying about everything. Let's just have fun tonight!"

We turned onto a side street and in a few minutes I could hear the music blaring. The large Sigma Pi letters were nailed to the top of the house. A guy was peeing in some bushes off to the left.

"And so we have arrived," I mumbled.

"Ladies!" A classically tall, dark, and handsome boy walked over to us. "Welcome to Sigma Pi. Looking for anyone in particular, or just here for something new to do?" He winked at Melissa. Her arm unwound from mine as she introduced herself to him. I didn't hear their exchange.

"Tyler invited us," I said to him.

He turned around to the house. "Yo, Tyler!" He added a whistle. "Tyyyyyler!"

"Find me before you leave," Melissa said as she was steered away by her new acquaintance.

I was left standing there alone in my skimpy outfit. I looked back toward Main Street. *Maybe I should just leave.* Melissa would never even know.

I was about to walk away when someone yelled: "Penny!"

I turned around and saw Tyler strolling over to me. He had two red, plastic cups in his hands. He was wearing a black t-shirt with Sigma Pi printed across it in neon green letters. His jeans weren't too baggy or too tight. He looked good. When he reached me, I noticed that he was a few inches taller than me even with my heels.

"I didn't think you were coming, Penny," he said and handed me a cup. "But I am so glad to see you. You look amazing, babe."

I flinched when he called me "babe." Austin always used to call me that. I took a long sip of the beer.

"You clean up well yourself," I replied.

He smiled at me. "Want to come inside?"

"Of course," I said. He wrapped his arm behind my back and his hand lingered on my waist as he led me toward the frat house.

The music was booming and it almost seemed like the house was shaking. I drank my beer while he gave me the tour. When we finished walking around the first floor I needed a refill. We headed into the basement and both refilled our glasses.

"Do you want to dance?" He almost had to yell so I could hear him.

"And by dance, do you mean that?" I asked and pointed to a couple who was grinding.

"Well, if you want to dance like that I might need another drink."

I laughed. "Probably something stronger than beer." I smiled up at him.

"Well that, babe, I can arrange." He grabbed my hand and brought me back over to the bar. He walked behind the counter and brought out a bottle of vodka. "If I'm going to dance crazy, so are you." He poured the vodka into two shot glasses. "We should probably finish these first," he said and held up his red cup. "It would be a shame to waste."

I rolled my eyes and drank the rest of my beer. I tossed him my empty cup. "Satisfied?"

"Not yet," he said and stared at me playfully. He lifted up his shot glass and I did too. The alcohol burned my throat as it went down. I slammed it back down on the table. Tyler looked back at the people dancing. "I don't know, still looks pretty provocative. Maybe one more?"

"Tyler, are you trying to get me drunk?"

"Me? You're the one that wants to dance like that. You, Penny, are trying to get me wasted. I don't know what I'm going to do with you."

"Fine, one more shot each. Then I'll see what moves you have."

Tyler grinned and poured more vodka into the shot glasses. "Here's to a fun night," he said and raised his glass.

Here's to forgetting Austin. My head was beginning to grow foggy, but I downed the second shot as well. Tyler grabbed my hand and we ran into the sea of people dancing. He turned me around and pulled my hips into him. I let my body move to the beat.

"Penny," he whispered into my ear. "What are you trying to do to me?"

I reached my hand up behind his neck and let him control my hips. He turned me around so that I was facing him.

"You're a great dancer."

"Tyler, this is not dancing," I laughed.

"Oops, alcohol must have worn off." He quickly picked me up and lifted me over his shoulder.

"Tyler!"

He walked me over to the bar and placed me back on my feet. Everything seemed a little blurry. He grabbed the bottle and wrapped his free hand around my waist. He led me toward the staircase. When we reached the first floor he led me to another set of stairs.

"I haven't shown you the second story yet," he said as we made our way upstairs.

"You mean your room?"

"Penny, you are quite the cynic. Actually, no, not my room." He touched a tie on one of the doorknobs. "This room," he said, and opened the adjacent door that didn't have a tie hanging from the doorknob.

"I can assure you, Tyler, that you will not be getting lucky tonight."

"I don't even know what you're referring to. I just wanted you to show me how you prefer to dance. Without all those other people around." He took a swig from the bottle and handed it to me.

I took a small sip and set it on the bureau. I grabbed his hands and placed them on my hips. Then I reached up and wrapped my hands around the back of his neck. We slowly swayed back and forth. This was probably the sweetest thing a guy had ever done for me. I moved closer to him so that our bodies were touching.

"So you like it nice and slow?" Tyler said gently.

"If you are referring to dancing? Yes, isn't this nice?"

He leaned down to kiss me. I wanted to forget about Austin and I needed to forget about Professor Hunter. I grabbed the back of his head and pulled him closer as he kissed me deeply. His hands slid down from my waist and grabbed my ass. I let him squeeze for a second before reaching down and moving his hands back to my waist.

"Penny, please, you're killing me." He lifted my chin in his hand and kissed me again.

I liked how his hands felt on me. "We should take things slow," I said breathlessly.

He pulled back and lifted me into his arms. He set me down on the bed and lay next to me. "Then why are you lying on the bed? That's rather forward of you."

"Tyler. I like you." Melissa was right. He was funny and sweet, even if he was a little pompous. Maybe this could be more. Maybe Tyler was just what I needed.

He put his hand on my knee and slowly moved it up my thigh. "I like you too, babe."

I grabbed his hand and held it there to prevent it from rising anymore. "Tyler, we've had too much to drink." My body wanted him and he could tell.

He looked down at me with his blue eyes. He lifted his hand off my thigh and slid his fingers through my hair. "I believe that I'm thinking pretty clearly." He kissed me again and I let my hips rise into him. I did want him.

But at the same time my mind was screaming "no." Austin had always made me feel insignificant. All he had ever wanted was my body, and I had given it to him. I liked the feeling of Tyler wanting me, but I didn't want to sleep with him on our first date. My flirtations had gone too far.

He moved on top of me and pushed my skirt up a little.

"Tyler, please." I began to sit up.

"No need to beg for it, babe." He unbuttoned and unzipped his pants. He pushed me back down onto the bed and lifted my hands above my head, holding them firmly in place.

"Tyler, get off of me." My mind was suddenly beating my body.

"Don't be a tease. You know you want this as much as I do. I promise to take it slow. Just the way you like." He began to kiss my neck.

I pulled up my leg and kneed him in the groin. He rolled off of me, grabbing the spot I had hit.

"What the hell, Penny?!"

"I asked you to stop." Tears had begun to stream down my face. I got up off the bed, stumbling slightly.

"You're such a bitch!"

I made my way over to the door and slammed it behind me. A few people turned to stare as I ran down the stairs.

CHAPTER 4

Thursday

I stumbled out of the frat house. It was drizzling and I had no coat or umbrella. I silently cursed Melissa for making me wear this miniscule outfit. No wonder Tyler had acted the way that he did. This wasn't me. Austin had messed with my head and completely demolished my self-confidence. I was embarrassed and ashamed of what had just happened. The tears began to mix with the drizzle. I had to focus hard on not falling over because of my stilettos and the booze.

The drizzle turned into rain as I made my way onto Main Street.

"Miss Taylor, is that you?"

My whole body froze at the deep voice. I was wearing the most inappropriate outfit I had ever worn, and now my white tank top was drenched and completely see-through. "Um...no. You have the wrong person." I quickly started walking again, but my high heels prevented me from moving too fast.

"Penny, stop!"

I turned around and stared up at Professor Hunter, who was as unbelievably sexy as ever. He was wearing a pair of jeans that hugged him in all the right places, and a leather jacket with a plain white t-shirt beneath it. He looked the same as he did in class, except that he had a 5 o'clock shadow and an umbrella.

"Professor Hunter, I'm sorry..." I let my voice trail off and I folded my arms across my chest to help hide my most likely exposed breasts.

He lowered his eyebrows when I said his name, just like he had in his classroom. "You like to apologize when you've done nothing wrong."

I probably imagined it, but it felt like his eyes lingered for a moment on my legs. He moved toward me so that I'd be under his umbrella with him. "Is everything alright, Penny?"

My eyes were probably red from my angry tears. I was hoping he wouldn't be able to tell in the rain. "I'm fine."

"Then what are you doing out so late all by yourself?"

"I could ask the same of you." I rolled my eyes at myself for being so immature.

"I was just going for a walk."

"Me too," I responded quietly.

He laughed. It was an enticing sound. I drew a little closer to him and let my arm brush against his.

"Are you cold, Penny?"

Cold and mortified. I nodded up at him. I liked the way my name rolled off his tongue.

He handed me the umbrella as he slid out of his jacket. Then he held his jacket out for me and I slipped one arm in and then the other. The leather held the scent of his cologne. He took the umbrella and held it above both of us again. He was such a gentleman.

"Well you really shouldn't be out alone this late, Penny," he said. "Especially in those walking clothes."

"Neither should you."

He laughed again. "Is your dorm near here? It would make me feel much better if I escorted you home."

"I live in Sussex."

"This way then," he said, and placed his hand on the small of my back for just a second.

We walked in silence for a few minutes. Every now and then I'd stumble a little in my heels and his hand would briefly touch the small of my back again. Each time he did, I felt like my heart would beat out of my chest.

"I'm not good at giving speeches," I said, finally breaking the silence. "I feel like I should just drop your class."

"I wish you wouldn't. If you ever need extra help, I have open office hours. I really am a fairly easy grader for Comm."

"It's going to be extra painful when you fail me, though."

"Why extra painful?" He said "extra" slowly, almost seductively.

"Because you...I mean I. Well, you're..." I let my voice trail off. I wanted to say, "Because you're gorgeous and I have a huge crush on you." *I can't believe I almost let him hear me say that.*

"Well it does seem that you aren't great at giving speeches," he laughed again. "Like I said, you can come by any time."

We walked along the length of the green. I had dreamt of having a date escort me back to my dorm room. But I only dated immature boys, not men. Professor Hunter was a man. I found myself once again wondering how old he was.

"Have you been a professor here for long?"

"Not long at all. I do love it here, despite how much it rains. Besides, you never know what you'll find during a long walk in the rain." He smiled down at me.

Is he flirting with me? It seems like he's flirting with me!

Before I knew it, we were at my dorm. I stepped out from under his umbrella and let the rain fall on me again.

"Here," I said and pulled off his jacket.

His eyes drifted for just a second to my wet tank top. "No, you can keep it."

"I've been stealing all your clothes. Soon you'll have nothing left."

"That does seem to be your plan." He had a mischievous look in his eyes.

"I insist," I said as I held out the jacket to him.

He took it reluctantly.

"I'm not in trouble, am I?"

"You're a senior, you're of legal age to drink, and you're allowed to wear what you like. Why would you be in trouble?"

But I wasn't a senior, I was a sophomore. And I wasn't over 21, I was only 19. I took a deep breath. He didn't need to know that. "You're right. And I was only walking, after all. Thank you for escorting me home, Professor Hunter."

He lowered his eyebrows when I said his name, just like he always did. But this time the action made me hold my breath. I was wrong about how he looked. He didn't look angry, his eyes looked hungry. I had to remind myself to keep breathing.

"I'll see you at 8 a.m. sharp, Miss Taylor."

"It's a date." My eyes got huge and I put my hand over my mouth. *Had I really just said that out loud?* I turned quickly away from him and fumbled with my sensor pass to open the door. Finally it clicked. I threw the door open and quickly went inside. I turned around at the last moment to see Professor Hunter staring at me intently, surprisingly not at all perplexed. The door closed with a thud.

CHAPTER 5

Friday

I woke up a few hours later and threw up in the waste bin. Melissa had made it home at some point because she was lying in bed, but I must have been asleep when she came back. She was still dressed in her skimpy outfit.

The sun was starting to rise. I tilted my alarm clock and saw that it was almost 7. So that I wouldn't wake Melissa, I switched the alarm off. I took a makeup remover cloth from its case and wiped off what was left of my eye shadow and mascara. Then I grabbed my bathroom stuff and quietly exited the room.

I brushed my teeth twice and used triple mouthwash to help remove the awful taste. Then I jumped into the shower to try to wash away the awkward night. I couldn't imagine facing Professor Hunter. And I didn't even want to think about what awful assignment he had planned for today. Comm 212 was going to be the death of me. Then there was also Tyler who I had to try to avoid. I had made such a fool of myself last night. And I knew it was my fault. I didn't intend to lead him on, I was just so upset about Austin and then I wanted to make my awkward crush for my professor disappear. But I had told Tyler to stop. He was the one in the wrong.

I let the water fall on my head and took a deep breath and grabbed my stomach. It felt like I needed to hurl again. I swallowed hard and rinsed out my conditioner before switching off the shower. The cold air sent goose bumps up my legs and I quickly wrapped a towel around myself. I tucked the edge of it into the top of the wrap to keep it in place and headed back to my room.

After finally getting a comb through my unruly curly hair, I pinned back my bangs and put some makeup on. A little more than I would usually wear to an 8 a.m. on a Friday. I pulled on a pair of tight jean shorts and a tank top and slid my feet into flip flops. I glanced at my phone and saw that it was quarter to 8. Searching through my closet, I found a sweatshirt and pulled it over my head before grabbing my backpack and heading out the door.

The sun felt good on my face. I entered Smith, the building where Comm was held, and made my way up the stairs. Luckily I was one of the first to arrive again, and I went to my seat in the far corner. A few minutes passed before Tyler entered the classroom. I turned and looked out the window. I silently willed him not to sit next to me.

The seat next to me squeaked slightly and I closed my eyes. *Why me?*

"Penny?"

I looked over at Tyler. He had dark circles under his eyes. He was sitting on the edge of his seat, as close to me as possible.

"Geez, Penny, I'm sorry. I don't even remember what happened last night, besides for the fact that I obviously acted like an idiot." He gave me a small, forced smile.

"Well, I do remember." I wished I could just tuck my head into my sweatshirt and disappear.

"I really am sorry."

The door closed and I looked over. As Professor Hunter walked into the room, I couldn't help but stare. He was wearing black square rimmed glasses. His hair that was usually pushed up a little looked like it hadn't been touched. The top was even a little curly. He was wearing the same leather jacket that he had almost let me keep. He took off his brown satchel and put it on his desk, then unzipped the jacket and placed it on the back of his chair, revealing a green V-neck t-shirt . The casual air about him made him even more endearing, if that was possible.

He shoved his hands into his jean pockets. "Doesn't everyone look alert today?" He smiled. "So, I think the best thing to do is probably hear about your nights. The more comfortable we are with each other, the easier it will be to stand up here later in the semester and give fantastic speeches. Everyone up to share?"

Some of my classmates groaned. I looked around. I probably wasn't the only one that was slightly hung-over.

Professor Hunter glanced at me for a moment as he sat down in his chair. He pulled out the class list from his bag and called out the first name. The first few people swore they were just studying. Some people mentioned that they weren't lame and had gone partying.

"Tyler Stevens?"

Tyler stood up and stared straight ahead. "Honestly I got drunk and made a fool of myself. I was with this smart, beautiful girl, and I probably blew my shot with her." With one hand he reached up and scratched the back of his neck as he looked down at the floor.

"Sounds like an unfortunate series of events," Professor Hunter responded. I looked up at him and he was staring right at me. I gulped.

Tyler sighed and looked at me as he sat back down.

"Penny Taylor," Professor Hunter said. While I stood up, he pulled out a small ceramic pig from his satchel. "I came prepared today. You'll have to trust that I have some pennies in here."

I wish I could control my blushing, but I knew my face was turning red. My heart was beating so fast. "I went for a walk in the rain with a stranger I met at a coffee shop."

Professor Hunter raised his eyebrows. "Sounds rather enchanting, Miss Taylor."

"It was."

He looked at me for a second more before looking down at his paper and calling the next name. I quickly sat down and looked at my hands. I could feel Tyler's eyes on me.

After Professor Hunter had called every name, he stood back up. "Well, it seems as though we have quite a few interesting characters this semester. And now I have a feel for things that you can all use improvement on. Speaking of which..." He rummaged in his satchel and pulled out a stack of papers. "I forgot to hand out the syllabus on Wednesday." He pulled the top packet off and dropped the rest on a boy's desk in the front. "Take one and pass it."

The boy grabbed one and handed the stack to his neighbor. As the papers began to cycle, Professor Hunter sat on top of his desk.

"So your first presentation isn't for a few weeks, but you'll probably want to at least pick a topic soon so you can start mulling it over. All you need to do is pick a person that has inspired you in some way and tell us all about it. But please, I'm tired of hearing about everyone's grandparents, so try to think outside the box. And next week I'll start talking about how to give effective speeches, so you'll definitely want to incorporate that advice. Any questions?"

"A girl in the front row's hand shot up."

"Yes?"

"Do we need your approval for our topic?"

"Not for this one. For later projects though, yes. But if you do have any questions you can always email me. My email is on the syllabus. And my office hours are listed on there too, if any of you have any questions or need some guidance on an assignment."

The two girls in front of me giggled. I clearly wasn't the only one that was affected by his good looks.

The pile of syllabi had reached Tyler, but there was only one copy left. He kept it for himself. I cursed silently. *Why me?* Now I'd have to go talk to Professor Hunter. I looked up at him and he was still holding a syllabus in his hands. He had a smile on his face. *Had he purposely not let me get one?*

"Any other questions?" he asked.

A normal person would probably raise their hand right now and say they didn't get a syllabus, but my heart was beating much too quickly. He made me so nervous.

"Okay then. Make sure to brainstorm this weekend. If you have an idea in mind on Monday, then my advice will be more beneficial. Have a great weekend."

I heard the pull of zippers on backpacks and feet shuffling. I slowly put my notebook, which was still empty, back in my bag. I pulled my sweatshirt off and stuffed it in my backpack as well. As I was doing so, a shadow fell on me. I looked up and saw Tyler hovering next to my desk.

"Second chance?" he asked sheepishly.

"I'll think about it," I responded.

A smile spread across his face. "Give me your phone real quick."

I handed it to him and stood up. He typed in his number and handed it back to me. "Have a good weekend, Penny," he said and walked away.

I lifted up my backpack and made my way to the front of the class. Professor Hunter and I were the last ones in the room. He was sitting on his desk again now, flipping through the last syllabus. He didn't look up as I approached.

"Excuse me, Professor Hunter?" I said nervously.

"How can I help you, Miss Taylor?" he asked and looked up from the pages.

"I didn't get a syllabus."

"Well here you go then," he said and handed me the one he was holding.

"Thank you."

"So a walk in the rain with a stranger was a highlight to your eventful evening, was it?"

"It was the only good thing about last night, actually."

"I had my suspicions after you referred to this class as a date."

I placed my hand over my eyes, and then slowly let it slide from my face. "I thought I had dreamt that." I was completely mortified.

"I didn't realize I had made an appearance in your dreams, Miss Taylor."

"That's not what I...I mean you didn't. Well I meant..."

Professor Hunter laughed his enticing laugh. "Have a good weekend, Miss Taylor. Maybe on Monday I'll ask everyone to share a memorable dream they had over the weekend."

I felt my jaw drop slightly. The door creaked open and students for the next class started walking in. "Professor Hunter," I said, and quickly turned and walked out of the classroom.

CHAPTER 6

Sunday

Despite Melissa's protests, I had spent the weekend in sweatpants, holed up in our dorm room with occasional trips to the dining hall. On Sunday night Melissa had practice with her a cappella group. I had just finished putting large curlers in my hair for volume. I could pretend it was for Tyler, or at least someone my own age, but that would be a lie. I was trying to look good for Professor Hunter. He made me feel unbelievably self-conscious. If he really did ask the class to share a memorable dream from this weekend I would die. The only dreams I seemed capable of having were of kissing him under that umbrella in the pouring rain. And him pressing my body against his with his strong hands. *What is wrong with me?*

I sighed, lay down in my bed, and turned on the T.V. Instead of looking at the screen, I grabbed my phone. I scrolled to the "T's" in my contact list. Tyler wasn't listed. I went down to the "Y's" in case he accidentally forgot the "T," but he wasn't listed there either. I slowly scrolled up through the list until I found him: "Apologetic Tyler."

I laughed out loud. He was near the top of my contacts list. That had to be on purpose. I clicked on his name and then on the message option. "Apologetic Tyler?" I typed. "That's a start." I added a smiley face emoji and pressed the send button.

It would be awhile before he texted me back. That was just how texting seemed to work. He'd see it right away, but he'd want to pretend he was busy doing something else and text me back in a bit. Or if he was like Austin, I'd never hear from him again. I put my phone down on my bed. I hated these games.

My eyes wandered to the T.V. screen, but I couldn't seem to absorb the funny scenes from America's Funniest Home Videos tonight. I picked up my phone right when I heard it buzz.

Tyler: "I'm hoping you'll eventually drop the 'apologetic' and I can be normal Tyler again. What is the lovely Penny up to tonight?"

I had just complained about games and I found myself putting the phone down. *This is ridiculous!* I picked it back up and wrote: "I'm trying to decide on a topic for my speech. Have you chosen yet?" My finger hovered over the send button for a second, but I pressed it.

He would most likely think I was pathetic for answering right away. When my phone didn't buzz after a minute, I knew it would be awhile. I put my phone down, hopped off my bed, and found the Comm syllabus on my desk. I looked down at my desk chair. I usually used my computer and did most of my homework in bed, so Professor Hunter's sweater was still folded on the chair. He said his syllabus had his office hours, so I'd go as soon as I could to return it. My heartbeat quickened with just the thought of being alone with him.

I sat back down on my bed and looked down at the first sheet of the syllabus. Professor James Hunter. *James.* Even his name was sexy. I found myself wondering if he went by Jim or Jimmy. I decided against it though. Professor Hunter seemed sophisticated, and James Hunter was a very sophisticated sounding name.

I read through the first page of the syllabus. It was the same as every other professor's, outlining expectations and grading policies. I flipped to the assignments and read about the first speech. *Who am I going to talk about?* I didn't want my speech to be boring. I wanted Professor Hunter to notice me. So far my answers to his questions seemed to make him want to talk to me. And our awkward conversations made me feel alive. My gut told me to talk about something safe. For some reason though, I found myself brainstorming about how I could twist the assignment into talking about the stranger in the coffee shop. It was bold, probably way too bold. But I began to wonder if he would like it. He seemed to enjoy my answers so far. I wanted him to stare at me intently again.

My phone buzzed and I picked it up.

Tyler: "Thought I'd do it about my grandfather just to piss off Hunter. I'll make it real funny though. After all, there's this girl in class that I really want to impress."

I smiled as I reread his text. He was bold. And if he was willing to push the limits, maybe I should too. I texted him back: "I'm looking forward to hearing what you come up with. See you tomorrow, Apologetic Tyler."

I skimmed through the rest of the syllabus to find Professor Hunter's office hours. When I found the page, it felt like my heart stopped.

"Penny, are you okay?"

I hadn't even noticed that Melissa had come back. She dropped her keys on her bureau, walked over to her bed, and sat down on it cross-legged.

"Yeah," I said quickly and closed the syllabus. I tossed it onto my desk. "Just looking through some notes."

"Well you'll never believe who I ran into," she said.

"Who?"

"You're supposed to guess, Penny!"

"I have no idea."

"Austin."

"Please tell me you just ignored him."

"No, I went over and talked to him."

My eyes bulged. "You're joking, right? Melissa please tell me you're joking?"

"I walked over to confront him about being a huge jerk. I was going to stick up for you! And you know the first thing he said to me?"

"I don't want to know."

"He asked for your number."

"Why would he ask for my number? He has it. And even if he did lose it, I've called him twice since I've been back and he's completely ignored me."

"Well, he said he got a new phone."

"And you believed him? When people get new phones they usually keep their old numbers." I rolled my eyes.

"Well I don't know, he seemed sincere about it. Anyway, I did stick up for you. I refused to give him your number."

"Thanks, Melissa."

"So he gave me his new number instead."

"He gave you his number? He's so full of himself."

"No, not like that. He gave it to me to give to you."
She pulled a slip of paper out of her pocket and waved it in
the air.

"I don't want it."

"Geez, aren't you even going to see if it's a new number?!"

"It doesn't matter. There are a million other ways he
could have contacted me. If he really wanted to see me, he
easily could have." I folded my arms across my chest.

"Fine," Melissa said. "Well I will just leave this here,"
she placed the paper on her nightstand, "in case you
change your mind. You're welcome by the way. I'm going
to go take a shower." She hopped off her bed, grabbed her
shower caddy, and walked out of the room.

As soon as the door closed behind her, I jumped off
the bed. Instead of grabbing the piece of paper like I know
she wanted me to do, I picked up my syllabus and turned
to the page that had Professor Hunter's office hours and
read the note he had written in it:

Miss Taylor,

I hate to think that you make walking around in the
middle of the night a habit. But if you find yourself alone
in the rain again, please do not hesitate to call me if you
feel you are in need of an escort.

- J. H.

152-726-0133

After reading it for the fifth time, I pulled the paper to
my chest. *Oh my God!* I grabbed my phone and quickly

added his number. It took all my willpower to not text him. I flipped my syllabus back to the first page and placed it on my desk. It was hard to tell if he was being a responsible adult figure or completely flirting with me. I liked to think it was the latter. Part of me thought I had imagined the look in his eyes when he had walked me home. But maybe he was hungry...hungry for me. When I heard Melissa's hand on the doorknob, I quickly switched off the lights and pulled my sheet and comforter up over me and closed my eyes, pretending to be asleep. I hadn't told her about Professor Hunter walking me home on Thursday night. I wanted to keep just this one thing to myself and my fantasies.

I fell asleep thinking of Professor James Hunter kissing me under his umbrella.

CHAPTER 7

Monday

My alarm started beeping, disrupting the images of Professor Hunter that were swirling around in my head. I almost hit the snooze button, but then I remembered it was Monday. This morning I'd get to see the man himself. I turned off the alarm and slid out of bed.

Once I was done washing up in the bathroom I came back to my room and undid the rollers in my hair. The volume looked great. I pumped some mousse into my hands and tousled my hair slightly. Then I put on my makeup, which included some mascara and even a bit of eye shadow. After one glance in the mirror, I quickly wiped some away. I wanted to look sophisticated, not trashy. The look was surprisingly hard to accomplish. I pulled on a skirt that was short, but not inappropriate, and tucked my tank top into it. I grabbed a long necklace so that it would dangle between my breasts. Turning back to the mirror, I scrutinized my reflection. It was too much. I pulled on a jean jacket to make myself not look so provocative.

A quick glance at the time and I was out the door. I was relieved to see that it wasn't raining today. As I made my way to my seat, I noticed that Tyler was already sitting at the desk next to mine.

"Wow, you look great," he said as I sat down next to him.

I smiled and crossed my legs away from him. "How was your weekend?"

"Horrible."

I turned to him. "I'm sorry, Tyler, did something bad happen?"

"Oh, no. It was just horrible because you weren't a part of it." He shrugged.

He was trying hard. Too hard. I looked over at the door, but it was just a student that walked in. "What did you really do this weekend, Tyler?" I asked.

"Just hung out at the house. Actually your text was the highlight. Did it take you awhile to find my number?"

"I was definitely confused at first," I laughed. "Apologetic Tyler is right where you belonged though."

I turned away from Tyler as Professor Hunter walked into the room. He had ditched his glasses, and his hair was smooth again. He was wearing a dress shirt with the sleeves rolled up, and there were a few buttons undone at the top. His shirt was tucked into his khaki pants and he had a brown belt. I found myself wishing I could unhinge his belt.

"Today I thought it might be fun to talk about a recent dream we've had," Professor Hunter said as he put his satchel on the desk. He smiled to himself. "And I'll kick us off." He rubbed his hands together and bit his lower lip as he concentrated. "Ah, I remember one." He put his hands in his pockets. "Last night I dreamt that it was pouring outside. And I just had this feeling that I was waiting for something to happen. Something exciting." He leaned against his desk and looked down for a second, as if in retrospect. He slowly lifted his head and made eye contact with me.

I swallowed. When I did, my throat made a weird squeaking noise. It suddenly felt hot in the room. His eyes were smoldering. He turned his attention back to the rest of the class. No one seemed to notice that he had looked at me. *Does he look at everyone that way and I just don't notice?* I didn't think so. He was referring to the night we had spent together in the rain. He was referencing the note he had left me. It didn't seem like he had any intention of being a responsible adult. There was no denying that Professor Hunter was flirting with me now. I swallowed hard again.

My heart began racing, like it always did when I had to speak in class. He was already going through the names. A few people had funny dreams and I watched him laugh. His smile was intoxicating. I took a deep breath. I knew what I was going to say.

When he finally called my name, I quickly stood up. "I've actually been having the same dream now for several nights." I tucked a loose strand of hair behind my ear. "It's always raining, but there's a man there holding an umbrella above the two of us so that we don't get soaked." I stared into Professor Hunter's eyes. "And he kisses me." He lowered his eyebrows slightly as if what I said bothered him. Or was he giving me that hungry look again? Today I couldn't read him at all.

I heard someone in the room snicker.

I quickly sat back down.

Tyler leaned over and whispered in my ear: "You just can't stop dreaming about me, huh?"

I laughed quietly. *Did I take it too far?* My heart was racing. I didn't want Professor Hunter to think I was forward, because I wasn't. I was giving him the wrong idea. In my mind it was a game, but he wouldn't see it that way. I could feel my face turning scarlet. *I did take it too far.*

When Professor Hunter was done listening to the other students' dreams, he stood up and walked over to the board. He picked up a piece of chalk and wrote the word "emotion."

"The best advice I can give you is to make your speech personal. You want to draw emotion from your audience. You want to hook them." He made a fist when he said the last line.

He had me hooked. I listened intently to every word that escaped from his lips.

"That's why this first speech is easy. You're all writing about someone you admire, someone who has helped shape who you've become. It's personal. Make your classmates aware of that. Don't ever be afraid to show emotion."

He looked out at all of us. "Many psychologists will tell you that there are hidden meanings in your dreams, but I've never seen it that way. They're quite black and white. The first thing that comes to your mind when you think of your dream is what it truly means. And it's emotional. Fear," he looked at a boy on the other side of class. "Anger," he looked at the girl that had snickered at me. "Desire," he glanced briefly at me. "So when you think of who you're going to talk about, figure out the emotion that they make you feel." He glanced at the clock. "And I will see you all on Wednesday." He walked away from the board.

"Catch you later, Penny," Tyler said as he stood up.

A girl in the front row quickly got up from her desk and went up to speak to Professor Hunter. I delayed by rearranging things in my backpack for as long as possible, but the girl was still talking to him. She had long black hair and tan skin. She was wearing a shirt that revealed her stomach. *Is that the kind of girl he thinks I am?* I closed my eyes. That wasn't me. I looked down at the outfit I was wearing. Tyler was right, I was a tease. I was actually a good girl and Professor Hunter didn't even realize. *I blew it.* Besides, a girl like that had to be more his type. I didn't have that much to offer.

I had another class that I needed to get to. I got up and walked past his desk. I didn't want to look at him, but I couldn't resist glancing over. He tilted his head so he could see me over the girl's shoulder and we made eye contact for just a moment. He raised his left eyebrow as he watched me exit the room.

CHAPTER 8

Monday

I opened up my textbook and pulled out my notes. Statistics was not going to be my forte. I was great at math in high school. Calculus had actually been one of my favorite subjects. But the foreign professor who was teaching Stat was hard to understand. I was going to have to teach it all to myself.

Melissa came into the room with a huge smile on her face. "You will not believe the day I had!"

"What happened?" I turned to face her, pulled the notes off my lap, and placed them on my bed. I leaned over and grabbed my soda from my desk and took a sip.

"You know that professor you have a huge crush on?"

I almost choked on my soda. "I don't really."

"Yes you do! Come on, Penny. I mean...you kept his sweater for God's sake."

"I'm going to return it later this week." I was planning on it. But I truly did want to keep it. "Did you find out something about him, or what?"

"Well first of all that he's gorgeous. This girl in one of my classes was talking about this hot professor she has, and it turns out it's the same guy. You didn't tell me that he's basically a model."

"He is really handsome."

"You mean smoking hot! Anyway, apparently he got fired from his last teaching job."

"Why?" I tried to ask it nonchalantly, but I felt like I was begging for the information.

"The girl didn't know. Weird though, right? I mean what does a professor have to do to get fired? Punch the dean or something?"

"You're just making things up." But I knew what a professor could get fired for: having sex with a student.

"Well yeah, it's probably just a rumor." Melissa shrugged. "Thought you'd find it interesting. Anyway, and then I met up with that cute guy, from the party we went to last Thursday, and we had dinner. He's such a gentleman. He even pulled my chair out for me."

"That's nice." My mind was no longer on the conversation. There was no reason to jump to conclusions about Professor Hunter. He may not have even been fired. He looked so young; this was probably his first job as a professor.

Maybe Professor Hunter didn't have the wrong idea about me. No, I wasn't a bad girl, but I wanted to be bad for him. *Doesn't that make me bad?* I wanted to do things with him that would surely get him fired. I looked down at my phone. I could text him right now. He gave me his number. He flirted with me every day in class. He even confessed that he dreamed about me too.

I clicked on his number and typed out: "I enjoyed our first date. But you stood me up today." I smiled to myself. *Would he find it funny?* It didn't matter. I wouldn't send it. He gave me his number because he was worried about my safety. I was a pathetic girl walking around in barely anything in the middle of the night. Any normal adult should be worried about me. I needed to delete his number before I made a terrible mistake.

My phone buzzed and I fumbled it in my hands. It made a light bleeping sound to let me know that my message had been sent. I almost screamed "NO!" out loud. I gulped. *Oh my God, what did I just do?* I felt like I was hyperventilating. *Is there any way to undo a text? What if I get kicked out of school?!*

"I'm sorry, I didn't mean to send that," I quickly typed out. I was about to hit the send button when my phone bleeped to let me know I had received a message.

"Miss Taylor, that was never my intention."

I put my phone down on my bed and stared at it. He had responded to me right away. He even knew it was me. So that probably meant he didn't give his phone number out to everyone. I deleted the message that I had typed out. I pictured him sitting in sweatpants, lounging on a couch, waiting desperately to see what I had to say next. I was going to be bold and bad.

I texted back: "You dreamt about me."

A minute later he responded: "I can't control my dreams, Miss Taylor."

He wanted to control his feelings for me. He wanted me to pull back. But I didn't dare. I had confidence when I wasn't staring directly into his deep brown eyes. "I don't want you to." I pressed send.

I placed my phone on my bed and pulled my hair into a ponytail. My foot began to tap impatiently. I pulled my Stat book onto my lap again and began to read the page I had left off on. I had to stop halfway and start over because my mind was wandering.

"Trust me, you do," his response read.

I took a deep breath, completely flustered. *What did he dream of doing to me?* "I don't trust you," I texted. *Geez why did I say that?* That was a conversation ender, if anything is.

"Miss Taylor, are you in need of someone to walk you home?"

I sighed. He was angry. I didn't want to make him angry. I wanted him to think I was sexy and alluring. "I wish that I was, Professor Hunter," I responded.

I stared at my phone for ten minutes. No reply. I sighed and rolled over, away from my Stat work. Next time I wouldn't play with his temper.

CHAPTER 9

Tuesday

The following night I tossed and turned again as I tried to fall asleep. I had shoved Professor Hunter's sweater into my backpack that afternoon and marched over to his office hours. But there were three girls waiting in line to talk to him. I had rolled my eyes and stormed back to my dorm. I was kidding myself. He probably did get kicked out of the last college he worked at. He probably slept with every girl that batted her eyelashes at him. He was a tool.

But no matter how hard I tried, I couldn't get the image of him out of my mind. Whenever I closed my eyes I imagined his hands on me. I wanted to taste his lips. I wanted him in every way. I had never felt this primal before. I truly felt like I needed him.

***

When my alarm went off I slowly rose out of bed. I was exhausted from my fitful sleep. I quickly got ready for class. I pulled on yoga pants and a t-shirt and slowly made my way across campus. When I reached Professor Hunter's classroom, I took a deep breath and walked in the back door. Class had already begun. I passed by all the full desks and plopped down in my usual spot. Tyler was no-where to be seen.

I stared at Professor Hunter defiantly. He was wearing his glasses again, and he had left his hair alone. He turned to the board and underlined the word "emotion" that he must have written before I had arrived.

"Today we are going to drive this point home. And first we are going to share what emotion we are currently feeling. And say the word in the way that the emotion has affected you. For example, if I was upset, I'd probably frown a little and say it in a rather pouty way."

Most of the class giggled. He stared at me and I kept a straight face. *Had I made him upset?* He had certainly upset me.

"Very well," he said. He called out the first name and went through the list.

"Tyler Stevens?" Professor Hunter called. "Absent," he said to himself, and made a note on his paper.

"Penny Taylor?"

I stood up quickly. "I feel foolish." I closed my eyes. "And frustrated. Foolish and frustrated." I sat down without looking at him. I kept my eyes on my desk for the rest of class.

When Professor Hunter dismissed us, I hastily grabbed all my things and went out the back door so that I wouldn't have to walk by him.

***

After my final class of the day I made my way back to my dorm. I just wanted to lay down in my bed and disappear. When I opened my door I almost ran to my bed. I collapsed on top of it and buried my face in my pillow. I had completely ruined it with Professor Hunter. But I still wanted him. I wanted him so badly.

This was ridiculous. He was completely off limits anyway. I sat up and leaned off my bed to grab the piece of paper from Melissa's nightstand. It was a new number. Austin hadn't been lying. He still could have tried to email me or send me a message on Facebook or something though.

I grabbed my phone and slid my finger across the screen. Professor Hunter's name popped up. I clicked on the message. "Now I know how it feels to be stood up. Lesson learned." The text was time-stamped at 10 minutes after Comm had ended. That was over eight hours ago.

"Is that an apology?" I typed out. But I deleted it before I sent it. I put the slip of paper with Austin's number back on Melissa's nightstand. I knew what I had to do if I wanted Professor Hunter to want me as much as I wanted him. I was going to play hard to get. And that started with me ignoring him.

Melissa entered the room just as I was turning off my cell.

"Did you want to go get dinner?" she asked , putting her backpack down.

"Yeah, I'm starving." I jumped out of bed and grabbed my clutch.

We walked over to the dining hall. After waiting in line for pizza, I sat down across from her. I could have eaten pizza for every meal. Melissa was eating a salad.

"So..." Melissa said.

"So, what?"

"So...did you call him?"

"Did I call who?" My heart was beating fast. *Did she know about Professor Hunter? Was it that obvious?*

"Austin? Who else? Oh wait! Are you dating Tyler now? Penny that's so exciting! I saw him at the party, you two were really cute together."

"No. No, I didn't call either one of them."

"Penny, come on. I heard Sigma Pi is having another party this Thursday that we have to go to. Tyler likes you!"

"I know he does," I sighed. "I just don't know if I like him."

"Well you have a few days to decide between the two. Because we're going out this weekend no matter what. And you're going to want a date because Josh asked me to be his girlfriend!"

"Who's Josh?"

"What do you mean? Josh, Josh. The one I met at the party last Thursday. You met him too, he was the one who came up and talked to us right away."

"Oh, yeah, sorry. Mr. Tall, Dark, and Handsome, right?"

"That's the one. Anyway, I wanted to go on a double date with you and well, whoever. So who is it going to be?

"And when is this date taking place?" I could feel myself grimacing. I didn't want to ask Tyler out and send him the wrong message. And I didn't want to call Austin again. I didn't do well with rejection.

"Saturday night."

"Okay, I'll think about it."

"That's all I can ask."

We ate our meals quietly for a few minutes. Then we started complaining about our new classes and laughing. As we walked back to the dorm I tried to impersonate my foreign Stat teacher. Melissa laughed so hard she dropped her ice cream cone on the ground.

"I know, that's how I feel listening to him. How am I supposed to learn anything?"

"You just have to hope everyone else can't understand him either, and that there will be a huge curve."

CHAPTER 10

Thursday

A few minutes before Professor Hunter's office hours ended, I peered around the corner and looked into his office. He was sitting at a desk with earphones on. His door was open and there weren't any girls waiting to see him, except for me. I took a deep breath and walked to the door. He didn't seem to notice me. He was wearing a white dress shirt. The top few buttons were undone and he had a loosened tie around his neck. The sleeves were rolled up, revealing his tanned, muscular forearms.

I tapped on the door.

Professor Hunter looked up and his eyes bulged slightly. He pulled the headphones off and set them on his desk.

"Miss Taylor, come in," he said. He walked over to the door and closed it behind me. His office smelled strongly of his cologne. He shoved his hands into his pockets. "I didn't expect to see you."

"I didn't expect to be here."

"You're angry with me," he said slowly.

"I'm not." I pulled off my backpack and leaned against his desk.

He looked at his watch. "My office hours are almost over."

I was making him uncomfortable. "I tried to come the other day when they first start, but you had quite the line."

He reached his hand up and ran it through his sleek hair. I wanted to do that for him. He walked over so that he was only a few feet away from me. "Part of the duties of being a professor," he shrugged.

"Right." I picked up my backpack and pulled out his gray sweater. I had pathetically snuggled up to it in bed last night, but he didn't need to know that. All he needed to know was that I was brave enough to waltz into his office hours and bring it back. "I came to return this."

He stared down at the sweater and then let his eyes slowly wander up to mine. I could feel my face flushing.

"You can keep that."

"It's yours," I responded. I hadn't expected him to reject it. That wasn't part of my master plan.

"Certainly it looks better on you."

I gulped and placed the sweater on his desk. He drew closer, reached around me, and picked it up. He grabbed my hand and placed the sweater on my palm. His hand stayed on mine as he stared down at me. This wasn't what I had expected. It was way better.

"It's a gift, Penny."

"I like when you call me Penny."

His breathing sounded heavy. "Miss Taylor, you should probably go."

I wanted to grab his tie and pull him toward me. But he had just called me Miss Taylor instead of Penny. *Did he want me?* I gripped the desk with my free hand to stop it from shaking. A wave of his cologne hit me. It was growing hard to breathe.

A knock sounded on his office door.

Professor Hunter's hand fell from mine instantly, and he took a step back. He looked at the ground for a moment, and put his fingers through his hair. With his hand still in his hair, he slowly tilted his head back up and looked at me from under his thick eyebrows. *The hunger.* Then he glanced back down at the sweater.

I swallowed hard, picked up my backpack, and shoved the sweater inside.

He walked casually over to the door and opened it as I zipped my backpack and pulled it over my shoulder.

A girl walked in. She was wearing a charcoal pencil skirt and a matching blazer. Her high heeled shoes made her almost as tall as Professor Hunter. She was wearing bright red lipstick. "Ready to go, James?" she asked, and then spotted me. She glanced down at her watch. "Sorry, I thought office hours were over. I can wait outside." She smiled at him.

"We just finished up," he said to the mystery girl. "I'm ready to go." He was tightening his tie when he turned back to me. "See you tomorrow, Miss Taylor." He said the words without really looking at me.

I walked over toward them. "Thanks for your help, Professor Hunter," I said and made my way out of his office. *Who the hell is she?* I glanced back at them. She was laughing about something and she touched his arm. My stomach churned. She wasn't a girl, she was a woman. And clearly, she was his girlfriend. They were both dressed for a fancy date.

***

I added Austin's new number into my phone and then tossed the scrap of paper in the trash. Melissa insisted that I needed a date for Saturday. Austin was a good option. Tyler was persistent and I didn't want to string him along, whereas I could just go on this one date with Austin and I'd probably never hear from him again. Two days seemed like a good amount of time to ask for a date. Not so far in advance that I seemed like a lonely loser, and not too close to the date that I seemed desperate.

Or maybe I should invite Tyler. I believed that he was sorry. Plus, he had been so sweet recently. I placed my face in my hands. This was so dumb. All I wanted to do was invite Professor Hunter. But he had a girlfriend. And he was my *professor.* I was so pathetic.

I looked up when Melissa walked into the room.

"Great news," she said excitedly.

"Will I think it's great?"

"That depends."

"On what exactly?"

"On if you already have a date for Saturday."

Oh no, what did she do? I just looked at her, hoping she would continue. When she didn't, I said, "I don't."

"Well you do now. I ran into Austin again, and he's coming."

I didn't want to see him. I felt sick to my stomach. "Where do you even keep running into him?"

"First of all, you're welcome. Coincidence? Fate? You can decide on Saturday." She sat down at her desk and opened up a book. She seemed mad at me.

"Sorry, Melissa. I'm sure Saturday will be fun. Thanks for asking Austin for me."

She turned around with a big grin on her face. "No problem," she shrugged, and went back to studying.

Crap! I lay back on my bed. I should have invited Tyler when I had the chance. Josh and Tyler were in the same fraternity. They were probably friends. There was no way Josh would fail to mention to Tyler that I had been on a date with another guy. Tyler was going to hate me. For a second I thought about calling Austin to un-invite him. That would feel so rewarding! I smiled to myself. I wanted him to feel rejected like I had all summer. Too late now, though. A part of me, even if it was rather small, did want to see him again.

CHAPTER 11

Friday

I couldn't compete with the mystery woman from Professor Hunter's office. There wasn't anything to really suggest that they were together, though. Maybe it was just one date. *Could I compete? Did I even want to?*

The woman had been sophisticated. She had even been wearing nylons. I rolled my eyes to myself. She had been sophisticated, but that didn't mean that I needed to be. I opened up my backpack and pulled the sweater out. Luckily Melissa was still sound asleep, because I didn't want her to judge me.

I pulled his sweater over my head. It was pouring outside, so I slipped my red rain boots on and grabbed my matching red umbrella. He had implied that he thought the sweater looked better on me. I took a deep breath and walked out of my dorm room.

When I reached class, Tyler was already sitting in the desk next to mine.

"Are you feeling better today?" I asked him as I sat down.

"I didn't miss class because I was sick. I just needed a day off."

"Classes only just started," I laughed.

"Well I needed an excuse to get together with you so I could copy your notes." He was leaning on the edge of his desk, staring at me rather seductively.

I laughed again. "Professor Hunter basically just defined the word emotion. You're supposed to make your audience feel something when you give a speech. I didn't take notes."

"Penny you're making this impossible. Do you have plans this weekend?" There was something endearing about the way he was looking at me. Confident yet eager at the same time.

I sighed. "My roommate is forcing me to go on this strange double date with her." Hopefully that would make it seem rather innocent. And it was true, I didn't want to go.

Tyler smirked at me. "If you want to ditch it, I'll take you out to dinner."

"If you knew Melissa, you would know that that isn't an option. Sorry Tyler," I said and smiled at him.

"The rejection hurts," he said with a smile. He placed both his hands on his chest and let his head fall back like I had just hit him with a fatal blow.

"Oh, come on," I said, and lightly shoved his shoulder. "Rather dramatic."

"Rain check?" he asked.

I nodded. I looked up as Professor Hunter entered the room. He was wearing his glasses and his hair was sexily disheveled. A tight black t-shirt and light jeans made him look so casual and approachable. I tried not to think about the fact that he may be dressed casually because he was up late with the mystery woman.

It was hard to pay attention to what he was saying. His sweater that I was wearing smelled like him and it was like I was in some kind of trance. *Does he notice that I'm wearing it?*

Today's assignment was to talk about our weekend plans.

On Tyler's turn, he looked down at me while he spoke: "I will be spending the weekend wallowing in my room, because this girl I'm crushing on is too busy to hang out with me."

"Oh my God," I mouthed silently to him.

"Penny Taylor," Professor Hunter called.

When I stood up, it looked like his jaw dropped slightly. He quickly closed his mouth and looked down at his paper.

I wanted to make him jealous. Tyler had already set me up. "This weekend I'm going on a double date with my roommate and her new boyfriend."

Professor Hunter seemed to wince when I said "date."

I quickly added, "But I'm absolutely dreading it," before sitting back down. I was bad at playing hard to get.

Tyler leaned over. "I wish you didn't have to go either," he whispered.

Professor Hunter called the next name on the list without looking back over at me. When he was finished listening to the other students, he walked over to the board. He wrote "lust" on the board in all caps.

"You want your audience to hang on every word that comes out of your mouth. It's kind of like in a relationship. You want that instantaneous lust you sometimes get."

I doubted anyone else noticed it, but during his speech he seemed to be blatantly staring at me.

"I don't necessarily mean it in a sexual way. Although, there is a reason that sex sells."

I heard a few girls giggle.

"You want to capture your audience's attention. You want them to yearn for more. And that, in my opinion, is the hardest thing about giving an effective speech. Because you can't force lust. It has to come naturally."

Am I forcing it? It didn't feel forced to me.

"Anyway, something to ponder over the weekend. Class dismissed."

"I guess I'll see you on Monday. If you change your mind, you have my number." Tyler winked at me.

I smiled back at him as he walked away. Wearing Professor Hunter's sweater to class had taken a lot of courage. But now it was time for the hardest part. I tried to walk as seductively as I possibly could in rain boots, and slowed down slightly when I passed by his desk so that he'd notice me.

"Miss Taylor, if you would, please wait a moment."

I froze. He had noticed. I never expected him to talk to me after yesterday, though.

"You're wearing my sweater."

"I've been told I look good in it."

He was silent for a moment. "You have a date this weekend," he said casually. He didn't ask it as a question, but said it as a statement. I felt like there was a trace of anger in his voice.

I gulped. That was none of his business. Especially since he had a girlfriend. "And how was yours?" I replied, with more sass than I intended.

"Hmmm?" he said, and raised his left eyebrow.

"I have another class I need to get to."

"So do I."

My heart was racing.

"Well then." I turned.

"Penny?" The tips of his fingers brushed the back of my wrist.

It sent shivers through me, and my body actually shook. *Play hard to get!* I went toward the door. Before I walked out I turned just my head, and said, "Have a good weekend, Professor Hunter."

CHAPTER 12

Saturday

I looked down at my phone one more time. For some reason, I had this hope that Professor Hunter would text me and beg me not to go. Or show up and whisk me away. I carefully clicked on his name, trying not to smudge my nail polish. Even though it was foolish, I couldn't help wanting to text him. He was most likely on a date with his girlfriend. The thought made me want to text him even more.

"Penny, you need to get ready to go. We need to leave in just a few minutes if we're going to be there on time."

I hopped off my bed. "I am ready."

"What the hell are you wearing?" Melissa said as she looked at my outfit. I was wearing jeans and a tank top. Apparently I was underdressed because she was wearing a new dress. It had a high neckline in the front, but there was no back until just above her butt.

"You look great, Melissa," I said, trying to change the subject.

She sighed in response and walked over to her closet. "Penny, you need to look hot. Don't you want Austin to be upset about what he's been missing?"

"I don't care about what Austin thinks."

"Just a second. Here," she said and tossed me a black dress.

"But..."

"Penny, you're not wearing jeans to dinner. You'll make me look ridiculously overdressed. And I bought this specifically for tonight."

"So bossy," I mumbled under my breath.

"Yep, now change."

I pulled on the dress, strapped on my black stilettos, and stood up. "Fine, now I'm ready."

"Perfect. That'll make him drool."

I couldn't help but smile when I looked in the mirror. The super short, sleek black dress I was wearing had a neckline that plunged to my belly button. The designer must have had a vague sense of modesty, because the dress had a black mesh material between the neckline so that I wasn't completely exposed. There was a slit up the side, and if it was any higher, the dress wouldn't be suitable to wear out. I completed the look with a pair of dangly earrings that helped elongate my neck. I felt sexy.

"Ah, I'm excited! Let's go," Melissa said.

We made our way out of the dorm. We walked arm in arm along the brick walkway, as was our custom, so that neither one of us fell over in our heels.

"So, are you nervous to see Austin?"

"I'm still mad at him."

"And you should be. But he clearly misses you, or he wouldn't have agreed to come."

I felt myself starting to sweat. "Melissa, I am nervous. Do I really have to do this?"

"You cannot back out at the last minute!"

"I feel like I'm going to be sick."

"Well, just don't get sick on him."

"Melissa!"

"Okay, okay." We stopped for a moment and she turned to face me. "Here's what you have to do. Just remember to act confident. And most importantly, don't say that you've missed him. That gives him all the power. You need to make him want you, not the other way around."

I took a deep breath. "Play hard to get?"

"Exactly." She grabbed my arm and we started walking again.

We stopped again in front of Kildare's, the restaurant we were going to. It was only 8 o'clock, so even though we were underage, we'd still be allowed in.

"You ready?" Melissa asked.

"As ready as I can be."

Melissa stepped into the restaurant first. "Hi," she said to the hostess. "We're looking for two...oh, never mind. I see them!"

Josh was waving for us to come over to a booth. He stood up as we approached and so did Austin. My stomach started to churn. I couldn't be confident. This was Austin. *The Austin.* The one that strung me along all of last semester and "didn't do labels." With his short, light brown hair, grayish blue eyes, and that sexy scruff on his chin, he had this way about him that made me act foolish.

He had me wrapped around his finger, and he knew it. I had slept with him, hoping that would get him to stay. But that wasn't the case. He just wanted me for my body. So I kept giving it to him. His position on "labels" never changed. And then when the semester ended, I stopped hearing from him. All summer I waited. When I got his, "Babe, it's hard being here without you. I miss you," text, I came back to campus as soon as I could. And he had completely disappeared. I felt my knees trembling. I knew I was hurt, but I hadn't realized how angry I was.

Be confident, Penny. I thought about the way I'd been acting with Professor Hunter. Austin had nothing on Professor Hunter. If I could act sassy and confident and strong around him, then this should be a piece of cake. *I can do this.*

When we reached the boys, Josh pulled Melissa close and kissed her passionately. This was already awkward. I looked up at Austin.

"Babe, that dress..." Austin said. He grabbed my waist and pulled me to him. He leaned down for the kiss but I turned my head. It didn't seem to deter him. He pecked my cheek. "Penny, where have you been hiding?"

"I've just been really busy. How are you, Austin?" *How could he ask me that?* He was the one that had been ignoring me. I wished he would let go of my waist.

"Better now that you're here." He reached down, grabbed my chin, and tilted it toward him. "I've missed you, babe. It was a long summer without you." He smelled like strawberries and beer. I had used his strawberry scented shampoo before on the occasions that I had spent the night at his apartment.

"I..." I stopped myself before I told him that I missed him too. I needed to take Melissa's advice, and that meant not telling him that I missed him. "I had a great summer. Well, crap job, but you know how it is," I shrugged.

He let go of my chin. Ignoring my comment, he said, "You really look stunning. You always did know exactly what I like."

I restrained myself from rolling my eyes. This wasn't even my dress. He slid into the booth and I sat next to him. Josh and Melissa sat down across from us.

"How long have you two been dating?" Josh asked Austin and me.

"A little over six months," Austin replied.

His words were hard to make out, because at the same time, I said, "We're not really."

Austin and I looked at each other. I turned back to Josh.

"It's complicated," I said.

"Ah." Josh turned to Melissa and made an apologetic face. I could tell that he was flustered that she hadn't told him the situation.

"It's not that complicated," Austin said and wrapped his arm around my shoulders. He scooted closer toward me so that our bodies were touching. I looked up at him and he looked down at me. "I'm sorry," he mouthed.

I gave him a small smile. That's what I had wanted. For him to apologize. I sighed with relief. Maybe now I could relax a little and enjoy the night.

CHAPTER 13

Saturday

I took another bite of the chocolate cake and glanced up at Austin. The two of us were alone in the booth because Melissa and Josh were still dancing. We had taken a break to have dessert. Austin was starting to stare at me, with his cloudy blue eyes, in that way that made my knees weak. He had already been through a few beers and I knew what was on his mind. I looked back down at my plate. I didn't know how much longer I'd be able to resist him.

"I got a new place," he said.

"Same roommates?"

"No, actually." He had started rubbing the back of my neck with his thumb. The familiarity of it was soothing and somehow arousing at the same time.

Austin knew that I didn't like when he smoked. It made him act like an idiot. And his old roommate, Benji, was usually the one persuading him.

"How's Benji doing?"

"I haven't seen him."

I hadn't expected that. He had apologized to me, plus he was done hanging out with his loser friends? Maybe he had changed. Being a senior seemed to make him take things more seriously now. I took another bite of cake, and Austin suddenly started laughing.

"What's so funny?"

He just kept laughing. "You have chocolate on your face."

"Where?" I wiped the side of my mouth with my hand.

He leaned toward me and slowly wiped the other side of my mouth with his thumb. He then placed his finger in his mouth and sucked off the chocolate. I could feel my heart rate accelerating. *Why is that so hot?*

"Did you want to come see my place?" he asked.

I gulped. He didn't really want me to come see his place. He wanted me. And I loved when he wanted me.

"Let me run to the ladies room real quick," I said, and slid out of the booth. I closed the stall door and just stood there. I didn't actually need to use the restroom, I just needed a second to think. Melissa had told me to be strong and I was about to cave. I needed to go back out there and tell him I wanted to call it a night. If he really had changed at all, he'd respect that. I walked out of the stall, washed my hands, and fixed my hair in the mirror.

When I exited the bathroom, Austin was still sitting at our booth alone. But he was turned around, talking to the booth of girls behind him. All four of the girls laughed at something he just said. I felt my heart rate accelerating. I walked back over to our table. He continued chatting to the booth of girls and didn't even notice my return.

Without even realizing what I was doing, I grabbed my glass and tossed what was left of my water in his face.

"Penny, what the hell?"

"Have a good life, Austin." I turned around and walked briskly out of the restaurant.

I heard footsteps behind me. "Penny, wait," Austin pleaded.

I ran down the stairs outside the entrance of the restaurant. My heels clicked on the brick sidewalk of Main Street.

"Penny, I'm sorry."

"Yeah I know, you already said that tonight." I turned around to face him. "What exactly are you apologizing for anyway? Are you trying to say that you somehow 'accidentally' ignored me all summer? Or are you referring to the girls you were just flirting with on our date? Or maybe all the times you've stood me up? Or are you just sorry for being an arrogant asshole in general?"

"Just..."

"Just what, Austin? Just give you another chance? Why, because you didn't mean all those things you said about 'labels'? You've changed and you want to be my boyfriend now?"

"You know that's not what I want. But I do want you."

"And every other girl on campus?" I was seething. I turned to walk away again.

"That's not what it's like. Damn it, Penny, won't you just listen to me?" He grabbed my arm.

My heel got stuck in a gap between the bricks as he pulled me. It snapped off and I fell to my knees. His hands were on me in an instant to help me to my feet.

"Get off me!" I yelled and pushed him away. I stumbled to my feet. The tears were starting to well in my eyes.

"Geez, Penny, lighten up."

"Save your advice, Austin. I don't care. We're done."

"Until you call me again, begging to see me."

He did get my calls! It took every ounce of restraint in me to not slap him.

"Well, until then," he said. He turned away and walked back up the restaurant steps.

"Grow up, Austin!" I yelled. Without turning around he put his hand up in the air to acknowledge he had heard me, and disappeared back inside the bar. He hadn't changed at all.

I was done with boys. I wanted a man. And I wanted that man to be Professor Hunter. It was time to find out if he wanted me. Before I could chicken out, I took my phone out of my clutch and texted Professor Hunter. "Any chance I can get a lift?"

CHAPTER 14

Saturday

Not even a minute passed before I got his response: "Where are you?"

"Outside of Kildare's."

My phone bleeped. "I'll be right there."

I put my phone back in my clutch and sat down on the curb. My knees were bleeding and I was holding my broken heel in my hand. I smiled when it began to drizzle. It was like my fantasies were coming true. After several minutes of nervous waiting, a black Audi coupe rolled up next to me. Even his car was sexy.

Professor Hunter leaned over and opened the car door from the inside. I climbed inside and shut the door.

"Did I wake you?" I asked. He put the car in drive and drove off. His hair was sleek from the rain. He was wearing dark jeans and a gray hoodie. The zipper of his hoodie wasn't pulled up all the way, and he clearly wasn't wearing a shirt underneath. His outfit made him look even younger. He really couldn't be much older than me.

"Yes," he replied.

The rain quickly picked up. In the silence, the drops began to splash loudly on the windshield. I could tell he was a little grumpy from me disturbing his sleep.

"You live near here?" I asked.

"Yes."

"Where?"

The car pulled to a stop at a red light. He leaned across me and opened up the glove compartment. I gulped. I wanted to kiss him so badly. He grabbed a tissue and placed it gently on one of my cut knees. Ignoring my question, he asked, "Do you want to talk about what happened?"

"I fell, that's all," I whispered. His breath smelled minty. I had woken him up and he had taken the time to brush his teeth. *Was he going to kiss me?* He let go of the tissue and sat back in the driver's seat. I blotted my knees with the tissue.

"That's all?" he said, staring at me.

I lifted my stiletto from my lap and shrugged.

When the light turned green he stepped on the gas. "You enjoyed your date then?"

"No."

We drove on in silence again. We were almost back to my dorm.

"Is that what you wanted to hear?" I added.

"I don't desire for you to be unhappy, Miss Taylor."

"Why did you give me your number, Professor Hunter?"

He pulled to the curb outside of my dorm and turned the car off. "You seem keen on putting yourself in dangerous situations." He glanced quickly at my outfit and then got out of the car.

My face flushed. Professor Hunter ran through the rain and opened up the door on my side. I slowly stepped out, not wanting for this moment to end. I kept blowing all my chances with him.

Instead of turning to walk me to the door he just stood there, staring at me. It was like he was waiting for something. I remembered the dream he recounted in class. He was waiting for something exciting to happen. And it was pouring.

"Professor Hunter..."

There was that look again. It took my breath away. And for the first time I realized that it wasn't anger or hunger. It was hunger and anger. He leaned down and placed his hands on the car, on either side of me. Our mouths were less than an inch apart. He opened his lips slightly like he was about to say something. I could feel the heat of his breath in the rain. He drew a fraction of an inch closer.

"I can't seem to stop thinking about you," I whispered.

Instead of responding, he quickly grabbed the back of my neck and let his lips meet mine. His kiss was full of passion, passion that he had been holding back just as much as I had. He pressed his body against mine and light-ly pushed me so that my back was on the cold, wet steel of the car. He leaned into me. The contrast of the heat from his body and the coolness of the car sent a spark through me. I had never wanted someone so badly before. I let my hands wander beneath the back of his hoodie. His skin was so soft.

His lips pulled away from mine and he groaned softly in my ear. "Penny, you need to try to stop." He stepped back and lifted the hood of his hoodie over his head. He rubbed his forehead as he walked around the car. With one last smoldering glance, he got into his car.

I stood in the rain as I watched him speed off.

CHAPTER 15

Sunday

"Penny?" Melissa nudged me. "Penny it's nearly dinner time, do you want to get up and get something to eat with me?" Her voice was etched in concern.

"I'm tired," I groaned and tried to turn over.

"Penny, you have to get up. Tell me what happened last night." She pulled the sheets off of me. "Oh my God, Penny, are you bleeding?!"

I looked down at my knees. The rain had made the blood trickle down my shins. It looked like something out of a horror film. I started laughing.

"Penny you're freaking me out."

"I'm fine," I sat up. "I just fell last night."

"Penny I have to ask you a serious question, so stop laughing. Did Austin hurt you?"

"No," I said immediately. "Geez, no."

"Okay, good. Then get up. We're going to the dining hall." She tossed a pair of workout shorts and a tank top at me. "You can tell me all about last night while we eat."

There was never any reasoning with her. I wasn't even upset about Austin. I just didn't want to get up. I wanted to relive Professor Hunter kissing me over and over again. As soon as I got up I knew I'd have to face the truth. He didn't want me to pursue him anymore. It was our first and last kiss. I touched my lower lip with my index finger. The fairytale was over.

I sighed and got out of bed. After cleaning my cuts with peroxide, Melissa and I made our way to the dining hall. I walked around aimlessly with an empty plate. Nothing seemed appetizing. I finally copied Melissa and got a salad.

"So tell me what happened," she said right when I sat down. "We came back to the booth and you were gone. I had assumed it meant you two had made up." She raised both eyebrows. "But now that I've seen you...not so much."

"He had me, you know. Like he always does. I went to the bathroom to try and talk myself out of going back to his place. And when I came back out, I saw him talking to these girls and I just snapped. I don't even know what came over me."

"So you had a fight?"

"I threw a glass of water in his face." I cringed.

"Seriously?! I can't believe I missed that. Great move, by the way. What did Austin do? Geez, I can picture his face." She laughed to herself.

"I ran out of the restaurant and he followed me."

"You know that you're basically describing a romantic comedy, right?"

"Yeah, except we had a huge fight. We both said some pretty horrible things."

"Hence the staying in bed all day?"

"No. It's weird but I'm actually okay with it. I just felt so tired afterward, you know? But I'm not sad or upset. I'm so over him."

"Well look at you. I'm proud of you, Penny. You finally stood up for yourself."

"Ha, yeah." I took a bite of my salad. I began to wonder if I should talk to her about Professor Hunter. She always had great advice. But I couldn't do it. There was something between me and Professor Hunter that seemed so private. I felt like I'd be betraying him if I told her. If I told her it almost seemed like it would be over. *But it is over.*

***

When I got back to my room I opened up my laptop. I had to finish my psychology paper for tomorrow. I pulled up the document and finished typing about the implications of Pavlov's experiments with his dogs. "You can potentially twist someone into something they are not. The implications are dangerous." It wasn't my best writing, but I hit the print button.

While my paper was printing, I opened up my email. There was an unread one from Professor Hunter titled "Comm 212 cancelled." *Oh my God, I made him quit?* I quickly clicked on it.

The first line read: "Comm 212 will be cancelled tomorrow."

I breathed a sigh of relief. My heart was racing. I read the rest of the email:

"Please read the attached article about the importance of improvising during a speech. You have to react to your audience, so it's important to be able to think on your toes. I know that originally speeches were supposed to start next

Monday, but I've decided to throw a wrench in things. Speeches will start this Wednesday instead. The speeches are only supposed to be two to three minutes, so it shouldn't take more than two days of class. Everyone with last names beginning with A through M will be going Wednesday, and everyone else will go on Friday. So, you still have plenty of time to prepare, but I wanted to give you more of a sense of thinking on your toes. I'm looking forward to hearing about the influcntial people in your lives."

- Professor J. Hunter

He had kissed me like I had never been kissed before, and then told me to stop thinking about him. Was class cancelled because of me? I pulled out my phone and clicked on his name. "I hope that everything is alright, Professor Hunter." I knew I was being defiant, but I pressed the send button anyway. He was sending me mixed messages, and I preferred to believe that the kissing me part of last night was what he really wanted too.

I climbed onto my bed, pulled my computer to my lap, and opened up Facebook. I clicked on the search bar and slowly typed James Hunter into the box. A photography company from Maryland, some grunge band, and several guys that were certainly not Professor Hunter popped up. I pressed the backspace key until his name disappeared.

I was about to ex out of Facebook when a message came up at the bottom of the screen. I clicked on it.

Tyler: "Mixed feelings about tomorrow. Class cancelled = awesome. Not getting to see you = major suckage."

I wrote back to Tyler: "What really sucks is that we have to give our presentations on Friday."

Tyler: "That's not really what I'm worried about."

Me: "So what are you worried about then, Tyler?"

Tyler: "Well, I'm waiting for you to spill the beans about your date. Let me down easily."

Me: "Honestly, it was a complete disaster."

Tyler: "Sorry, that sucks."

Me: "I feel like you aren't sorry."

Tyler: "Yeah, not even a little. Actually I think I can make you feel better. I wanted to cordially invite you to dinner...any night of your choosing."

I looked down at my phone. Professor Hunter hadn't responded.

Tyler: "And I won't take no for an answer."

Me: "How about lunch one day?" *As friends.*

Tyler: "Let's do it Wednesday. And then we can make fun of all the speeches."

Me: "Haha, okay, Tyler."

Tyler: "I'm going to go before you change your mind. Night!"

I smiled to myself and shut down my computer.

CHAPTER 16

Wednesday

As soon as my alarm sounded Wednesday morning, I was out of bed and getting ready. I needed to look super casual for lunch with Tyler so that he wouldn't get the wrong idea. I took off the baggy t-shirt that I had slept in and replaced it with a tank top and an off the shoulder, light-weight sweater. I pulled on a pair of old skinny jeans with holes in the knees and slipped on my favorite Keds.

I put a little frizz control lotion in my hands and scrunched my wavy hair to give it some added texture. When I looked in the mirror I felt a tiny bit of hope. Pro-fessor Hunter had never returned my message. But maybe he just didn't like the flirtatious version of myself. This was the real me. I felt uncomfortable wearing short skirts and revealing dresses. So I'd try and see if he liked this side of me better.

After eating a bowl of cereal, brushing my teeth, and applying minimal makeup, I locked the door behind me. I went into Professor Hunter's class and sat at my usual spot in the corner. Tyler walked in with a huge smile on his face.

"So where do you want to go for lunch?"

"Can I meet you at Russell Dining Hall at 12:30?"

"We don't have to go to the dining hall, Penny. I'll take you somewhere, my treat."

"But it's steak sandwich day."

Tyler laughed. "Okay, I guess I can't pass that up."

I smiled. Professor Hunter walked into the room. He was his usual handsome self, but it looked like he hadn't shaved in a few days. This morning he didn't even glance at me. He had told me to stop thinking about him, but I couldn't. Clearly he had stopped thinking about me, though. It stung.

"It's presentation day!" He pumped his fist into the air.

Most of the class groaned.

"It's not going to be that bad. Okay, first up is Raymond Asher. Let me just fix this." He grabbed a podium from the corner and placed it in the middle of the room. "And I'll get out of your way." He made his way to the back of the classroom, and I watched his every step. The only empty seat was the one right in front of Tyler. He sat down and placed his satchel on the floor, still not glancing at me at all. I hadn't realized that I had been holding my breath.

Raymond walked confidently to the podium. He placed both hands on either side of the top of it and leaned in a bit. It looked like he had done this hundreds of times. Was I unaware of a prerequisite to this class? I was getting nervous and I wasn't even presenting until Friday.

Raymond gave a funny presentation about his grandfather who was "clearly better than any of Professor Hunter's grandparents" and deserved a proper shout-out.

Tyler leaned over a little to me. "Crap, he stole my idea."

I laughed quietly. It looked like Professor Hunter's back stiffened.

Without commenting on Raymond's speech, Professor Hunter called out the next name. He never spoke after any of the speeches, just finished writing his notes and called the next name on his list. I heard a wide array of stories about friends, siblings, parents, and significant others. They started to all blur together.

At the end of the last speech, Professor Hunter said, "Great job today. Class dismissed." He was still scribbling notes.

"I'll see you at lunch, Penny," Tyler said and stood up.

Crap. Now Professor Hunter knew I had a sort of date.

Professor Hunter looked down at his paper and tilted his head a little to the left. He wanted to hear what I had to say. It was the first time all day he had acknowledged my existence.

"Don't be late, I have a class at two," I said.

"I wouldn't dare." Tyler laughed and walked out of the back door of the classroom.

I stayed seated. My heart rate was accelerating. When the class had emptied, Professor Hunter turned and put his papers into his satchel.

"I'm sorry about the other night, Miss Taylor. I was out of line." He still wasn't looking at me, just fumbling with his notes.

"I'm not sorry."

He shook his head back and forth. "You don't need to be, it was my mistake."

"I mean that I'm not sorry that it happened."

Sitting in that desk made him look just like a student. Why couldn't he have just been a student? He finally turned his head to look at me. He looked angry. For some reason I could tell he wasn't mad at me though. He was angry at himself.

"Enjoy your lunch date, Miss Taylor. I will see you in class on Friday." He abruptly stood up and walked away.

I wanted to get up and walk with him, but something kept me in my chair. I gulped. There was something about that anger in his eyes. I suddenly felt extremely cold. The realization hit me hard. This wasn't a game. Flirting with him wasn't the same as it was with guys my own age. Professor Hunter had an air of danger around him. He was intriguing because he terrified me.

CHAPTER 17

Wednesday

Tyler and I met outside Russell Dining hall at 12:30, which was a horrible mistake on cheese steak day. The line was already ridiculously long.

"Hey."He gave me a big hug.

"We better get in line," I said and pulled away.

We went into the dining hall and stepped into the back of the line.

Tyler turned to me. "Wanna play 21 questions?"

"Yeah, sure. You can go first."

"Okay. Why did you agree to have lunch with me?"

I laughed. "Because your persistence is charming. Why did you want to have lunch with me?"

"Well isn't that obvious? Because I like you. You're cute and funny, and you can be pretty assertive when you need to be."

I cringed. "I'm sorry about kneeing you in the crotch."

"Ha, I deserved it. Please. Next question. How many boyfriends have you had?"

"One. No. Well, yes. But not really..."

He laughed. "Simple question."

Why did I agree to play this game?! "It's a complicated answer."

"Fair enough. Your turn."

"How many girlfriends have you had?"

"Three. What's your major?"

"Marketing. What's your major?"

"Penny you're cheating. You're not supposed to just repeat every question I ask."

"Oh. Okay. Well, then. What's the most embarrassing thing you've ever done?"

"I don't get embarrassed easily."

"Well you're the exact opposite of me then. But if you had to just choose one thing that a normal person would probably find embarrassing?"

He laughed. "Well, one time at camp I wet my pants while I was sleeping. And my sleeping bag got completely soaked. So after everyone woke up I switched it with my bunkmates so that everyone would think he did it."

"Tyler! That's not embarrassing for you. That's embarrassing for the boy you played the prank on."

"I don't know...I mean, I just told you I used to wet my bed."

I laughed. "Okay, fair enough. Next question."

"What's the most scandalous thing you've ever done?"

I thought about my back against the car and Professor Hunter pressing against me. "Pass!" I almost yelled. I knew my face was turning red.

"Ooohh," Tyler laughed. "Jackpot. Penny you have to tell me, it's part of the game."

I was bad at thinking on my toes and even worse at lying. "Errr...one time I...Oh, please, Tyler..."

"Okay, fine. You don't have to tell me now. But I will get it out of you eventually." He was smiling.

"Do you have another question?" I asked.

"Which sounds better to you: sweatpants, popcorn, and a movie? Or a dress, great food, and dancing?"

"Sweatpants and a movie, hands down."

"Okay, that's going to be our next date then."

I smiled. Why couldn't I just forget about Professor Hunter? Tyler was sweet and funny. And he wasn't my teacher. I studied his face. He was handsome. Actually, he was really handsome.

"What do you want to do after you graduate?" I asked him.

"Geez. I don't know." He rubbed his chin. "You'll have to hold me to answering that later too."

"Fair enough. We each only get one pass, though."

He nodded in agreement.

Since he had already used his pass, I needed to think of something juicy to ask him. We were at the front of the line so I used the extra time to brood over different questions I could ask him. Once we both got our sandwiches, we sat down across from each other.

"Still your question," he said.

A girl walked up to our table and touched Tyler on the shoulder. She had long, straight blonde hair and huge breasts. They were basically falling out of her shirt.

"Hi, Tyler," she said.

"Hey, Claire," he said quietly. She leaned down and whispered something in his ear. His face remained expressionless and then the girl walked away.

I couldn't help myself, I was a little jealous. I guess I liked Tyler more than I had realized. But it no longer seemed like I was his type.

"Are you dating anyone else right now?" I asked.

"Anyone else? Are you saying that we're dating?"

My face flushed. "Just answer my question. Are you dating anyone?"

"I wouldn't say that."

"What would you say, then?"

"That I've gone on a few dates this semester."

I took a huge bite of my steak sandwich. It was good, but not good enough to make me forget about the blonde bimbo. I had gone on a date with Tyler. One date. And he'd tried to go all the way with me. *Had he had sex with her?*

"Is she one of the girls that you've been seeing?"

"Yes. Okay, you've asked a bunch of questions in a row. I believe it's my turn. In your words, have you been dating anyone else?"

"I thought we weren't supposed to repeat questions."

He shrugged. I knew that he was trying to make a point. He already knew that I had a date last weekend. And despite that, I wouldn't say that I was dating anyone else. But I began to wonder if Professor Hunter counted too. I certainly wanted to be dating him. And I had kissed him.

"I haven't really been seeing anyone, no," I replied slowly.

"But you've gone on a date. So...I don't really under-stand why you're upset. We're on the same page here."

I leaned forward. "Exactly how many girls have you slept with, Tyler?"

He leaned forward. "I'm going to pass."

"You're not allowed to pass."

He stared at me.

"That many, huh?"

"Look, I know why you're asking. You want to know if I've been with anyone since I started talking to you."

"So...?"

"Penny..."

"Oh my God, Tyler. You're such a slut," I whispered.

He gave me a mischievous smile. "I'm just messing with you, Penny. No, I haven't slept with anyone this semester. And only three girls total. There, that's not so bad, right?"

"What is wrong with you?" I leaned across the table and lightly shoved his shoulder.

"You're fun to mess with. You're so gullible."

"Very funny." I shook my head at him.

"Besides, now I got a question answered without even having to ask it," he said.

"Oh, yeah? And what is that?"

"You like me."

I kept my mouth shut.

"You got so jealous. You should have seen your face, Penny."

I put a stray strand of hair behind my ear. "Look, Tyler, I just broke it off with this jerk, and I feel like I'm not really in a place to date anyone right now. I'd love it if we could be friends, though."

"Yeah, I know."

"Wait, what?"

"Josh told me. I guess Melissa told him about it or something."

Damn it, Melissa! She had such a big mouth.

"I like you, though. So I hope you can forgive me, because I'm just going to keep trying. Besides, I've heard that you think my persistence is charming."

"Okay, Tyler."

"So what is your speech going to be about?" I asked him.

"Well that asshole stole my idea. But I think I have something else planned. You'll have to wait and see. What about you?"

"I have no idea."

CHAPTER 18

Friday

I looked down at my notes. My hands were already shaking. I had chosen to wear casual clothes again today, jeans and a tank top. But I was probably wearing an inappropriate amount of eye makeup and I had taken the time to straighten my hair. I wanted Professor Hunter to listen to my speech and think I wasn't just some clumsy, flirtatious girl.

"Penny," Tyler said and grabbed my hand.

I looked up at him.

"Don't be nervous, you're going to rock it. And try to pay attention today. I think you're going to like my speech." He winked at me.

When Professor Hunter walked in I moved my eyes back to my notes. Seeing him would just make me even more nervous. I felt like I was going to throw up. Being nervous was way worse than a hangover. Professor Hunter called out the first name and made his way to the back of the room. Again, he sat down in front of Tyler.

I completely spaced out during all the speeches. I just stared at my notes, hoping that someone would pull the fire alarm. I even began to wonder if I should go to the bathroom and pull the alarm myself. Ultimately I decided against it because I figured everyone would be able to deduce that it was me.

Before I knew it, Professor Hunter called Tyler's name. My heart started racing. I was next. For a second I put my nerves aside so I could listen to Tyler's speech.

He didn't look at all nervous when he reached the podium. Tyler looked at me and began his speech:

"I've gotta be honest with all of you. I'm going to be incredibly sappy for the next few minutes, because I have met THE most amazing girl. She's sweet and funny and super cute."

I put my hands over my mouth and began shaking my head back and forth. *Oh my God!*

"And she is quite inspirational. Let me give you some examples. She usually says no when I ask her on a date."

The whole class started laughing.

"But it's okay, because she does laugh at all my jokes. She also kneed me in my junk that one time."

Everyone laughed again.

"But she's apologized. So that was nice of her. As you can see, she's a handful. Wow, now that I think about it, is she really that inspiring? I know it sounds crazy, but I really think so. And hey, at least she's inspiring me to be persistent."

His speech garnered a good applause. He walked confidently back to his seat. After he sat down, he leaned over and said, "You're up, Penny. By the way, your face is bright red."

Professor Hunter called my name a moment later and I felt like I was going to faint. I grabbed my paper and stood up. When I walked past his desk, I smelled his cologne and felt even more light headed. Forgetting to watch where I was going, I tripped over a backpack in the aisle and fell sideways into someone's desk. The desk screeched a few inches to the right and the girl sitting there looked like she had just been woken up. I was surprised she didn't scream.

"I'm so sorry," I said quickly, and finished walking to the podium. The screeching sound seemed to echo as the girl moved her desk back where it belonged.

The majority of the class was still laughing at me once I reached the podium. *Why me?!*

Professor Hunter rubbed his forehead and looked up at me slowly. I felt my knees begin to shake. It looked like he wanted to laugh at me too. I closed my eyes and took a deep breath. I heard someone cough. *Crap, how long had I been up here already?!*

"Okay so that was embarrassing." *Good, own it!* "Anyway, I...," my throat caught. I swallowed and began again. "I have been inspired by so many people that it's hard to choose just one. Which got me thinking that we actually choose the people that are going to influence our lives. It's our choice. We're able to choose who is going to influence us because we choose which strangers become more than acquaintances. We get to choose that. So really, aren't we all as individuals the ones that inspire ourselves the most?

"Acquaintances come in and out of your life all the time. And yes, we can certainly be influenced by mere acquaintances, because some are a positive force and others are a negative energy. Sometimes I think that pain is what defines you; the way you react to adversity. I actually have been inspired by many strangers in my life. The elementary school bullies. They helped me grow. They made me stronger. The professor who gave me my first D last semester."

A few students laughed at my joke.

"I've learned to study harder," I smiled to myself. "Acquaintances can be impactful. But there's usually a reason that they remain at a distance. Whether it's because you're uncomfortable with the idea of befriending them, or they just hate you." I shrugged. "I'm stronger because of the acquaintances that have come in and out of my life.

"But it's the people that become more than acquaintances that really inspire us. The people we choose to grow with. Sometimes it's best to remain strangers. But more often than not, if you choose to let them in, they'll inspire you in more ways than you can possibly imagine."

Professor Hunter's lips were parted. He closed them and I saw his Adam's apple rise and then drop as he swallowed. He looked down and began scribbling on the piece of paper in front of him. I stood there awkwardly until he called the next student's name. I looked down as I walked back to my desk to make sure I didn't trip on anything.

Before I reached Professor Hunter's desk, I quickly glanced up and saw him smirking. He looked at me and raised one eyebrow. When he did that it almost felt like a challenge. He liked my speech. Maybe I wouldn't have to forget about him after all.

Tyler put his elbow on the edge of his desk and leaned over. "You decided to talk about me too, huh? I liked it."

I stared over at Professor Hunter. Tyler had whispered, but Professor Hunter was right in front of him. *Did*

Professor Hunter hear that?! I was talking about him in my speech, not Tyler.

Professor Hunter's shoulders slowly rose as he took a deep breath. When they fell back down, I heard a sigh escape from his lips. He ran his hand through his smooth hair and started scribbling on the next piece of paper.

After the last speech, he dismissed the class. I said goodbye to Tyler, but remained seated, fiddling with things in my backpack. When the class was empty, I stood up and walked in front of Professor Hunter's desk.

"Did you enjoy my speech, Professor Hunter?"

He looked up at me. "Miss Taylor, you'll have to wait until Monday for your grade, just like the other students."

Great, I was now lumped with all the rest of his students in his mind. I looked down so that he couldn't see that I was hurt by his words.

He lightly touched my elbow. I looked back up at him.

"But I will say that it was rather enlightening."

I almost melted under his touch.

His fingers lingered for another moment and then he let his hand fall to the desk. He stood up so that he was now towering above me. He leaned forward as he went to grab his satchel. When his head was level with mine he paused. Our faces were only a few inches apart. He flashed me a smile. "Have a good weekend, Penny," he said and then grabbed his satchel and quickly exited the room, leaving me speechless. His intoxicating scent lingered in the air for a few moments after he disappeared.

CHAPTER 19

Monday

I had eagerly waited for the weekend to end, but now that it was over I was incredibly nervous. Professor Hunter had definitely liked my speech. I had made him smile. Originally, I thought that Tyler's comment had upset him, but then Professor Hunter had acted the way he had before our kiss. He seemed to like me again.

I took great pains getting ready for class. I added a few curls to my hair with my curling iron, and then ran my hands through them to give them a looser, more natural look. After scrutinizing my closet, I ended up wearing a turquoise high low skirt and a black tank top. It was casual, yet still chic. I wanted Professor Hunter's eyes on me, and he didn't seem opposed to the more casual look. I strapped on a pair of sandals, and without another look in the mirror, I went to class.

Tyler was already in his seat. When I sat down he was all smiles. "Well, you look fantastic," he said.

"Thanks, Tyler."

"So, do you want to have lunch again on Wednesday?"

"Yeah, I'd like that. Do you think we'll get our grades today?"

"Probably. I think he was just grading them while everyone presented. Why, are you nervous that you failed?"

"Should I be?" My jittery nerves were taking a quick turn into panic mode.

"No, Penny, it was a great speech. You seemed a little nervous presenting, but so did everyone else. Besides, you did exactly what he wanted, you thought outside the box. I wouldn't be surprised if you got an A."

A moment later, Professor Hunter walked into the classroom. I turned to face him. He was wearing his usual sweater and dress shirt combo with a pair of dark jeans. He seemed to get sexier every time I saw him. His hair was sleek and sticking up a little at the top today. He was clean shaven again.

"So I have the grades here," he said and lifted a stack of papers out of his satchel. "You'll get them at the end of class. The main problem that I saw with the first speeches was the amount of eye contact."

He grabbed the podium from the corner and placed it in the middle of the room. "Okay, I'm going to give you two examples, and I want you to tell me which speech is better." He pulled out a piece of paper from his pocket and began reading it word for word without looking up:

"My older sister always inspired me growing up. She did everything first, fearlessly. And I admired her for that. Her insane courage was something that I lacked, but reveled in. She always pushed the boundaries and knew what she wanted. And she was determined enough to go after all her dreams. I just wished she had rubbed off on me a little more. Don't get me wrong, I love being your teacher. But I like to follow the rules. I like to play it safe. Because of her, though, sometimes I feel compelled to take those risky chances. Sometimes I make huge, stupid mistakes and don't look back. She inspired me to be strong."

Am I one of those huge, stupid mistakes? He wants to move forward with me!

"Okay, let me try that again. And let's see if you can see a difference." This time he gave the same speech, but only looked down once. For most of it, he gazed around the room. He made gestures with his hands. He delivered his joke a little louder and smiled to himself afterwards. He paused as the class laughed, clearly reacting to them. And he added another joke in since the class seemed to enjoy the first.

"So, which speech was better?"

A hand shot up in the front of the room.

"Yes, Miss Lang?"

"The second one. In the first one, you didn't make any eye contact. And you were pretty monotone throughout."

"Right. Was there anything else about the second one that was better?"

Another hand shot up.

"Mr. Potter?"

"You emphasized different parts of the speech and also had more personality during it. You used hand gestures and stuff."

"Right. So how many of you preferred the first speech over the second one?"

No one raised their hands.

"So why did half of you give me a speech like that first one, if you can so easily tell that the second one is better?"

Again, no one raised their hands. He turned around and wrote "fear" in all caps on the chalkboard. "Not everyone was lucky enough to have a sister like mine growing up, to help teach you how to be fearless. It's completely normal to get up here and stutter and have your knees shake. But what's there to be scared of? Me? Certainly not. Like I told you before, I'm a fairly easy grader."

I had forgotten that he had said he was an easy grader. Maybe Tyler was right. Maybe I would get an A.

"So are you scared of your peers? You shouldn't be. You'll never see the majority of them ever again after you graduate. And chances are, they aren't even listening. They're probably daydreaming about their next class or that guy or girl they have a crush on. Not that I'm encouraging this behavior. We should all be listening to each other's speeches so you can get ideas on how to improve your own. But I'm getting sidetracked. My advice for you all for your next speech is simple. Stop worrying so much. Take a walk on the wild side and be fearless."

He walked away from his podium and lifted up the stack of papers on his desk. "As soon as you get your grade, you can leave. If you have any questions about it, feel free to email me or stop by my office hours. I went easy on everyone this time, but make sure to take the advice I give to heart and try to improve for the next project. And most importantly, don't forget to make eye contact."

He began to wind around the classroom handing out the papers. When Tyler got his he said, "Score!"

"What, did your weird speech about me earn you an A?"

"Well, an A-. I guess I've found my muse." He winked at me. "See you Wednesday, Penny."

I continued to watch Professor Hunter walk around the room. Every now and then he'd call out a name that he wasn't sure of. Finally he walked to the back of the room and placed my paper face down on my desk.

I turned it over and my eyes skimmed for the grade. At the bottom of the page, in bold letters, a C- was scrawled.

What the fuck?! I quickly read through the whole sheet:

Student: Penny Taylor
Topic: Yourself/Acquaintances
Miss Taylor,

It didn't seem like you were properly prepared for this presentation, despite being one of the last students that had to present. You stumbled over your words. You failed to make sufficient eye contact with the audience. You failed to harness your audience's attention. And the general lack of confidence you portrayed left your audience wanting.

You only loosely followed the topic of the presentation, and the topic that you did choose did not seem constant. Your examples were scattered and unrelated. The presentation as a whole was unfocused. You failed to nail your point home, Miss Taylor, mainly because it was unclear what that point even was.

Grade: C-

Bullshit! I rubbed my fingers across the words and felt the raised texture of the whiteout beneath them. The original words and grade had clearly been changed. I could still see traces of the A underneath the C-. What had he originally written? I read his comments again. I could feel my anger rising. I looked up, but Professor Hunter was gone.

CHAPTER 20

Monday

After my second class of the day, I stormed over to Professor Hunter's office. I knew that like me, he had a class after Comm 212. But maybe he didn't have another one after that. I needed to talk to him now. It couldn't wait until Tuesday's office hours.

When I arrived, his office door was closed. I looked down at my phone to check the time. I had basically run over here. He could still show up. I started to pace outside of Professor Hunter's office, fuming. After several minutes passed, I went back up to his door. Just because it was closed didn't necessarily mean that he wasn't inside. I banged on the door with the fist that was holding my grade.

No answer. I knocked once more, but had the same result.

I sighed and looked down at my phone once again. It had been nearly a half hour since my last class had gotten out. He wasn't coming. I sighed and put my phone back in my bag. This was stupid. I needed a day to calm down. Then I'd come to his office hours tomorrow like a normal person, instead of whatever crazy, angry person had temporarily taken over my body.

I was just about to leave when I heard footsteps approaching. I looked behind me and saw Professor Hunter strolling toward me with a cup of coffee in his hand.

"Can I help you, Miss Taylor?"

I stayed by his door. When he reached me, I held up the paper with my grade on it. "Yeah, what the hell is this?"

He gave me a sharp look. "My office, now." He pulled out his keys from his pocket and unlocked the door. I stormed inside and he calmly followed me. He closed the door behind us and casually strolled over to his desk. He took a slow sip of his coffee and placed it on top of the desk.

"What can I do for you?" he asked.

I was still standing near the door. My hands were on my hips. "You said you were tired of hearing everyone talking about the same people in their lives. You said to think outside the box. That's what I did. This," I held the paper up again, "is bullshit, Professor Hunter."

"Please take a seat," he replied calmly.

I ignored him and walked behind his desk so that I was right next to him. I picked up the paper and quoted him: "You failed to harness your audiences' attention. I was one of the last people to go, and I still made them laugh!"

"Penny..."

"It was unclear what your point was," I quoted him again. "My point was that I choose who gets a chance at inspiring me. I said that several times, Professor Hunter. Maybe you weren't listening."

"Penny..."

"And this C- used to be an A. I can see it through the whiteout. You changed my grade. You changed it because you overheard Tyler say that the speech was about him. Well it wasn't about him. It was about you." I poked him hard in the middle of his chest. "I don't know why I ever let you kiss me. Is this a game to you, Professor Hunter?"

He drew closer to me. He looked so angry. "Penny, I'm fully aware that this isn't a game. This is my career that we're talking about."

"And this is my G.P.A." I crinkled the paper in my fist and threw it on the ground. My heart was beating fast. He was glaring down at me from under his thick eyebrows. The hunger in his eyes was a temptation I could no longer resist. I had been lying to myself this whole time. I wasn't a good girl. I was bad. And boldness suddenly came easily to me.

I reached up behind his neck and pulled his head down. Without hesitation, he tilted his head the rest of the way down and kissed me deeply. When our lips touched my whole body tingled. He placed his hands on my back and slowly let them drift to my ass. I loved his hands on me. He squeezed my ass hard and lifted me up. I wrapped my legs around him as he shoved my back against the adjacent wall. He buried his face in my neck and let his lips trace my collarbone. It sent shivers down my spine. I slid my fingers through his thick hair.

He lifted his head. "I told you to stop thinking about me." His breathing was heavy. He pressed his body even more firmly against mine.

"I can't possibly."

"You're infuriating, Penny," he whispered into my ear.

"Then punish me, Professor Hunter."

He moaned slightly at my words and pulled me off the wall. His arm bumped into a filing cabinet and sent a vase toppling off the top. It smashed against the ground, but he didn't flinch. Holding me firmly against him with one hand, he shoved the contents on his desk to the floor with his free arm. A stapler and a container of pens crashed to the floor. Papers slowly drifted to the ground as he dropped me down on top of his now empty desk. He immediately reached up my skirt and grabbed my thong. In one swift movement, he pulled it off and let it slide down my legs and onto the floor. He bent down and kissed the inside of my knee. Slowly, he let his lips trail up my inner thigh. I wanted him. I needed him inside me.

And right when his kiss would have answered my needs, he pulled me to a seated position and grabbed the sides of my tank top. I raised my hands over my head and he slowly lifted it off of me, pushing against my bare skin with his palms. With one hand he undid my bra and threw it across the room. The anger remained in his eyes. He tugged his sweater off and let me clumsily undo the buttons on his dress shirt. I reached up to his shoulders and pulled the shirt off his muscular arms, revealing his perfectly sculpted torso. I couldn't believe this was actually happening. I gulped as he leaned over top of me and pushed my naked back onto his wooden desk. I could feel his erection on my leg, trying to break free of his jeans. My hands wandered down his rock hard abs to his erection. I unbuttoned and unzipped his pants. Oh God, his cock was huge, almost falling out of his boxers. I wanted him so deep inside of me.

He leaned over and lightly sucked one of my nipples as he squeezed the other, then he brought his lips to my ear.

"You're going to want to scream," he whispered. "But don't make a sound." He moved back down to my other thigh. Again he traced his lips along my inner thigh, torturing me. I felt his warm breath lingering. And the next second his tongue answered my needs in one slow stroke.

Oh my God! No one had ever done that to me before. I felt my hips rise, wanting more. But he pressed me down and spread my thighs even wider, letting his tongue explore even deeper inside of me. I felt his tongue circling me. His left hand slid up my thigh to join his tongue. Before it did, he leaned up to me and whispered in my ear.

"Just this once, Penny." He bit my earlobe as he pressed down firmly on my clit with his thumb.

I gasped. I hadn't expected that, but it felt so good. My hips rose, wanting him inside of me, but he pushed down on me forcefully.

"Do you understand?"

"Yes," I replied breathlessly.

He grabbed my thighs and pulled me to the edge of his desk so that my legs were dangling off the sides. His finger slowly entered me and I began to writhe under his touch. He was teasing me. It was just the tip of his index finger, encircling me. I groaned softly when his tongue once again found my clit. He slid his finger all the way inside of me, and before I realized it another of his fingers had joined in. He moved them in and out, slowly, torturing me even more. Faster and faster. His tongue was in tune with his fingers. He was driving me crazy. My whole body shook as he took me over the edge.

When his fingers pulled out I moaned again. I was greedy. I wanted more. His thumb drummed against my clit as he leaned toward me.

"I know how to please, Penny," he said slowly, licking his fingers that had been inside of me. God was he sexy. He walked around the desk, trailing his fingers along my naked torso. He lifted my arms above my head.

I groaned. I couldn't stand it anymore. I had wanted this ever since meeting him in that coffee shop. I needed his huge cock inside of me.

"But you asked me to punish you." He pulled on my hands and my back slid across his desk. My head dropped off the edge so that I was looking at him upside down. He let his boxers fall to the ground and brought his dick to my face. I opened up my mouth, inviting him in. If this was only a one time thing I wanted to taste him. His pre cum was salty and delicious. I let my tongue caress and enjoy. He was too big for my mouth but all I wanted was to satisfy him. He thrust himself in and out. I tightened my lips and enjoyed the moan that escaped from his. I was wet all over again, wanting him more than ever. He leaned over and squeezed my breasts. I knew he was close. Soon he would explode in my mouth.

He climbed up on top of the desk, leaned over, and sucked my clitoris. If I didn't have his dick in my mouth I would have screamed with delight. He landed a few strokes with his tongue that sent shivers through me. Before I realized it, I was no longer giving him head. He was in total control, fucking my mouth. And I loved every mind-blowing second of it. I wanted to surrender myself completely to him, but I couldn't resist reaching up and grabbing his ass. I needed to touch him everywhere while I had the chance. It was as firm as his abs. There wasn't an ounce of fat visible on Professor Hunter's body. He pulled his delicious cock out of my mouth, climbed off the desk, and spun me around so that my ass was on the edge of his desk again. He leaned down and grabbed a condom out of his wallet. I could barely breathe.

"Profess Hunter," I panted.

"I've wanted you ever since you fell into my arms at that coffee shop." He slid the condom in place, grabbed my hips, and quickly thrust himself inside of me.

I moaned. It wasn't slow and loving. It was fast and rough. He was in complete control of me and I wasn't protesting. My back arched as his fingers dug into my hips. He went faster and faster, deeper and deeper. I loved being punished. My toes curled. I was just about to feel complete release when he stopped.

"Please," I begged.

"I asked you to be quiet," he said.

He pulled out of me and turned my body so that my stomach was now on his desk, with the tips of my toes barely on the ground. I let him pull my skirt off. I felt his hands cup my ass as he admired my naked body. No one had ever made me feel this sexy before. He parted my legs, grabbed my hips forcefully, and entered me again. My breathing hitched. He slid himself slowly in and out. His fingertips traced the back of my thighs.

"Professor Hunter," I moaned.

He grabbed my hair and pulled my head back. The sensation made me tense and Professor Hunter moaned as I tightened around him. He slid his free hand along the arch in my back, giving me chills. I couldn't wait another second. I placed my hands on the side of the desk and pushed so that he'd be deep inside me once again.

He grabbed my breasts and squeezed them. I arched my back so that I was no longer on the desk as I reached one arm back and let myself pull on his hair. He kissed my raised arm gently and then pushed me back onto the desk.

"Stay still," he said forcefully.

He held me down and spanked me hard. I wouldn't resist his dominance again. I wanted him to own me. He placed another hard slap on my other ass cheek. I wanted him to claim every inch of my body. The sensation of pain and pleasure was bringing me to the tipping point. Then it was suddenly faster and harder than before. I could feel my hips digging into the edge of his desk. No one had ever been this deep inside of me. His fingernails dug into my skin. He spanked me again and I clenched myself around him.

He groaned and reached one hand down to find my clit.

"Yes!" I moaned.

He stroked it possessively. I let myself come as his cock seemed to harden even more in its release. My whole body shuddered as my orgasm washed over me.

He was panting. "Mmmmm," he sighed. He pulled out and turned me over. He stared down at me. I suddenly felt unbelievably exposed. He bit his lip and ran his hand through his hair.

"Penny."

"Professor Hunter."

His Adam's apple rose and fell. He pulled the condom off and tossed it in the trash.

"I like being punished," I said.

"I like punishing you." He pulled his jeans back in place and slowly buttoned his shirt, leaving the top few buttons undone. He rolled up the sleeves.

I didn't want it to end. I didn't want his body to be hidden underneath his clothes.

"I have a class that I must get to or I'd be tempted to have you again." He lifted his satchel over his shoulder. "By the way, you gave a fair argument. I'll reconsider your grade."

I felt my jaw drop slightly as he let his eyes rest on my exposed breasts. I wanted to say something enticing and sexy but my mind was foggy. This had surpassed even my wildest fantasies of him.

"Please lock the door when you leave." He let his eyes linger on my body for one more moment before walking out of the office and closing the door behind him.

He left me naked and alone in his office, more addicted to him than ever.

PART 2

CHAPTER 21

Monday

It looked like a tornado had just swept through the small office. Papers were scattered all over, some seeping in the coffee that had spilled on the floor. A broken vase lay on the ground in fragments. *Just this once.* How could he expect me to give him up now?

I put my arms across my naked body to cover myself and climbed off of Professor Hunter's desk. My bra was in the corner next to a filing cabinet. I maneuvered around the obstacle of pens on the ground and quickly clasped it back on. My skirt, tank top, and underwear were lying by his desk. The shirt was partially wet from landing in the pool of coffee on the floor. I put it on anyway.

I let my breath escape after I had finished dressing and looked around the room. This was the only professor's office I had ever been to, but I assumed it was similar to everyone else's. The only thing that seemed out of place, besides for the office supplies strewn all over the floor, was the suitcase in the corner. Was he planning on going somewhere? I ran my finger along the edge of his desk as I walked behind it and sat in his chair. His scent was everywhere. I took a deep breath. *Just this once.* Why did I agree to that? Looking at the desk, thinking of what we had just done, made me want him all over again.

I stared at the closed drawers. Every inch of me wanted to go through them and his suitcase. But I didn't want to snoop. I wanted him to trust me. If he trusted me then maybe this could be more. I leaned back in his chair and felt the softness of the sweater he had left behind. A smile spread across my lips. It didn't need to be just this once. It couldn't be just this once. When I stood up I was a little sore. A chill ran up my spine as I remembered him inside of me. I grabbed a sheet of paper and a pen from the ground, sat back down, and wrote him a note:

Professor Hunter,

Thank you for listening to my argument. But I don't think I've learned my lesson. You might need to show me that again.

P.S. I borrowed your sweater.

Just in case someone came in before him, I decided against signing it. I pushed the note into the middle of his empty desk and placed the pen on top of it. I got up and shoved his sweater into my backpack. I turned the lock on the inside of the door, smoothed my tank top, and then walked confidently out of Professor Hunter's office, closing the door behind me. *Just this once my ass.*

***

I was sitting on my bed daydreaming. The T.V. was on so that Melissa wouldn't grow suspicious of the glazed look over my eyes. She was too good at identifying my

TEMPTATION

different moods. Just thinking about what had happened earlier made my heart race.

My phone buzzed. When I looked down I gulped. It was Professor Hunter. I had been hoping all day that he'd text me, and now he finally had. The message read: "I see that you've taken another one of my sweaters."

I felt the smile spread over my face. I typed out, "I was a bit chilly after you left me naked and alone in your office, Professor Hunter," and pressed send.

Professor Hunter: "I apologize for my abrupt departure. But you barged into my office at a rather inconvenient time."

Me: "And when would be a convenient time?"

I heard Melissa's book slam shut, and I jumped slightly.

"You should see the look on your face, Penny. Who on earth are you talking to?!" Melissa asked and flung one of the pillows off her bed and at my face.

I dodged the pillow and looked up at her, but I couldn't get the stupid smile off my face. "No one," I said, and quickly exited out of my message thread with Professor Hunter and slid my phone under my covers.

"Oh my God, Penny. I've never seen you like this. Tell me!"

"No one, Melissa. I was just looking through some old messages." I could feel my face blushing. I was such an awful liar.

"Bullshit! If you were looking at old messages then I would have seen you acting like this whenever you got them in the first place. Give me your phone." Melissa hopped off her bed and ran over to me.

- 111 -

Oh crap! I couldn't let her see the messages that I had been sending to Professor Hunter. "Tyler!" I almost screamed. "It's Tyler, okay."

Melissa squealed and jumped onto my bed. "I was hoping this would happen! You and Tyler are so cute together. And this is so perfect. Since Josh and Tyler are friends, now the four of us can hang out all the time!"

I tried to hide my sigh. "Right now we're just having fun flirting, okay? No double dates yet. Please, Melissa? I'm begging you."

"Fine," she rolled her eyes and hopped off my bed. "But you'll be happy to know that Sigma Pi is having another party this Friday. So we can at least get ready together."

"He hasn't asked me to come," I protested.

"Then just ask him about it."

"But we're taking things slow. If he hasn't asked me, he probably doesn't want me to come."

"Don't be ridiculous, Penny. Just ask him then. Clearly you're both into each other."

"But..."

"If you don't do it, I'll text him for you." She had that stubborn look on her face. She always seemed to get whatever she wanted.

This was a complete disaster. I didn't see a way out of this one. If Melissa got my phone she'd open up my messages and see that I had been texting Professor Hunter. *Game over.* But wasn't it already over? I silently wished that *just this once* really meant *this is just the start.*

"Okay, fine," I conceded. "We're going to lunch on Wednesday, so I'll ask him then." I had planned on canceling lunch after what had happened this afternoon. Now, not only was I not canceling, but I was making yet another date with Tyler. I felt awful.

Melissa seemed content with my response. "Let's go shopping sometime this week, okay? I don't think you have anything appropriate for the party's theme."

"Oh God, what is the theme?"

"Guess."

"Conservative outfits throughout the ages?"

"Toss me that pillow back so I can throw it at you again!"

"Just tell me the theme."

"It's going to be a luau!"

"You mean like tiki torches and everyone running around in bathing suits?"

"Yep." She clapped her hands together in excitement.

"Yeah, I'm not going to that."

"I swear, Penny, you're going to end up being a lonely cat lady if you keep acting like that. Take a risk every now and then." Melissa sighed and sat back on her bed.

I couldn't help but smile. If she had any idea what I had done with Professor Hunter she'd be high-fiving me instead of scolding me. I had to resist the urge to tell her.

"I'll ask Tyler about it on Wednesday like I said. Goodnight, Melissa." I switched off the light on my desk and pulled the covers up under my neck. Pretending to be asleep, I closed my eyes and listened to Melissa turn off her light and get in bed. When I heard her light snoring, I lifted my covers over my head and pulled out my phone.

There was a message from Professor Hunter. "It would be most convenient after you graduate in the spring."

I held my breath. The lie of me being a senior was looming over my head. He had assumed I was a senior like everyone else in his Comm class seemed to be. And he had escorted me home one night because I was drunk. I couldn't tell him the truth. But what would he do when he found out I was only a sophomore? Maybe he wouldn't care. He liked me. He didn't want it to be just a one-time thing either. He wanted to date me after I was no longer a student.

"What happened to just this once?" I replied.

A minute later I got his response. "We can discuss it over dinner. I will pick you up on Saturday at 8."

I pulled my phone to my chest and smiled. I had a date with Professor Hunter. *A date!* I liked how affirmative he was. I gulped, remembering his lips on my neck.

"I'll be waiting," I typed back and pressed send. He was as addicted as me. I fell asleep dreaming about our tryst.

CHAPTER 22

Wednesday

On Wednesday morning I was twenty minutes early for class. I drummed my fingers across my desk as I impatiently waited for Professor Hunter to come through the door. As the clock slowly ticked forward, students eventually started to arrive.

Tyler sat down next to me. "So how did you do on your first speech?" he asked.

I felt my face blushing. "Really well, actually." It didn't feel like a lie. Hopefully Professor Hunter would change my grade to the A it originally was.

"I knew it," he said and nudged my shoulder playfully. "What are you feeling for lunch today?"

I had been so consumed by Professor Hunter that I had nearly forgotten about lunch. And Melissa. *Oh no, the luau.* "Do you want to just get pizza somewhere?"

"Pizza sounds perfect. How about Grottos?"

"I was hoping you'd say that. It's my favorite." I smiled.

The class drew quiet when Professor Hunter entered the room and I stopped breathing momentarily. He pulled his satchel off over his head and placed it on his desk. He was more dressed up than usual in dress pants and a button down shirt. A tie was tucked behind a vest that matched his pants.

"I only had a few people complain to me about their grades, so I'm glad that we're all on the same page. I think we'll all be seeing even better speeches for the next assignment. Speaking of which, have any of you read ahead in the syllabus to find out what the next speech is about?"

A girl in the front center of the classroom raised her hand.

"Yes, Miss Snyder?"

"We're supposed to tell you about why we chose our majors."

"Precisely. There's usually a pretty personal reason why we choose the majors that we do. Whether it's about who you want to become, impressing your parents, or maybe just not knowing what the heck you want to do after you graduate. I find this topic to be quite beneficial for seniors, because maybe a look inside that true reason will help you decide which jobs you should be starting to apply to. So today let's go around and state what your majors are and one thing you love about them. Raymond, you're up." Professor Hunter sat down in his chair.

When Tyler stood up, I realized that I had been daydreaming. I had been staring at Professor Hunter and had completely tuned out everyone. When he called my name I slowly stood. I loved the feeling of his eyes on me.

"I'm majoring in marketing."

Professor Hunter seemed to sit up straighter as he listened to me.

"And mostly I love the creativity behind it." I sat down. I couldn't think of anything super exciting and interesting to enchant him with today. Hopefully I'd be able to think of something better for the actual speech.

When class was dismissed I dillydallied as usual. Before Tyler left he asked, "Meet at Grottos at 12:30?"

"Sounds good."

He smiled and walked out of the room. I went straight for Professor Hunter's desk once the class had emptied out.

"I'm surprised to hear that you're majoring in marketing, Miss Taylor."

I didn't want to be formal. I wanted him to kiss me, but I knew that he couldn't. Not here. But I could barely control myself when I looked at his lips. "Why does that surprise you?"

He stood up and pulled his satchel over his shoulder. "I'm just surprised that it's taken us this long to run into each other, since I'm a marketing professor."

I gulped. I was only taking my first marketing class this semester. *Should I tell him I'm only a sophomore?* No. I didn't want him to call off our date. I'd tell him soon, though.

"I guess we weren't supposed to meet until now," I replied.

"I take it you're a believer in fate then?"

I nodded. "And you?"

He took a step closer to me. "I don't know what I believe. But I know what I want."

I was about to ask him what he wanted, but I didn't need to. I stopped breathing as he stared at me with his intense brown eyes. He wanted me. Again.

He was making me so nervous. "I'm going to be late for my next class, Professor Hunter."

"I'm not stopping you."

But he was stopping me. When he looked at me like that I couldn't move. I just wanted to enjoy having his eyes on me.

"Why are you so dressed up?" I couldn't resist the temptation to ask him. He looked like he was dressed for another date with the mystery woman from his office. If he was hiding a girlfriend, I could hide my age.

"I have a work function after I'm done classes today."

"Oh?"

He lifted up his arm and looked at his watch. "You don't want to be late, Miss Taylor. And neither do I." He smiled at me, shoved his hands in his pockets, and casually strolled out the door.

He was being so secretive. I couldn't help but feel jealous of the mystery woman as I quickly tried to make it to my next class on time.

CHAPTER 23

Wednesday

I walked up to Grottos' entrance and found Tyler leaning against the wall outside and looking at his phone.

"Hey," I said.

He smiled up at me and shoved his phone in his pocket. He put his arm out for me. I laughed and put my arm through his, and he escorted me into the restaurant.

"Table for two," he said to the hostess.

"Right this way," she replied.

We followed her to a table and I sat down and picked up the menu.

"What kind of pizza do you like?" Tyler asked.

"I guess I really don't need to look at this," I laughed and put the menu down. "Cheese. I always order just cheese."

"Sounds good to me."

When the waitress came over I ordered a cherry Coke and Tyler ordered a Sprite and a large cheese pizza.

"So," Tyler said and scooted forward a bit on his chair. "I guess I'm going to have to figure out the answer to the question I passed on."

"Hmmm?"

"You had asked me what I want to do after I graduate. I'm going to need to figure that out for our next speech."

"Oh, right!" I smiled. "What did you say your major was again?" I should have already known the answer from class today, but I hadn't been paying attention.

"Do you always daydream during Comm?"

I laughed. "I don't daydream. If you haven't noticed, I get incredibly nervous talking in front of the whole class." It was a lie. I always seemed to be daydreaming about Professor Hunter. During Stat I hadn't even tried to make out what the heck my foreign professor was saying. I was just picturing the hunger in Professor Hunter's eyes.

"Yeah, which is incredibly cute."

I couldn't help blushing.

"I'm double majoring in finance and economics," he said.

I was a little surprised. "Really? I wouldn't have guessed that in a million years. You must be really smart."

He laughed. "Does that surprise you?"

"It doesn't surprise me that you're smart. It's just that you're really funny and endearing. Why such serious majors?"

"Yeah, I don't know. They just seemed like logical choices I guess. And I really don't have a clue what I want to do when I graduate."

"You'll need to do some soul searching before your speech then."

"I guess so. Anyway, this was leading me to the fact that you're going to need to answer the question that you passed on."

"What was that again?" I asked, pretending to look confused.

The waitress came over and placed our drinks on the table.

"I know you remember the question."

I took a sip of my soda and stared innocently at Tyler.

He laughed. "I asked you what the most scandalous thing you've ever done was."

When he had first asked me the question in the dining hall, I completely freaked out. Professor Hunter had just kissed me. But now it was so much more than that. A kiss didn't seem nearly as scandalous. Before I even knew what I was doing I was answering his question:

"I kissed a professor once." I tried to say it nonchalantly.

Tyler laughed. After a few seconds of silence he said, "Wait, are you serious?"

"Well, he kissed me, actually."

"Which professor was it?" I could hear a hint of jealousy in his voice.

The waitress arrived and placed the pizza down on the rack in the middle of the table. "One cheese pizza," she said with a smile. "Anything else I can get for you?"

Tyler continued to stare at me.

"No thanks," I said to her and she walked away.

"Penny? Which professor?"

Why couldn't I keep my mouth shut? It just felt so good to finally tell someone. "Yeah, I'm not going to tell you that. That's the most scandalous thing I've ever done though. Consider the question answered." I grabbed a slice of pizza and put it on my plate.

"Where did you kiss?" Tyler asked.

"Not answering that."

"How long ago was it?"

"Not answering that."

"Were you trying to get your grade changed or something?"

"No!" *Kind of.*

"Was it just the one kiss?"

"Tyler!"

"Fine. But for a scandalous story, you left out a lot of the scandalous details."

"I think kissing a professor counts as scandalous enough." I took a bite of the pizza. "Sooo good."

Tyler smiled at me and grabbed a slice for himself. "You are quite intriguing, Penny."

As I ate my pizza, I thought about the luau I was supposed to ask him about. I couldn't say no if he invited me, or Melissa would be suspicious of me. Would Professor Hunter be mad if I went? He couldn't be. He was probably dating other people too. And were we even dating? I was so confused. And I could always say I was sick at the last minute.

"So my roommate, Melissa, is getting along really well with your friend Josh."

"Yeah, Josh really likes her." Tyler was looking at me curiously.

"What?"

"Well. I know you're still getting over your ex. And I completely understand that that takes time. But it physically hurts me to know that someone as beautiful as you is just sitting in your dorm room every weekend. It's a sin."

I blushed. "I like staying in."

"How about you make an exception this Friday?"

"What did you have in mind?" Oh good, he was going to ask me. Asking him just so I could cancel later seemed horrid.

"My frat is having this luau thing. I was hoping you could come."

"As friends?"

"As my date, Penny. God you're infuriating."

That's what Professor Hunter had said to me right before our second kiss. Right before the mind-blowing sex that I was sure could never be topped. *Am I really that infuriating?*

"I'll come as your friend," I replied.

Tyler smiled and shrugged. "It starts at 10. Did you want to meet me there?"

"Yeah, I can walk over with Melissa."

"Great." He looked pleased with himself despite my denying it was a date.

My stomach churned with guilt. Tyler was so sweet. I always laughed with him and had fun. I felt like I could always be myself around him. And he really was handsome. His crystal blue eyes always made me smile. But he deserved someone who wasn't daydreaming about their professor half the time.

When the check came I rummaged through my backpack for my share. Tyler pulled out a twenty and placed it on the table.

"I'll pay for half," I protested.

"Don't be ridiculous." He stood up and put his hand out for me to grab.

I took it and let him pull me up out of my chair.

"Thanks for lunch," I said.

"Hey, what are friends for?" he said with a smile.

CHAPTER 24

Friday

My new bikini was hanging in my closet. I already knew I was going to cancel, but pretending to be excited and shopping with Melissa would hopefully only help make my sudden upset stomach more believable. I didn't like deceiving her, but she could be so relentless. If she ever became suspicious of me she'd easily be able to get the truth out of me. And Melissa couldn't find out. I didn't want Professor Hunter to get in trouble. And I certainly didn't want to get in trouble.

I lay down in my bed and tucked the covers under my chin. During class earlier I had watched Professor Hunter's lips move but I couldn't seem to concentrate on the words that he spoke. Instead, I pictured him shoving everything on his desk to the ground and having sex with me right in the classroom. I pictured him pressing my naked back against the chalkboard.

I gulped. He said we could talk about it tomorrow night at dinner. But if he really was just going to end whatever it was that was going on between us, he could have done it already. He wanted to have dinner because he wanted to keep seeing me. Or start seeing me. I was already nervous just thinking about it. If he took me to a fancy restaurant he would order wine or something and wonder why I was just drinking water. I'd have to tell him I was only 19. This was going to be a disaster. I needed to see what he had to say though. Because I couldn't stop thinking about him. If Professor Hunter felt the same, maybe there was some way we could make this work.

Melissa walked in the room with a huge smile on her face. But as soon as she saw me in bed she put her hands on her hips. "Penny, what are you doing?"

"I don't feel well." I tried to make a pained expression.

"You just don't want to wear that bikini. You'll live. Get up."

"Melissa, my stomach is really upset."

"Are you throwing up?"

"Well, no, but..."

"Good. There's two hours until the party starts. Have some Tums." She tossed me a bottle from her bureau.

I unscrewed the cap and popped two in my mouth. Fortunately they were also a calcium supplement or I'd have to spit them out when she wasn't looking.

"You're probably just nervous to see Tyler. It's called butterflies. There's absolutely nothing wrong with you."

She wasn't going to let me get out of this easily. I quickly got out of bed, clutched my stomach, and ran for the door. Melissa looked up at me from her desk.

"Penny, are you..."

I didn't hear the rest of her sentence because the door had closed behind me. Keeping my hands on my stomach I walked to the bathroom. If there was one thing Melissa hated it was hearing about bodily fluids. This would make her stop bugging me. I sat in the bathroom stall for ten minutes before heading back to the room.

I groaned as I entered our room and plopped down on my bed.

"Penny?" Melissa sounded concerned.

"I really don't feel well. I just ruined a toilet," I lied.

"Oh my God, Penny. You're disgusting. Please spare me the details."

"I don't even understand how all of that was in me."

"Ew! Stop. Please, Penny. You're grossing me out."

"Sorry, I just really don't feel well."

"Okay, okay. Just stop talking." Melissa walked over to the fridge and pulled out a ginger ale. "Here, hopefully this will help." She opened up the top and placed it on the desk by my bed.

"I'm really sorry I can't come." I lifted the soda and took a small sip.

"Don't even mention it. Look, you should probably get some sleep. I'm just going to get ready there." She tossed some things in her backpack and lifted it over her shoulder. "Anything you need before I go?"

"Will you let Tyler know I'm sick? And that I'm sorry that I couldn't come?"

"Yeah of course."

"Thanks, Melissa."

She picked up the trashcan and put it next to my bed. "Just in case. Feel better, Penny!" she said with a smile and hurried out of the room.

***

Shark Tank was all I needed to be happy on a Friday night. Well, that and thoughts of Professor Hunter. I had already picked out my outfit for tomorrow night. And Melissa was right, there were butterflies in my stomach. They just weren't for Tyler. I was a little nervous to see Professor Hunter again, but mostly I was worried about dinner. I had practiced saying "I just want water" in the mirror. He couldn't know I was under 21. Not yet. Not before we had explored what this really was between us. I just hoped he wouldn't press the issue.

The sharks were starting to get irritated with each other. Just as Kevin O'Leary went on a rant about his elite wine club, my phone buzzed. I picked it up and swiped my finger across the screen.

Tyler: "Hey, I'm sorry to hear you can't come tonight."

"Yeah, I'm sorry too, Tyler," I responded. "Some other time," I added and pressed send.

Tyler: "There is something you can do to make it up to me."

I laughed. "And what might that be?"

Tyler: "Come let me in."

Me: "Wait, what?" *Shit, is he here?* He was supposed to spend the night having fun at the luau and meeting someone else. What was he doing here?

Tyler: "I'm standing outside Sussex. Melissa told me this was your dorm. Hopefully she didn't lie to me."

I jumped out of my bed, pulled on a pair of sweatpants over my pajama shorts, and put a bra on under my tank top. I was such a bad liar; this was going to go horribly. He would probably know I wasn't sick. I pulled a few tissues out of their box, wadded them up, and tossed them around the room.

Crap. I had an upset stomach, not a cold. I grabbed all the tissues and shoved them in the waste bin. I picked up the dirty clothes off the floor and put them into the hamper. I smoothed my hair down and looked in the mirror. This was a disaster. I quickly slid on my slippers and went to go let him in.

Tyler smiled when I opened the door. "Hey, Penny," he said.

"Hi, Tyler. I really don't feel well."

"That's why I'm here. Friends help each other feel better when they're sick." He emphasized the word "friends."

"But I don't want to get you sick."

He pretended to cough. "I haven't really been feeling very well either."

"It's my stomach," I laughed.

"Oh. Well, my stomach has been really upset too. So we can just be sick together." He walked through the door I was holding open for him. "So, where's your room?"

I laughed. "If you insist." I walked back up the stairs and he followed me. I opened the door to my room and let him in.

"So remember when I promised you that our next date would be sweatpants, popcorn, and a movie?"

"Tyler..."

"Yeah, yeah, I know. This isn't a date. But..." he rummaged in his backpack and pulled out a bag of un-popped microwave popcorn. "I figured since you were sick you might be wearing sweatpants." He looked down at my legs. "And I was correct. I made sure to wear some too." He was wearing dark gray sweatpants and a white t-shirt. He put the popcorn in the microwave and pulled a DVD out of his bag. "And I brought a movie."

He really was a sweet guy. "Tyler, I can't ask you to miss your party for this. Melissa made it seem like it was going to be lots of fun."

"Trust me, there is nothing I'd rather be doing." He handed me the disc. I looked down and saw that it was The Princess Bride.

"This is my favorite movie."

"Yeah. I'd be lying if I didn't confess that Melissa told me. But I already owned it, because I like it too." He smiled at me as he pulled the popcorn out of the microwave, then sat on the end of my bed.

I put the movie in and sat down next to him.

"Popcorn?" he asked and put the bag down between us.

"You're a really good friend, Tyler."

"Yeah I know." He laughed and put his arms behind his head and leaned against the wall.

"No seriously. I've never really had a guy friend that was genuinely nice just because he cared."

"Honestly, I'm just paying my dues." He winked at me. "But I like being friends with you too. And since we're just friends, I can do stuff like this and not get in trouble." He slid over and put his arm around my back.

"Is that right?"

"I'm just here to take care of you." He tapped his shoulder that was closest to me.

"So I guess since we're friends I'm supposed to rest my head on your shoulder?"

"Well, I mean if you want. I just had an itch. But I promise I won't read into it."

I leaned my head on his shoulder. In the movie, Westley was just saying goodbye to Buttercup so he could go off and find a fortune so that they could get married.

"I never understood why she was always so mean to him at first," Tyler said.

"Because she didn't realize that she loved him yet."

"Right," Tyler said. He rested his head on top of mine.

CHAPTER 25

Saturday

My head rose and fell with his breath. I was dreaming about Professor Hunter again; dreaming about being wrapped in his strong arms. I listened to his slow, steady heartbeat. I could lay here forever in his embrace. I let my hand wander beneath his shirt and felt his abs. His body seemed to tense from my touch, which made his muscles even more pronounced. He was so sexy.

"Are you feeling any better?" he whispered.

I almost jumped out of my skin. Tyler. I was with Tyler, not Professor Hunter. We must have fallen asleep watching the movie. I pulled my hand out from under his shirt and sat up.

"You lovebirds must have been exhausted. It's almost noon," Melissa laughed.

Oh my God, Melissa's here? All I wanted to do was disappear back into my dream. I felt my face flushing. "We fell asleep watching a movie," I said quietly. I didn't want to look down at Tyler and I didn't want to make eye contact with Melissa so I just stared at my lap.

"Sure," Melissa said.

I heard Tyler yawn as he sat up beside me. "Good morning, Melissa."

He rubbed his hand on my back. "Penny?"

"Yeah. I do feel better. Thanks, Tyler." I still didn't look at him. What had I done? This was the opposite of what was supposed to happen last night. And why had I just touched his abs? *He had really nice abs. What the hell is wrong with me?*

"Did you want to get something to eat?" Tyler asked.

"Yes, we'd love to," Melissa answered for me. Her coming to the dining hall with us was going to be a disaster. Everything was a disaster!

Tyler hopped off the bed. "Do you mind if I borrow this?" He lifted up the mouthwash from my dresser.

"No, go ahead." He took a swig and walked out of the room.

"Oh my God, Penny! Spill it."

"Nothing happened." I slid off the bed and quickly changed into jean shorts and a t-shirt. I tried hard not to make eye contact with her.

"I don't believe that for a second. You both slept so long. Like you just had sex long."

"I was sick."

"Yeah sure. Why aren't you giving me the details? Was he small or something?"

"No!"

"So he's big?"

"Melissa!" I smoothed my hair and pulled it back into a ponytail. "We're just friends."

"He doesn't look at you like you're his friend."

I grabbed my shower caddy and went to the bathroom without hearing what else she had to say. I brushed my teeth and washed my face without looking in the mirror. This was getting out of hand. I needed to find Tyler a girlfriend so that I could stop lying to both him and Melissa. My addiction to Professor Hunter wasn't going anywhere. I was already breaking rules if I was going to date him. I didn't want to have to feel bad about anything else on top of that.

***

"Okay, Tyler," Melissa said as she sat down across from us in the dining hall. "I can't get the truth out of Penny, so I'm going to ask you instead. You guys had wild sex last night, right?"

"Not wild sex, no." Tyler laughed.

"But you did have sex?" Melissa asked. My face was turning scarlet.

"No. We're just friends." He shrugged and smiled at me.

"Ugh, you're both ridiculous."

Tyler laughed again.

"I hate to break it to you, Tyler, but friends don't usually sleep together."

"We didn't sleep together sleep together. We just fell asleep together."

"So, you're trying to tell me that you don't like Penny?" Melissa never backed down easily.

"No, I hate her guts. She's the worst."

"Hey!" I said and nudged his shoulder.

"So, Penny, you're telling me that if you found out Tyler was dating someone you'd be okay with that?" Melissa was staring at me.

Tyler silently took a bite of his bagel.

"Yes. I'd be happy for him."

"Prove it," she replied.

"Wait, what?" Tyler asked.

"Go ask a girl out. There are at least fifty in here right now. I'm sure one of them would say yes. I can point out a few that have definitely checked you out since you've sat down."

"Look, I don't want..."

"See. That's because you like Penny. Boys and girls can't be just friends. It doesn't work. I have homework to do. I will let you two soak in your denial." Melissa left the table.

"Your roommate doesn't like to be wrong," Tyler said once Melissa was out of earshot.

"Tell me about it," I sighed.

Tyler finished his bagel and turned to me. "So is that what you really want? For me to be dating other people?"

"Well we're friends. I want you to be happy."

"Right." He pushed his scrambled eggs around with his fork. "Well I actually have lots of homework I have to get to too. I'm glad you're feeling better." He stood up and grabbed his tray.

"Tyler?"

He walked away without looking back at me.

CHAPTER 26

Saturday

As I got ready for my date with Professor Hunter, I tried not to think about hurting Tyler's feelings. I truly did want him to be happy. And I wasn't the person that could do that for him. He deserved better. I just hoped we could remain friends because he had become one of my closest friends since we had met.

Professor Hunter hadn't told me where we were going, but I assumed we were going out to eat. Fortunately Melissa was out to dinner with Josh, or else I would have had to sneak around and get ready in the bathroom. I put on a strapless, summery dress and added a brown belt above my waist. I strapped on a pair of high heeled sandals and looked at myself in the mirror. I added some red lipstick because I liked to think that it made me look a little older.

My alarm went off, letting me know that it was 8 o'clock. I grabbed my clutch and made my way to the curb behind Sussex where Professor Hunter had dropped me off before. His sleek black car was already waiting there. Before I reached the car Professor Hunter stepped out. He was wearing a perfectly fitted black suit with a white dress shirt underneath and a black tie. Just seeing him made my knees shake.

He walked around the car and opened up the door for me.

"Hi, Professor Hunter."

He grabbed my face in both his hands, leaned in, and kissed me deeply. We were supposed to discuss us, but instead all I wanted to do was rip off all his clothes again. He pulled away far too soon.

"Good evening, Penny." He tilted his head, motioning for me to get in the car. "We should get going. We have a reservation." I slowly stepped back and got into the car. He closed the door behind me.

He sat down in the driver's seat and we sped off into the night.

"Where are we going?"

"Someplace where we can be alone."

His words sent chills down my spine. "But I haven't had anything to eat." He made me so nervous.

He had a funny look on his face. "Yes, I'm taking you to dinner."

I was a little confused, but I decided to wait and see. I always loved surprises. "So you wanted to discuss what you meant by just this once?"

"I meant what I said."

"Oh." I turned to look out the window. We were on I-95, cruising by all the other cars. The trees were a blur. I felt like I was going to be sick. "I don't understand why you asked me to dinner then."

"Because I've changed my mind."

I tried to slow my breathing. "Why?" I turned back to look at him.

He took his attention away from the road for a second. "Because I can't stop thinking about you, Penny."

I gulped. "I can't stop thinking about you either." We drove in silence for a few moments. I couldn't believe this was happening. "Did you grow up around here?"

"No. I'm from New York."

"What made you come here to teach then?" I was reminded of Melissa saying that he had gotten fired from his last job. Had he worked as a professor in New York?

"I needed a change."

"Did you live in the city?"

"Yes."

"I understand why you needed a change then."

He laughed. "Not a fan of New York City?"

"Everything is so loud and busy all the time. And everyone seems so depressed on the subway."

"I wouldn't know, I rarely rode the subway."

"I'm sure the taxi's aren't much better. And there's not enough grass."

He laughed again. "Well it is very different from here. Is this where you grew up?"

"I live about an hour away. Well, an hour from school. I don't really know where we are now."

We pulled up to a huge building. There was a tennis court to the right and a pool beside it. Behind them I could just make out a golf course in the dark. A valet quickly came to my door and opened it for me.

"Welcome, madam," he said and put out his hand for me to grab. No one had ever called me madam before. I took his hand and he pulled me out of my seat and closed the passenger side door. Professor Hunter stepped out of the car and the valet walked over.

"Hello, Mr. Hunter," the valet said with a huge smile. "I've heard so much about you."

Professor Hunter handed the valet the key. "Thank you." Professor Hunter walked over to me and put his hand on the small of my back. He escorted me into the building.

My heels clicked on the white marble floor. The biggest chandelier I had ever seen hung above us. A woman with her breasts pushed up to almost her chin walked up to us. "Mr. Hunter. Your table is ready." She seemed nervous to be talking to us.

We followed her down a hallway and entered an elegant restaurant. I wasn't dressed nearly fancy enough. Most of the women wore lace dresses and the men were in suits like Professor Hunter. It felt like they were all staring at me. But as we made our way to the back of the restaurant I realized that they were staring at Professor Hunter. I didn't blame them, he was so handsome. But I felt a little jealous.

The woman showed us into a private room in the back. There was a roaring fire and an elegant loveseat to one side. In the middle of the room was a table with a beautiful flower arrangement in the center. A bottle of wine and two glasses were already on the table. *Oh no, they are going to ask me for my I.D.*

Instead of questioning my age, the woman said, "Your waiter will be right with you," and walked out of the room, closing the door behind her.

I turned to Professor Hunter. "Where are we?"

"My country club."

Memberships for country clubs were usually extremely expensive. I hadn't realized that Professor Hunter was wealthy. That was probably why he never rode the subway. Professor Hunter walked over to the table and pulled my chair out for me.

"No one's ever pulled out a chair for me before." I sat down and stared at him as he sat down across from me. I was experiencing a lot of firsts tonight.

"Then you haven't been dating the right people."

Dating. Were we dating? "And I've never been to a country club before. Do you come here often?"

"This is actually only the second time that I've been here."

"Oh, so you just joined?" That explained why people were staring. They had never seen him before. They were wondering who the new person was.

"Yes. Earlier this week actually."

Just at that moment the waiter walked in and hurried over to the table. "Good evening. My name is Jerrod. It is my pleasure to be serving you tonight, Mr. and Mrs. Hunter."

I was about to tell Jerrod that we weren't married when Professor Hunter gave me a mischievous smile. Jerrod started telling us about their daily specials but I couldn't stop staring into Professor Hunter's eyes. Jerrod uncorked the bottle of wine and poured us each a glass while he was talking.

After Jerrod was done his spiel, Professor Hunter said we would need a minute to look at the menu. I skimmed through mine, trying to find the cheapest thing as Jerrod left the room. Most of the meals were as much as the used textbooks I always bought for classes. I didn't feel comfortable letting Professor Hunter pay for this.

"Penny?" He reached over and grabbed my hand.

"Professor Hunter, I've never had food that costs this much. What did you say this place was called? The name isn't even listed on the menu." I picked up my glass with my free hand and took a sip of the wine.

"I was thinking Hunter Creek Country Club."

I coughed, choking on my wine. *Hunter.* The way he was greeted, the way that people stared. I already felt like he was out of my league, but now I felt completely inferior. What was he doing with a girl like me? "Professor Hunter, do you own this country club?"

"It seemed like a good place for a first date."

So you bought it? "What exactly did you do in New York?"

"I was a professor."

"For how long?"

He lowered his eyebrows slightly as he looked at me. "Less than a year."

"And before that?"

"I owned a startup. Would you mind if I ask you a question?"

The mystery of who Professor Hunter was had barely started to unfold and he wanted to talk about me? I wasn't the one that was interesting. "What did you want to know?"

"Everything."

The way he said it made me blush. He had already seen me naked. He had already had me in the most intimate way. "There really isn't that much to know," I said.

"I don't believe that's true. You enjoy challenging me and aren't afraid to speak your mind. I find you unbelievably refreshing ."

I took another sip of wine. I felt so nervous under his gaze.

"So why is it that you don't feel like you're interesting?" he asked.

I gulped and looked up at him. It was because of Austin and all the times that he made me feel insignificant. "Honestly, you're the first person that's ever made me feel like I'm the only girl in the room. I'm not used to feeling like I matter."

Jerrod came in to take our order. I looked back down at the menu. I scanned the menu for something that wouldn't get stuck in my teeth. Professor Hunter reached his hand out and grabbed mine again.

"Penny, I've heard that the crab cakes are wonderful here."

I smiled, relieved that I didn't have to choose. "That sounds perfect."

Professor Hunter ordered for us. When Jerrod left the room, Professor Hunter put his elbows on the table and leaned in slightly. "When we're together, I can assure you that I don't see anyone else in the room. You always have my undivided attention."

"That must make grading other student's speeches quite difficult."

Professor Hunter laughed. "It does."

His words should have comforted me, but all I seemed to be able to focus on was when he had said "when we're together." I was reminded of the woman from his office. I wasn't necessarily the only person he was dating. If we even were dating.

Professor Hunter reached in his pocket, pulled out a penny, and slid it across the table. "A penny for your thoughts?"

I smiled up at him. This was why we were here. To talk about what we wanted. "The last guy that I dated didn't believe in labels. So really, I'm just wondering, where it is that we are? I mean, I'm not trying to pressure you. It's only because I'm curious. I just want to know where you stand on things."

Professor Hunter started laughing. He was laughing *at* me. I could feel my face turning scarlet.

"Where I stand on things? Penny, I don't relish the idea of sharing you, if that is what you're referring to."

"I don't relish the idea of sharing you, either, Professor Hunter."

The expression on his face grew serious. "What do you mean?" he asked slowly.

"I know that you have a girlfriend. That woman from your office. You were going on a date. It was obvious."

He sighed and smiled at me. Did he look relieved?

"That wasn't a date," he said.

"No?"

"We had a work function that we were both attending. I am not interested in Professor Keen. I am only interested in you. But since you've brought it up, if I were dating Professor Keen, you'd prefer that I'd stop, yes?"

"Yes," I replied instantly.

"Then you won't mind me asking you to stop dating Tyler Stevens." He raised his left eyebrow as he looked at me.

"Tyler and I are just friends."

He sat back in his chair. "Then I guess neither of us have anything to worry about."

CHAPTER 27

Saturday

"There is one more thing, Professor Hunter."

Jerrod opened the door and brought in our entrees. I took a bite before he had even left the room.

"This is amazing." I had completely forgotten that I had asked Professor Hunter a question. I took another bite of the crab cake.

"What is it that you wanted to ask me?" Professor Hunter asked.

I finished chewing. "My roommate, Melissa. She can be rather, well, persistent. She always wants me to go out on the weekends and tries to get me to go on double dates and stuff."

"And?"

"And what am I supposed to tell her?"

"That you're dating someone."

"But she'll want to know who it is."

"So tell her about me. Maybe leave off the professor part though." He smiled at me. He had no idea how hard this was going to be for me to do.

"You want me to tell her I'm dating an older, wealthy, unbelievably handsome gentleman who is way out of my league?"

"And you'll want to say my name is James, not Professor Hunter. Which you should probably start doing in public as well."

I was wondering when he'd ask me to call him by his first name. "She won't believe a word of it."

"Hmmm. You'll have to mention that it's the best sex of your life as well. Maybe you can distract her with those details."

I felt my face begin to flush. I hoped he thought it was because of the fire. I had been wondering if sex was on his mind. I still barely knew him, but I knew I wanted him again. He was right, it was the best sex of my life. It wasn't even comparable to anything I had with Austin. Austin was like a jackrabbit. He always finished in just a few minutes. I didn't even know what an orgasm felt like until I met Professor Hunter.

And I think I knew how to get what I wanted. "Thank you for dinner. That was one of the most amazing things I've ever put in my mouth."

His Adam's apple rose and then fell. "Certainly not the best, though. Do you need to be reminded?"

He was making me wet with just his words. I remembered him ramming his huge cock in and out of my mouth. I gulped. "I may need a refresher."

Jerrod walked in holding two dessert menus. "Are either of you interested in dessert this evening?" He placed the menus down in front of us.

"I'd absolutely love some dessert," I said, looking at Professor Hunter.

"Could you give us a while to discuss our options?" He smiled politely at Jerrod. As soon as Jerrod closed the door Professor Hunter was on his feet. He pulled out my chair for me. I was about to stand up.

"Sit back down," he growled.

I quickly obeyed. There was hunger in his eyes. It was the same intensity he had back in his office.

"I already know what I want for dessert," he said and dropped to his knees. He removed my panties and spread my thighs with his strong hands.

"But Jerrod will be back in just..."

His tongue found my clit and my words quickly turned into a moan. He sucked on it hard and then let his tongue enter my wetness.

My hips rose slightly, wanting him deeper inside of me. He moved his mouth back to my clit and let his fingers fill me. I gasped at the sudden pressure.

"What were you saying, Penny? That you want me to stop?" He pulsed his fingers faster.

"No. Please, don't."

"Don't what?" He was teasing me. He wanted me to beg for it.

"Don't stop. Please don't stop," I moaned.

He let his fingers go deeper still. I wasn't going to be able to hold on much longer. The door creaked and Professor Hunter quickly stood up. He lifted his hands above his head and yawned, pretending to stretch. *Damn it, Jerrod!*

Jerrod walked over to us. I was having trouble slowing my rapid breathing. I was awkwardly panting. *Oh, shit.* My panties were dangling around my ankles. *Does Jerrod notice?* I quickly tucked my feet under my chair.

"What is it that you decided you wanted again, Penny?" Professor Hunter asked me.

My face was flushed. It had to be obvious what we had just been doing. I looked at Professor Hunter in horror. I hadn't even looked at the menu. He had a challenging look in his eyes.

I gulped. I knew what he wanted me to do, but I could feel Jerrod staring at me. *Oh please don't notice my panties!*

I took a deep breath. "I'm actually in the mood for something warm and salty." I raised an eyebrow at Professor Hunter. *Game on.*

Professor Hunter bit his lip.

"Well, we have salted caramel squares," Jerrod said. "If you'd like, we can heat them slightly. I'll have to ask the chef though. I'm not sure if they'll melt."

I felt like I was the one that was melting, trying hard not to unravel under this awkward exchange.

"I'd rather have something sweet," Professor Hunter interjected.

"Well our lava cake is made from scratch and it is warm and sweet. Best of both worlds then."

"That sounds perfect," I said. Jerrod needed to leave the room right that second.

"We'll split the chocolate lava cake then," Professor Hunter said, without taking his eyes off me, and handed Jerrod the menus.

"Very good choice, sir," Jerrod said. He collected the menus and walked back out of the room.

"Your juicy cunt is the most amazing thing I've ever had in my mouth. And I'm not done with it yet." He got back down on his knees, grabbed my ass, and pulled me into him. One long, slow, stroke with his tongue brought me to my breaking point. I let the orgasm wash over me as his tongue still slowly encircled me. He placed one gentle kiss on my clit that sent shivers down my spine, and then slid my panties back up my legs. He stood up and pulled me to my feet with him.

"We almost got caught," I said breathlessly.

"We're not out of the clear yet." He unzipped his pants and unbuttoned the flap in his boxers, letting his enormous erection spring to life. "I still need to remind you what the best thing that's ever been in your mouth is."

Ever since his office all I ever wanted in my mouth was him. I wanted to suck on his length and bring him to orgasm this time. I wanted to taste him. I sunk to my knees between his legs and let my tongue slowly trace around his tip. I let my lips slide down his shaft. This was my chance to show him I knew how to make him groan too. I could feel myself growing wet again as his dick throbbed against my lips. I held my breath as I went all the way down, letting his massive cock enter my throat.

"Penny," Professor Hunter moaned.

When his fingers intertwined in my hair and he began guiding me I didn't mind. I wanted him to come. And I liked when he fucked my mouth. I loved how in control he was. His cock throbbed against my lips again as he thrust in and out of my mouth, faster and faster.

Hot, salty liquid shot into my mouth. I drank him down, lapping up every ounce of it. I licked my lips and locked eyes with him as I zippered his pants. He pulled me to my feet.

"Are you convinced now?" he asked.

"There's nothing I'd rather do than that."

"Are you sure about that?" He grabbed my ass and pulled me in close. I could feel his muscles underneath his shirt. And he was right. There was something I wanted more. I wanted him deep inside of me. I wanted him to make me scream his name.

"No." I felt my body trembling.

"Tell me what you want then." He lifted my legs and wrapped them around him. He carried me over to the loveseat and laid me down on its silky cushions.

I gulped. What did he want me to say? Everything in my mind was dirty and unspeakable.

He leaned over me and whispered in my ear. "I think I know exactly what you want. Because you like a little danger. You liked having Jerrod's eyes on you when you were seconds away from coming. You like breaking the rules and the idea of getting caught turns you on even more. And right now all you want is my dick so deep inside of you that you scream."

My heart was pounding.

"But I have no intention of giving you what you want. At least, not yet."

"Professor Hunter," I panted.

He got off the loveseat and put his hand in front of me. I didn't want to get up. I wanted him on top of me, pushing my dress up my thighs.

"I think we need some fresh air, Penny."

I didn't know what he had in mind, but I grabbed his hand and let him pull me to my feet. I'd follow him anywhere. He kept my hand in his as he led me out of the private dining room. It seemed like everyone in the restaurant turned to look at him as we walked through. He squeezed my hand and smiled down at me. God was he sexy.

We exited the restaurant in the back and stepped onto a huge terrace. It was chilly and there were only a few people standing by a fire with glasses in their hands, enjoying an after dinner drink. Professor Hunter escorted me past them and we made our way down a set of stairs. His strides were longer than mine and it was hard to keep pace with him. If I walked any faster I'd be jogging.

We reached a row of golf carts. He leaned in and turned the key. "This will do." He smiled at me.

"Are we allowed to use those? We're going to get in trouble."

Professor Hunter laughed and got behind the wheel. "Get in."

Of course he could use them. He could do whatever he wanted. He owned the place. I climbed in next to him and as soon as my butt hit the seat he pressed down on the gas pedal. He stuck to the small paths and wooden bridges on the course for awhile and then veered off into the grass. We rolled up next to a small waterfall and he cut the engine. Lightning bugs flittered in the dark sky around us. It felt like I was in a dream. And even though we were surrounded by fresh grass and beautiful flowers, all I could smell was his sweet cologne. Every inch of me felt alive when I was next to him.

I got out of the cart and walked over toward the little waterfall. The water splashing against the rocks was surprisingly loud. I saw Professor Hunter's reflection in the rippling water as he came up behind me and wrapped his arms around me. He moved my hair to one side and kissed the back of my neck. My whole body tensed. *Oh my God, he wants me right here. In the middle of the golf course.* But he was right. I liked the danger of it. The thought of getting caught made it even more exciting. One of his hands slipped down the front of my dress and his fingers wrapped around my breast. His other hand crept up my thigh and under my dress. He moved my underwear to the side and slid a finger inside of me.

Oh, God yes. Fuck this is hot. I pushed my hips back and let my ass rub against him. It didn't take long before I could feel his dick harden.

"Don't pretend for a second that you don't get excited by the idea of someone catching me deep inside of you." He slid another finger inside of me and began to pump his hand. "I can feel how much you love it. The way you clench around me. But at least now you can scream as loud as you want and no one will hear over the water." He moved his fingers faster.

Yes! How could I feel so much satisfaction with just his hands?

"Tell me what you want."

But I wanted more. I wanted his hard cock inside of me again. It was all I could think about. "More."

"More what?"

I wasn't used to talking dirty. But I wanted to please him. And I wanted him to please me. "I want your dick inside of me."

He removed his hands from me. My knees felt weak as I turned to face him.

"James," I said breathlessly.

"Oh, Penny." He cupped my chin in his hands and lifted my face so that I'd be looking at him. He was shaking his head back and forth. "We are not in public right now."

I gulped.

He had a wicked look in his eyes. "You have a lot to learn."

"Then teach me, Professor Hunter."

He dropped his hand from my face. "Take off your clothes."

I looked around. I could see the fire on the terrace. We were far away, but could they see us? "But..."

"Take off your dress before I rip it off," he growled.

I undid the belt around my waist and pulled the dress off over my head. The cool air made me shiver.

"Take off all of it."

I unhinged my bra and let it fall to the ground. I bent down, pulled my panties off, and stepped out of them. I reached down to un-strap my shoes but Professor Hunter lifted my naked body over his shoulder.

"Professor Hunter!" I laughed.

He responded by lightly nipping at my exposed ass cheek. I felt the leafy limbs of the weeping willow tree on my back as he carried me beneath it. There was only a little light, dancing around as the breeze made the branches sway. I began to sit down. I wanted him to take me right now; right here under this tree.

"Don't sit down." He quickly grabbed my hand.

"Why?"

"The fertilizer will give you a bad rash."

I laughed. "Wait are you serious? Why do you know that?"

He shrugged.

"Professor Hunter!"

"Put your hands on the trunk of the tree."

"Have you had sex on a golf course before?"

"Penny, put your hands on the trunk."

His voice was serious. God, he was so sexy when he talked like that. Demanding. Forceful. He was glaring at me from under his thick eyebrows. *So sexy.* I followed his instructions.

"Spread your legs." His voice sounded tight. I could tell he wanted it just as badly as I did.

I spread my legs. The cool air against my wanting pussy was invigorating and somehow made me crave him even more.

"Arch your back," he instructed and pulled my hair, making me follow his instructions.

The wind blew and I felt the goose bumps rise all over my naked body. But I didn't shiver. All I felt was the ache of desire. I heard the rip of foil and before I could even process what was happening, he grabbed my hips and thrust himself deep inside of me.

I groaned. I was still sore from the last time his huge cock had been inside of me. But the pain slowly mixed with pleasure until I no longer knew where the line was. His dick was relentless, fucking me harder than last time, harder than I knew I could take.

"Yes!" I screamed.

My swollen breasts bounced with each powerful thrust. I pushed my palms against the trunk of the tree, moving my hips in time with him. His fingers dug into my flesh. I liked it rough and he knew it. He reached around my waist and grabbed my clit between two fingers and squeezed. Hard. *Fuck yes!* I felt myself clench around his throbbing cock as a wave of release washed over me.

He pulled out and turned me toward him. I knew he wasn't nearly done with me yet. I wanted to make him come. I wanted him to lose control for once.

I grabbed his tie and pulled his face down to mine. "James," I said as seductively as I could muster and bit my lip.

He grabbed my ass, lifted me up, and pushed my back against the trunk of the tree. He raised one eyebrow and thrust his length back inside of me. My bare back rubbed against the rough bark of the tree but I didn't cry out. I didn't want him to stop. I never wanted him to stop.

"What are you trying to do to me?" he moaned. He pushed into me and pinned me in place as he let his hands wander away from my ass. I wrapped my legs firmly around him as he squeezed my breasts and rubbed my hard nipples. He grabbed my arms and raised them above my head. I was immobilized by his touch. His dick began to move in and out again, slowly this time. He leaned in and kissed me. He bit my lip playfully and then slammed his cock into me hard.

"Professor Hunter!" I whimpered.

He went faster and faster, making my bare ass bounce against the bark. *So raw. So intense. So right.* I felt his cock throb inside of me as our orgasms collided. My whole body was trembling as he pulled me into his chest. Even after his release, his cock was huge inside of me. His breathing was as ragged as mine. I liked the feeling of his hot breath on my neck. He pulled out and set me down on my feet.

He zipped up his pants. He was still in his full suit. I suddenly felt so naked and exposed. I put one arm across my chest and my other hand in front of my aching pussy.

"You have nothing to hide from me," he said and moved my arms to my sides. And he was right. I was exhausted. Spent. His.

CHAPTER 28

Saturday

I ran my fingers through my hair. "Do I look okay?" I asked as I stepped out of the golf cart.

"Penny, you look stunning."

"I mean, does it look like we just had sex?" I whispered, even though no one was around. My dress was wrinkled and a little damp from the dew on the grass. I tried to smooth the fabric with my hands, to no avail.

He tucked a loose strand of hair behind my ear. "Penny, it looks like I just fucked your brains out."

"Professor Hunter!" I lightly pushed on his chest.

"That's how I prefer you to look." He tightened his tie. "Now, I believe I owe you a piece of cake." He lifted me into his arms and carried me back to the terrace. I loved how strong he was. One couple was seated next to the fire and the man smiled and nodded at Professor Hunter. Professor Hunter put me back on my feet and draped his arm across my shoulder as he escorted me back into the restaurant.

I kept my eyes on the ground. I couldn't bear to see anyone looking at us, especially if what Professor Hunter said was true. If anyone knew what we had just done, we'd be kicked out. Or I guess we wouldn't. I was having a hard time getting used to the situation. It seemed like if you owned a country club you could basically do whatever you wanted without consequences. Just because he owned this place, though, didn't make what we had just done appropriate.

"Let's eat dessert out here," Professor Hunter said and slid into a booth.

Was he trying to torment me? I sat down across from him. I could feel the eyes on me, but at least there weren't that many diners left in the restaurant. It only took a minute for Jerrod to find us.

"Ah, I thought I'd lost you two." Jerrod was smiling. Did he know? I ran my fingers through my hair again.

"I just wanted to give the Mrs. a tour," Professor Hunter said and winked at me.

"Of course. Did you two still want the chocolate lava cake?"

"Yes, Jerrod, thank you."

"We kept it warm for you. I'll be right back."

A moment later Jerrod came back carrying the cake and two glasses of water.

"Anything else I can get for you?"

"That will be all for us this evening."

"It was a pleasure meeting you both. I hope to see you again soon."

"Have a good night, Jerrod," Professor Hunter said.

I watched as Professor Hunter took a bite of the cake. How was it possible that he could even make eating look sexy? I grabbed my fork and took a bite. *Delicious.*

"There is one more thing we need to discuss," I said.

"And what is that?"

I leaned forward slightly. "My grade," I whispered.

"What about it?" He had a devilish grin on his face.

"You gave me a C- when I deserved an A."

"Penny, it would be very unprofessional of me to give you favoritism."

"As unprofessional as what you just did to me on the golf course?"

He put his fork down on the plate. "Touché."

"So you'll change it back?"

"Penny, I've always had it recorded as an A."

What? "But. My paper. It said C-."

"And you think if I wanted to whiteout every single word on a sheet of paper I wouldn't just get another one?"

"You were just trying to upset me?" I could feel my temper rising.

"No, I was trying to seduce you."

A shiver went down my spine. The danger that I felt when I was with him was real. Had he been planning this whole thing ever since we had met in the coffee shop?

"So everything played out just like you wanted?" I felt a little hurt. This had been a game to him this whole time.

"No. Not at all. Like I told you before, I can't stop thinking about you. I thought if I let myself give into the temptation then I could move on. But I'm more addicted to you than ever."

He pulled out a hundred dollar bill from his wallet and placed it on the table. "I guess I should get you home. Your roommate is probably wondering where you are." He grabbed my hand and pulled me to my feet.

I almost asked him if we were supposed to wait for the check. But he owned the place. Certainly he got free meals.

The money he left on the table was probably just Jerrod's tip. Professor Hunter was very generous.

Professor Hunter escorted me out of the restaurant and back toward the entrance of the country club. The woman with the large breasts was still standing at the reception desk. "Have a good evening, Mr. Hunter."

"You too," he said to the woman and nodded at her.

It was annoying how she didn't even acknowledge my existence. As if sensing this, Professor Hunter squeezed my hand.

As soon as the valet saw us come out of the country club, he hurried off. I began to shiver as we waited for him to get the car. Professor Hunter took off his suit jacket, draped it over my shoulders, and pulled me in close.

"Maybe your roommate will find your story more believable if you wear this back to your dorm."

I leaned into him and took a deep breath of his cologne. *Is this really happening?* "I barely believe that I'm dating you, so it'll be hard to convince someone else that it's true."

He rested his chin on the top of my head and only moved away when the valet handed him the keys to his car. He opened up the door for me and walked over to the valet.

"Thank you," he said and slipped some money into the valet's hand. Professor Hunter climbed into the driver's seat. The car started before I even buckled my seatbelt.

After he turned out of the country club, he put his right hand on the center console. Without hesitation I let my hand slide into his, and his fingers intertwined with mine.

"What will happen if someone finds out that we're dating?" I asked.

"It's frowned upon, but the university's policy isn't explicitly stated in their handbook. It's more a question of ethics than anything else."

"You've looked it up?"

He looked at me. "Yes."

"So you won't actually get in trouble?"

"That depends on a lot of things."

"Like what?"

"Well, if there was even a whisper of sexual harassment, I would get fired. Or if someone in your class found out about us and thought you were getting favoritism, they could file a complaint. Or..."

"I'm not going to tell anyone, Professor Hunter."

"Then I don't think we have anything to worry about."

"Would you still have pursued me if the university's policy was explicitly against it?"

He paused for a moment. "Yes," he finally said. He squeezed my hand.

"Even though you could get fired?" I realized the question was ridiculous as soon as I let it slip. Professor Hunter clearly didn't need this job. If he could randomly buy a country club, he probably didn't need to work at all.

"I know that you want this just as much as I do. I believe that my ethics are sound, so no one can make me question them."

We drove in silence for a few minutes.

"What did your startup company do?"

"Tech."

He was being so vague. "What happened to it?"

"I sold it. But I still have a seat on the board."

"Then why are you teaching?"

"For the same reason I left New York. I needed a change."

"And if it wasn't because of how loud and busy the city was, then what was it? A midlife crisis?"

"How old do you think I am, Penny?" he laughed.

"Actually, I thought you were probably a grad student when I met you in the coffee shop. You can't even believe how shocked I was when I found out you were my Comm professor."

He laughed again. I wasn't sure there was a sound in the world that I liked better than his laugh.

"So take a guess," he pressed.

"Well, Professors have to go to grad school and then get their master to teach right?"

"Yes, but I didn't do that. I was busy running a company in my early twenties. They granted me an honorary degree at the last university I worked at if I agreed to teach a few entrepreneurship classes in their masters program. I have the same arrangement here."

"So, maybe you're 29?" *Please don't be over 30.*

"Close. I'm only 27."

Only 27. If I was 22 like he thought I was, there would only be five years difference between us. An eight year difference seemed worse. But my birthday was soon. I'd be twenty in a few weeks. I needed to tell him. This was the perfect opportunity.

He pulled up outside of my dorm and cut the ignition. "What, you're sad that I'm not older?"

I laughed. "No. No, that's not it. I just..." I took a deep breath. I needed to tell him.

He leaned in and kissed me. "Like I said, you have nothing to worry about."

CHAPTER 29

Sunday

As soon as I locked the door, Melissa switched the lights on.

"Where the hell have you been?! I texted you like ten times, Penny!"

I pulled Professor Hunter's suit jacket tighter around myself. I just wanted to be back in his arms. "I..."

"Oh my God. Oh my God! Were you on a date?"

"No." *Crap, why did I just lie? I'm so bad at this!*

"Penny, you're wearing a men's suit jacket."

"Yeah, sorry. I meant yes. Yes, I was on a date."

"I knew it! You and Tyler were being so ridiculous earlier, but you just needed a little persuading. He ditched that party on Friday night just to hang out with you. There were tons of girls there. He chose you. He's like the complete opposite of Austin. I'm so happy for you."

"No, not with Tyler."

"What?"

"I wasn't on a date with Tyler."

I could tell she was getting annoyed with me.

"Yeah, I heard you. I meant who were you with?"

"It was someone new."

"Penny, who?"

"His name is James." I could feel myself start to blush, remembering when I had challenged him and called him James on the golf course. I walked over to my dresser and pulled out a pair of sweatpants and a t-shirt and began to change.

"Well, where did you meet?"

I should have known I couldn't get off that easily. "My Intro to Marketing class," I lied.

"No wonder you like him," she said and picked up his suit jacket from the back of my chair. "He wears the same cologne as that professor you had a crush on. Yummy."

Oh shit! "Oh, really? I hadn't noticed."

Melissa laughed. "Don't pretend you didn't snuggle up to your professor's sweater at night."

I didn't know she had seen me do that. "Okay, fine, I did notice. That's actually what first attracted me to him." That seemed reasonable enough.

Melissa no longer looked mad at me, just super curious. I'd rather her be mad and not speak to me. I was going to have a hard time keeping track of all these lies.

"So tell me about him," she said and sat back down on her bed.

"I'm pretty tired. Can I tell you about him tomorrow?"

"Yeah, not happening. You made me worry about you till...what time is it? It's 2 a.m., Penny! I think I deserve at least a few details."

"Okay." I sat cross-legged on my bed and looked at her. If I stuck to true things, it wouldn't really be lying. "Well he's unbelievably handsome, apparently wealthy, and he's a little older than me." I thought about Professor

Hunter's suggestion of telling her how it was the best sex of my life, and blushed.

"Wait, how much older? I thought you said you met in class? Is he like a foreign exchange student or something?"

Why am I so bad at this? "I meant I met him after my marketing class. I ran into him on Main Street. Literally."

She knew how clumsy I was, so she seemed to accept that answer. "Why didn't you tell me you had a date with him?"

"I don't know. I didn't want to jinx it I guess. He's way out of my league, Melissa."

"Don't be ridiculous. You know that you're a catch. You probably made him drool in the dress you were wearing."

"Thanks, Melissa."

"So, where did he take you on your first date?"

"To this country club. It was at least half an hour from here."

"Well that's super fancy. I can see why you think he's wealthy. I don't know any other students who are members of a country club."

I didn't want her to assume he was a student. I wanted her to think that he was always busy so that she wouldn't be hurt if she didn't get to meet him. "He's actually not a student."

"So what does he do?"

"He founded some tech company."

"Impressive." She thought about that for a moment before adding, "How old did you say he was?"

"27," I said quietly. I shrugged like it was no big deal. My stomach was still in a knot from not confessing my age to Professor Hunter in the car.

"I thought you said he was only a little older than you. Penny, that's like...eight years."

It was time to take Professor Hunter's advice. "Melissa, you don't even understand how sexy he is. I can't even think straight when I'm around him."

She laughed. "Okay, I need some sleep. Next time text me back so I don't have to worry all night."

"Sorry about that, Melissa. I was distracted."

"I bet," she said and turned off the light.

I was too tired to go get ready for bed, so instead I lay down and pulled the covers on top of me.

"Poor Tyler," Melissa mumbled. I heard her turn in her bed.

I took a deep breath and closed my eyes.

CHAPTER 30
Monday

It was going to be so awkward to see Tyler. I hadn't spoken to him since he had walked out on me at the dining hall. I had encouraged him to see other people because I cared about him. He had become a really good friend. But he was probably never going to talk to me again. And I had basically molested his abs, which definitely gave him the wrong message. The cold shoulder would make me feel horrible, but at the same time I would be kind of relieved. I was sick of lying to him. Maybe it was better for both of us if he pretended I didn't exist.

When I walked into the room I was surprised to see that Tyler was already sitting in his usual spot. I had been expecting him to be seated on the opposite side of the room.

"Hey, Penny," he said as I approached.

"Is this from you?" I picked up the single red rose that was on my desk.

"Yes. Look, I'm really sorry about Saturday. I acted like an idiot."

I sat down and smelled the sweet aroma from the rose. *Why can't he just give me the cold shoulder instead?* He was so sweet.

"I'm sorry too, I..."

"You don't need to be. You've made it perfectly clear that you just want to be my friend. I just can't seem to resist making a fool of myself around you. But I'm going to try to start acting like your friend. No more hidden agendas. If that's really what you want. Because I just enjoy being around you."

"So you had a hidden agenda on Friday night when you came over? I had *no* idea."

"I mean, I did want to help you get better. But I'd be lying if I said I wasn't hoping for a kiss." He laughed.

"Okay, Tyler. Friends for real?" I stuck out my hand for him to shake.

"Friends don't shake hands, weirdo." He high fived me instead.

Professor Hunter walked into the room and locked eyes with me. And then he looked down at the rose on my desk and his expression darkened. He ran his hand through his hair as he put his satchel on his chair. I could tell he was mad. *Crap.*

"Speeches start next Monday. And this time we'll go backwards in the alphabet. So last names beginning with Z through N will go on Monday and M through A will go on Wednesday."

Is he punishing me? Now I'd have to be one of the first people to present.

"I don't want nerves to be as big of a factor for this speech. It's important to feel comfortable in this room. So let's all share something a little more intimate today." He paused. "Oh, I have an idea. I had an amazing date this weekend."

A few girls in the classroom sighed but I ignored them. I was dying to see what Professor Hunter had to say.

"Romance, dinner. The whole package. So how about everyone shares what their ideal first date would be. And let's switch things up today and start at the end of the alphabet so we get a feel for how next week's speeches are going to go. Adam Zabek, start us off."

I tuned Adam out and tried to think quickly of what I was going to say. Did Professor Hunter want me to talk about our date too?

"Penny Taylor."

I stood up and said the first thing that came to my mind. "I like piña coladas and getting caught in the rain. And the feel of the ocean and the taste of champagne."

Most of the class laughed. *Thank you, Rupert Holmes.*

Professor Hunter smiled and leaned back in his seat. "Tyler Stevens?"

Tyler stood up. "Hmmm. My ideal first date is probably making love at midnight in the dunes of the cape."

I couldn't resist laughing. Professor Hunter's smile immediately disappeared. *Damn it, Tyler!*

Professor Hunter cleared his throat. "Okay. Let's move past the song lyrics."

I smiled at Tyler and he stuck his tongue out at me. After everyone was done describing their ideal dates, Professor Hunter started talking about enunciation. But when he turned to write enunciation on the board, I stopped paying attention. Instead, I was looking at how his khakis hugged his ass. And how he bit his lip when he was concentrating. When class was finally dismissed, I said goodbye to Tyler and waited for the class to empty out.

Not knowing what to do about the rose, I grabbed it and held it down by my side. *Please don't be mad.*

"I see that you are continuing your relationship with Mr. Stevens, despite my request," he said as soon as I was close to his desk.

"I'm not."

He eyed the rose in my hand.

"It's just a friendship rose."

He rested back on the side of his desk and folded his arms across his chest. "Penny, there is no such thing as a friendship rose."

"But we really are just friends."

He gave me a challenging look. "I'll be picking you up at 1."

I hadn't expected him to change the subject. I was busy thinking of examples of how Tyler and I were just close friends. "Wait, what?"

"I'm taking you on your ideal date."

"But, I can't. I have a class at 2."

He put his satchel over his shoulder. "So skip it."

"You're a terrible influence, Professor Hunter."

"I don't think you really believe that. I'll see you at 1." He winked at me and walked out of the room.

CHAPTER 31

Monday

"A delivery came for you," Melissa said as she stood up from her chair. She was all smiles.

There were a dozen red roses in a vase on my desk. I put my backpack down and walked over to my desk. A bow was tied around the vase, and a card was attached to it.

Penny,

I know that you think roses symbolize friendship, but believe me when I say that these ones do not. I hope you're excited for our date. Thank you for skipping class.
-James

The roses were beautiful. No one had ever bought me flowers before today. Except for my parents when I graduated from high school. I read the note again. It was sweet, even if he was a little cocky. And even though he was just trying to show up Tyler. But Professor Hunter was right, I was going to skip class.

"When did these come?" I didn't even realize that flowers could be delivered that fast.

"Just a few minutes ago. So, who are they from?"

I laughed. "You expect me to believe that you didn't read the card?"

"I didn't!" she protested. "But I confess that I did read who they were from. *James*. So what did you do to earn those?" Melissa asked.

"Nothing." *I made him angry.*

"You are one lucky girl then."

I leaned in and smelled the roses. *I'm so lucky.* I thought about the date he was planning. I like piña coladas and getting caught in the rain? And the feel of the ocean and the taste of champagne? *What the hell was I thinking?* I was basically asking Professor Hunter to get me tons of illegal drinks.

"So what are you doing here anyway? Don't you usually just grab lunch and go to class?"

"Pro..." I coughed. *Shit. I almost said Professor Hunter!* I took a deep breath and tried to think of a quick recovery. "Probably gonna skip it." *Who the hell talks like that?*

Melissa stared at me. "Skip what? Lunch? We can go to the dining hall together real quick if you want."

"No, I'm going to skip my class."

"I can't even imagine you skipping a class. You never break the rules." She paused. "Are you feeling alright? Does your stomach hurt again?"

"No, I'm fine." I was tempted to tell her that I was about to go on a date with a professor. I knew how to break the rules too! But of course I couldn't. I could mention *James* though. "James had some free time this afternoon and I didn't want to miss getting to see him."

"He's turning you into quite the bad ass."

If only she knew.

"So where are you going?"

It was a beautiful, warm September day. And if we were going early, it was probably because the destination was far away. I eyed the new bikini in my closet.

"He didn't really say. But he dropped some hints. I think he's taking me to the beach."

"It's good that we went shopping last week then."

"I know. Thanks for helping me pick out a new bathing suit. I always appreciate your fashion advice."

"Mhm. So tell me more about him. I want all the juicy details."

"Well. He's spontaneous."

"Obviously. Last minute beach trip. But I mean like...what's he like?"

"He's funny, but serious. There's just something about him that's so intriguing." I stopped talking. The more vague I was, the better. "I honestly don't know him all that well. Hopefully I'll find out more about him today." I did have a lot of questions for Professor Hunter. It was true that I barely knew anything about him.

"So I guess that means you didn't do much talking on your last date then?" Melissa gave me one of her challenging looks.

I felt myself blushing. I knew what she was hinting at. And she was right.

"I've never seen you this flustered before, Penny! So when exactly do I get to meet this mystery man?"

I laughed awkwardly. "I'm sure you'll get to meet him soon." I changed into my new bikini and pulled on a pair of jean shorts and a tank top. I rummaged around in my closet until I found a canvas bag. After mentally checking off a beach towel, sunscreen, sunglasses, and a hoodie, I was ready to go.

"Well, have fun. I can't wait to hear all about it. Being whisked away to the beach sounds so romantic."

"It really does." *So romantic.*

"Oh! And you better take a picture with him today. Because I need to see what he looks like. He sounds so dreamy."

"Yeah, definitely," I lied. I grabbed my bag and headed out of my dorm. "See you later!"

I only had to wait a few seconds before Professor Hunter pulled up in a red convertible with the top down. His hair was mussed up and he was wearing aviators. He smiled as he leaned over and opened the door for me from the inside. He was wearing khaki shorts and a polo. His legs and arms were tan and muscular.

I took a deep breath as I got in. "New car?" I asked. It still had that new car smell.

"No. But I haven't driven it much."

I grabbed my sunglasses from my bag as he sped off. The wind rushed through my hair. I had never been in a convertible before. I pictured people in the movies standing up in their seats, spreading their arms wide, and screaming at the top of their lungs. I felt like I was already experiencing that feeling just by being next to Professor Hunter.

"So, where are we going?"

"I think you can probably guess."

"Well, it's not raining, so I'm not sure where we could get caught in the rain. But we've been caught in the rain before, so maybe you're skipping that portion. Which means you're probably going the feel of the ocean route. So I'm guessing that we're heading to the beach!"

Professor Hunter smiled at me.

"You should have warned me though. What if I hadn't worn a bathing suit?"

"I was actually hoping you would forget it."

I lightly pushed his shoulder as I laughed. He pulled onto I-95 and the noise of traffic filled my ears. Professor Hunter was now speeding past all the other cars on the road.

"You're going to get a ticket!" I yelled over the roar of traffic.

He slowed down a little, but was still going faster than most of the other cars. "You don't break the rules very often, do you?"

"Not really. But I do sometimes."

"Give me an example."

"You."

He laughed. "Besides for me."

"Well. One time...no, that was okay. Well there was another time...hmmm..."

"Maybe you're right about me then. I am a terrible in-fluence on you."

"Yeah, you're the worst."

"Then I'll have to learn to behave myself better."

"I guess so." I hoped he knew I was kidding. He was so hard to read sometimes. I liked that he was a bad influ-ence on me. I felt alive when I was with him. He was the best thing that had ever happened to me.

"I don't actually want you to behave around me, Professor Hunter. I like that you're a bad influence on me. I think you're just what I need."

"Penny, I couldn't behave myself around you even if you begged me to." The convertible sped up again and he turned on the radio.

***

We arrived at the beach in record time. He drove to the end of the boardwalk and parked on a side street.

"Have you ever been here before?" he asked.

"I used to come here every summer when I was growing up." I grabbed my stuff and stepped out of the car.

"All the more special then." He got out of the car, reached into the back seat, and pulled out a towel and a cooler. He put the towel over his shoulder and grabbed my hand.

"What about you?"

"I've come down here a few times."

"So this is where you take all the ladies to impress them?"

He laughed. "No, I've only ever been here by myself."

"You're kind of a loner, aren't you?"

"I guess you could say that I have a hard time trusting people."

One of the first times I had texted him I had told him that I didn't trust him and he had gotten mad. Everything was different now though. I did trust him. And I wanted to know more about him. No, I wanted to know *everything* about him.

"Why?" I asked.

He squeezed my hand. When we stepped onto the boards, I heard a buzzing noise. Professor Hunter dropped my hand and reached in his pocket. It looked like all the color drained from his face. "I'm sorry, I have to take this." He walked a few paces away from me. I could just barely make out his conversation.

"This isn't a good time." He sounded angry. "I don't even know why we're still talking about this." He paused and listened to the person on the other end of the line. "I told you I didn't care about any of the specifics. Just sign the damn papers." He ended the call and put the phone back in his pocket.

He put a smile on his face as he came back over to me, but I could tell that it was forced. "Sorry about that."

"Is everything okay?"

"Just a business call." He grabbed my hand again and we took the few steps down to the beach.

"Something with your tech company?"

"Well, it's not mine anymore. But yes."

I looked out at the ocean. I had always imagined how cool it would be to come to the beach when there was no one around. Today was that day. There wasn't anyone on the beach down here except for the occasional passerby. I slid off my flip flops and picked them up in my free hand. The feeling of sand underneath my bare feet was exhilarating. We began walking toward the water.

"Professor Hunter? You didn't answer my other question."

He ran his hand through his hair. "I'm sorry, what was your question again?"

"Why do you have a hard time trusting people?"

He took a deep breath. He seemed unsettled. "People have a tendency to wear many different masks. I've been bad at seeing people for who they really are until it's too late."

Shit. And he shouldn't trust me either. I was lying to him about my age.

He put his towel on top of the sand and sat down, pulling me on top of him.

"I barely know anything about you," I said breathlessly.

"You know that I like you and that you like me. What else does anything matter?"

He lightly tugged my hair so that our faces were only an inch apart. I wanted to tell him that it did matter. But I couldn't resist him when his lips were this close to mine. He was too good at distracting me. I leaned down and kissed him. After a minute, he rolled over so that he was on top of me. He gave me one last kiss and then sat up, pulling me into a seated position with him.

"So I couldn't bring the real thing, but..." he opened the cooler and brought out two bottles of piña colada cocktails. "I guess these are the next best thing." He popped off each top and handed me one of the bottles.

"Cheers," I said and clanged my bottle against his. I took a small sip. "This is so good."

Professor Hunter started coughing. "Ugh! It's disgusting."

"What? It's delicious."

"It tastes like the lovechild of a coconut and a bottle of Nyquil."

I started laughing.

"You can have mine too. I brought backup for myself," he said, handing me his bottle and replacing it with a bottle of beer.

"So piña coladas and getting caught in the rain aren't your thing?"

"I'm all about getting caught in the rain. But I prefer scotch."

"I like how sophisticated you are."

"Penny, nothing I'm going to do to you here is sophisticated."

I gulped. "What do you have in mind?"

He reached over and touched the strap of my tank top. "Well, I don't think you need this anymore."

I put down my drink and pulled my tank top off over my head. He reached over, undid the button on my jean shorts, and slowly unzipped them. I lifted my hips slightly and he slowly pulled my shorts down my thighs and off my legs.

I felt myself blush as he looked at me in my bikini. He stood up and took off his shirt. Now I was the one staring at him. He had an Adonis belt worthy of the god himself. He offered me his hand and pulled me to my feet.

"Want to go for a swim?"

"Yes, just let me put some sunscreen on first."

He laughed. "It's almost the end of September. I'm sure you'll be fine."

"Stop being a bad influence for one second. I get burnt crazy easily." I sat back down and pulled the sunscreen out of my bag.

He kneeled back down on his towel and took the bottle from me. "Let me do it for you then. Lay down."

I lay down on my stomach. He lightly touched my back.

"Penny, I'm so sorry."

I knew he was referring to the small cuts on my back. The bark from the tree had left a few marks. "The risks of having sex on a golf course I guess. It doesn't hurt, though."

He gently started to massage the sunscreen onto my shoulders and arms. "Are you sure it doesn't hurt?"

"I'm sure." I wanted to change the subject. I didn't want him to feel bad about what had happened on the golf course. It was one of the best moments of my life. "You know, when I was younger I used to be so envious of all the girls on the boardwalk that had boyfriends. I couldn't wait until I was older. Holding hands on the boardwalk seemed like the epitome of romance."

He rubbed the lotion underneath the strings of my bikini and began to massage my lower back. "So did you force your high school boyfriends to take you here? To show all the other girls up?"

All of my senses seemed on alert when his hands were on me. Except for my hearing. I had been too distracted to hear what he had said.

"Yes. I mean, no. I'm sorry, what did you say? I wasn't paying attention."

He laughed. "So you must have brought all your high school boyfriends here. Turn over."

"No. I wish." I rolled onto my back and propped myself up on my elbows.

"Couldn't get them to take you here, huh?" He rubbed his hands across my stomach. They dipped slightly below the top of my bathing suit bottom.

It was so hard to concentrate on what he was saying. His hands were so distracting. I took a deep breath. "No, I mean I didn't have any boyfriends in high school." I closed my eyes. *Why did I just tell him that?* He was going to think I was weird. *But I am weird.* I opened my eyes and was surprised to see him smiling at me.

"I wouldn't have guessed that, Penny. But I find it incredibly adorable." His hands rubbed across my collarbone and then right above my breasts. His hands lingered for a moment. "Your heart's beating so fast."

I gulped and sat up. "You make me nervous."

He looked satisfied with my response. "Ready for that swim?"

"It'll take a minute to dry."

"Okay, then do me."

"What?" My heart began to beat even faster.

He laughed and tossed me the bottle of sunscreen. "Get your mind out of the gutter, Penny. I'm trying to be a good influence here." He lay down on his stomach.

I liked when his hands were on me, but I was excited to get to really explore his body. I straddled him and began to massage his back. I had never seen such a perfectly sculpted body before, let alone gotten to touch it. His back was so muscular. And he had two small dimples on either side of his spine, right above his shorts. I let my hands dip slightly below his waistline.

"You're getting a little frisky there," he teased.

"I just don't want you to get burnt," I responded quickly. I moved my hands to his shoulders and then down his muscular arms. His biceps flexed slightly under my touch. He was so sexy. So perfect. How was I getting so turned on by this?

"Okay, roll over."

He followed my instructions and then put his hands under his head so he could watch me. I liked straddling him. He was staring at me. *Crap.* I completely forgot what I was supposed to be doing. I quickly squirted some sunscreen into my hands and massaged it onto his chest. I could feel his eyes on me and it was hard not to blush.

I moved my hands down to his abs. I could feel his cock hardening, slowly pressing harder against me. He thought this was hot too. I kept my hands on his abs way longer than necessary. The tip of my finger slowly traced down his happy trail. I looked up and saw his Adam's apple rise and then fall. I smiled at him.

"Enjoying yourself?" I asked.

"Very much so. I like being responsible."

I dipped my hand slightly below the waist of his shorts and his body tensed. He wanted me to touch him. I moved my hand a little lower and then quickly pulled it out of his shorts. "Ready for that swim?"

CHAPTER 32

Monday

He grabbed my hand and we both ran down to the water. As soon as my toes touched the icy water, I screamed and stopped in my tracks. "Oh my God, it's so cold. There's no way I'm going in!"

"You get used to it." He leaned down and splashed water up at me.

"Professor Hunter!" I ran away from him and back up to our towels. I quickly grabbed a small football from my bag. "Let's at least warm up some first!" I tossed it to him. He caught the ball and threw it back to me.

"I never would have guessed you could throw a football," he said. We continued to throw it back and forth.

"What? Why?"

"Has nobody ever told you that you're clumsy?"

I laughed. The next time I caught it he said, "Now try to see if you can run by me." He drew a line in the sand with his toe and stepped in front of it. "That's the goal line."

I ran toward him and did a few side steps, but he quickly caught me and twirled me around. I laughed as he twirled me in the air. When he put me back down he kept his arms wrapped around me.

"You lost. So now we both have to run in the water as fast as we can."

"Professor Hunter, you're not even wearing a bathing suit. How about a rain check?"

"Yeah, I thought it would be more fun without a bathing suit." He let go of me, unbuttoned and unzipped his shorts, and then tossed them into the sand. He was left standing there in his gray boxers. "Have you ever been skinny dipping, Penny?"

My heart was beating fast. "No."

"Well, I thought you might join me."

"You did, did you?" I glanced around me, but no one was nearby. Still, I couldn't possibly.

He grabbed me and kissed me passionately. His hands wandered up my back and untied my bathing suit top.

"Professor Hunter!" I screamed and held the front of my bikini in place. "It's the middle of the day."

"I dare you."

His words sent a fire through me. I could never say no to him. I looked around again. There really wasn't anyone around.

He pulled off his boxers. And there he was, in the middle of the beach, completely naked, with an erection that had already sprung to life. His eyes were challenging me. And I had never backed down from one of his challenges. I pulled my top off over my head and stepped out of my bathing suit bottom. My heart was beating so fast. I was standing naked on the beach with Professor Hunter. *I can't believe this is happening!* He grabbed my hand and we ran screaming into the freezing ocean.

I let go of his hand as a wave came toward us. I dove into it as it crashed down. When I came up, we were deep enough that my shoulders were under the water.

"I can't believe we're doing this," I said. My whole body was shaking. But I wasn't sure if it was because of the cold water or the thrill of what I was doing. We were in far enough so that the water was pretty still. He hugged me close. Despite how cold it was, he was hard. I wrapped my legs around his waist.

"Shit it's cold!" I said. My teeth were chattering. "How do you always get me to do such crazy things?"

He had a smile on his face. "Because you trust me."

"Well I don't know why. You've convinced me to do so many things that could get us in trouble."

"There's actually something else that I've always wanted to do." He placed a cold, wet hand on my cheek.

"And what is that, Professor Hunter?"

"I've always wanted to have sex in the ocean. Are you on birth control?" he asked, without giving me time to process what he had just said.

"Yes." I gulped.

"And is there anything I need to worry about?"

"You mean do I have any STD's?"

"Yes."

"No, I don't."

As soon as I said I was clean, his hard cock filled me. I hadn't expected it so soon. I let out a tiny cry. "Professor Hunter. We can't do this..."

He silenced me with a kiss. I let his tongue caress mine as he slowly started to move his length in and out of me. I wrapped my arms around the back of his neck and pressed my naked torso against his. He lightly bit my lip and then kissed me more passionately. His lips tasted salty from the ocean water. I moved my hands down his shoulders and felt his strong biceps. I let my hands wander to his back and felt the muscles beneath his soft skin.

"Professor Hunter," I moaned when his lips left mine. I tightened my legs around him. The initial panic I felt for doing this in the open was now overcome with the feeling of pleasure. I let my head fall back as he thrust deeper inside of me. He wrapped one arm behind me and made me arch my back. My hair dipped into the water and a chill went through my body. His other hand wandered to my breasts and squeezed each one. His hand then swept down my stomach and I felt his fingers brush against my clit.

My breathing hitched. He continued to thrust in and out of me, a little faster, as he matched the rhythm with his fingers.

"Yes!" I screamed.

He pulled me back up against his chest and squeezed my ass as he guided himself in and out of me, faster and faster. The sound of the waves crashing and the seagulls cawing suddenly disappeared. The only sensation I had was the feeling of him inside me, the pleasure building.

His cock throbbed and I felt a sudden heat course through me. *Oh my God.* I clenched around his throbbing cock as my own orgasm washed through me. He kissed me again as more of his hot cum filled me. The sudden warmth inside of me and the coolness of the water made my whole body shiver. I had never felt anything like that before. One last ripple of warmth shot through me. I felt so connected to him, so in sync. When he removed himself, it felt like some of the heat escaped from my body. The salt water stung. I rested my head on Professor Hunter's shoulder, wanting to be as close to him as possible. He kissed the top of my head.

"We have an audience," he whispered.

"What?!" I whipped my head to the shore and saw a few boys standing by my bikini. They looked like they were probably in high school. The tallest of the three gave Professor Hunter a thumbs up. "Oh my God," I put my head back on Professor Hunter's shoulder and closed my eyes tight. *This isn't happening.* He held my naked body tightly, protectively against his.

"Oh, shit. Hey!" he yelled to the boys.

I opened my eyes and saw them running off with my bathing suit. *Crap!*

His hands left my back and I realized he was about to run after them.

"Don't you dare leave me in this ocean!"

Professor Hunter started laughing harder than I had ever seen him laugh. "Penny, I'm so sorry," he was able to say, interspersed between his laughter.

"Stop laughing! This isn't funny, Professor Hunter! I just bought that." But I started laughing too. I couldn't believe someone had just stolen my bikini. Or that I was naked in the ocean in the first place.

"I'll buy you a new one."

I looked back at the sand and didn't see anyone. "Should we make a run for it? It's freezing." I unwound my legs from his waist and let him grab my hand. We began to run.

"Oh, wait. The coast isn't exactly clear." Professor Hunter pointed toward the boardwalk. "Boys don't steal bikinis and run away. They stay to look."

I was completely mortified. "What do we do?"

A wave crashed down behind us. It probably would have knocked me over, but Professor Hunter lifted me over his shoulder.

"Professor Hunter, put me down!" I was very self-conscious about my naked ass being up in the air on a public beach. The boys were probably snapping photos. I didn't need my ass to go viral.

He laughed and walked the rest of the way out of the water. When he put me down I quickly ran to our towels. I wrapped my towel around myself as he casually strolled toward me.

"Penny, those boys were far away, they could barely see you."

"But they could still see me! And they probably took pictures with their phones. And they...they saw us having...well, you know."

"The highlight of their young lives, I'm sure." He slowly began to dry off with his towel.

I slid my shorts back on and pulled my tank top on. Without my bikini top, my breasts had no support. And my body was so cold that my nipples were trying to poke through my shirt. I folded my arms across my chest and sat down. I should have been furious with him, but instead I just felt relaxed. *I just had sex in the ocean. With Professor Hunter.* None of this even felt real. It was just a crazy dream. A crazy, sexy, awesome dream.

Professor Hunter pulled on his boxers and shorts, but kept his shirt off. He sat down beside me and rubbed my back. Just his touch made my body tingle. "Are you ready for part two of our date?"

"That depends on what we're doing. I'm not exactly dressed to go anywhere."

"Well, how about we go to my place?"

He got up and pulled me to my feet. I was sad to see him put his shirt back on, but I couldn't be more excited to see where he lived. It would be the perfect opportunity to learn more about him.

"That sounds perfect."

CHAPTER 33

Monday

We pulled into the parking garage of the fancy new apartments that had been built on the edge of Main Street. "You live here?" I remembered seeing flyers advertising them. I think you could buy one of them for close to a million dollars. Professor Hunter was definitely loaded.

"Yes." He turned onto the third story of the parking garage. He pulled into a space next to his black Audi coupe and a line of several other cars.

"Your neighbors have really nice cars too." Of course they did. Anyone who could afford to live here was insanely wealthy.

He stepped out of the convertible. "Those are mine."

"Seriously?" I got out of the car and looked around. "All of them? One of them looks like the Batmobile!"

"Yeah. Turns out it's never very convenient to drive though. And it doesn't give me any superpowers." He put his hands in his pockets as he watched me take my hoodie out of my bag, zip it up, and lift the hood over my head.

"Okay, I'm ready," I said.

"What, do you think I'm sneaking you in? I don't believe that anyone from the university lives here."

"Well I don't want to get caught. Someone in the lobby might see us."

He laughed. "Okay." He put his hand on the small of my back and led me over to an elevator. I noticed that there were two other elevators in the parking garage. One was in the middle and one was on the opposite side from us. *Weird.* I was just about to ask why there weren't any buttons by the elevator when he opened his wallet and swiped a card where the buttons usually would be. The doors opened immediately and we stepped in. He touched the button for the top floor and the elevator doors closed.

"Penthouse, huh?"

"I guess you could say that."

I looked around the elevator. There was a door on the opposite side of the elevator as well. So maybe each floor had two apartments? I thought about the other two elevators. No, each floor probably had six apartments. I had seen elevators going directly to rooms before in the movies, but never in real life. But when the elevator stopped, the doors didn't open. Professor Hunter took out a different card and swiped it next to the buttons. The doors parted, he grabbed my hand, and we stepped into his apartment.

"Wow." I walked down the few steps from the elevator and looked around. I was standing in his living room, which was surrounded by windows that overlooked the small college town. Professor Hunter walked over to the fireplace, touched a button, and a flame burst to life. There was no T.V., no magazines on the coffee table, and the modern couch looked like no one had ever sat on it. The kitchen to the right had granite countertops and shiny new appliances. And there was a dining area with a vase of fresh flowers in the center of the table.

I had completely forgotten to thank him for my flowers. "Oh, Professor Hunter. Thanks for the friendship roses."

He laughed. "You're welcome."

"But really, thank you. How did you know I was going to agree to skip class anyway?"

"I just hoped you would. And I know that I can be pretty persuasive."

"Yes, you can."

It was hard to pull my eyes away from his, but I was still curious about the apartment. I looked around again. I wasn't sure what I had expected. I just thought by being in his place I'd get a sense of who he was. The apartment was immaculate, but there were barely any decorations. It felt cold. It didn't look like anyone lived here at all. It looked more like a sample apartment that people could come look at when they were deciding if they wanted to buy one.

"Okay, so this is the living room." He walked over to me, grabbed my hand, and steered me to the windows all along the back of the apartment. I looked left toward Main Street. The lights from the small shops made it look beautiful. He wrapped his arms around me.

"It's beautiful."

"You're beautiful," he whispered into my ear.

I laughed. "I'm a mess." I was sweaty from the beach and my skin was tight from the salt water. I ran my fingers through my hair.

"Well, I was thinking maybe a quick shower could be the rain portion of the date you requested."

"Actually, that sounds perfect. Are you sure that's okay?" I turned around to face him.

He was smiling down at me. "Come with me." He grabbed my hand and led me to one of the closed off rooms next to the kitchen. He turned on the lights and I felt my body tremble slightly. It was his bedroom. I couldn't help but imagine all the things that he might do to me in here. Professor Hunter's bed was in the center. His sheets were pristine white and the bed was made perfectly. I never made my bed. *Ever.* Not even when my mother bugged me about it.

He turned on another light and stepped into his walk-in closet. There was a whole row of white collared shirts and suit jackets. And below it, all his pants were folded on hangers, even his jeans. *Who hangs up jeans?* I thought about the clothes all over the floor in my dorm room. He'd be horrified.

He had more shoes than even Melissa, and they lined the bottom of the closet. And the whole closet smelled like his cologne. It was like I had died and gone to heaven.

"You really don't need your sweaters back." I stepped beside him and looked at the dozens that were folded on shelves next to his dress shirts.

He laughed. "I'm afraid I don't really have anything for you to change into." He opened up a few drawers.

"Could I just borrow one of those shirts?"

He handed me one of the v-neck t-shirts from the drawer he had just opened, switched off the light, and led me to his bathroom. There was an elegant bath to the left with a few steps up to it. And attached was a shower with three glass walls. The vanity was to the right and the only things that were on it were his toothbrush and some toothpaste. How could anyone be this neat and organized?

Professor Hunter switched on the shower as I was looking around. Then he came up to me and slowly unzipped my hoodie. His hands touched my shoulders and slowly slid down my arms, pushing my hoodie until it fell to the ground. I had never felt so sexy in a hoodie before. He pulled my tank top up my sides and over my ribcage. I lifted my hands in the air and he pulled it off over my head. He unbuttoned and unzipped my pants, and then slowly slid them off my hips. Since I wasn't wearing a bra or underwear, I was left completely naked in the center of his bathroom.

"Do you mind if I join you?"

I shook my head no.

Professor Hunter pulled his polo off over his head. After spending the day at the beach he was even tanner. He shed his shorts and boxers. He was already starting to get another erection and I felt a shiver of electricity go through me. I wanted him again. I wanted him here, in his apartment, in his shower. I wanted to be his. He stepped into the shower and I followed him.

His hands were on me as soon as I was under the water. The water fell on our heads as we kissed under its constant stream. He reached over and grabbed a bottle from the ledge. I had never heard the brand name before, but when he poured some of the liquid into his hands I realized that it was part of what made him smell so good.

"Face the wall," he said. I did what I was told. He pushed me lightly so that my breasts were taut against the tile. He slowly rubbed his hands up the back of my legs, massaging my thighs. He cupped my ass in his hands. His fingers wandered over my ass and between my legs. My heartbeat quickened. I knew that I was wet. His fingers could easily slide inside of me. I moved my hips back slightly. But instead of answering my needs, he swept his hands away from my wetness and across my back. He massaged my shoulders. He ran his soapy hands up my arms and across my clavicle. He pulled me away from the wall slightly and his hands fell to my breasts. He massaged them gently. I could feel his erection pressed against the small of my back. I knew he could feel my heart beating fast. He had to be aware of what I wanted, but he wasn't giving it to me.

"Professor Hunter," I groaned. "Please."

He pulled me underneath the water. Chills went over my body as the soap washed away.

"Is something wrong, Penny?"

"No." It felt like my heart was going to beat out of my chest.

He pushed my back against the tile. "Is there something that you wanted?" His voice was so seductive.

I gulped. "Yes." His torso glistened from the water flowing down it. And the steam from the shower surrounded him. God he was sexy. He looked almost ethereal.

He leaned over and took one of my nipples in his mouth and bit it lightly. He pinched my other nipple between two of his fingers. I writhed under his touch.

"And what is it that you want?" He left a trail of kisses down my stomach and stopped right where I wanted it the most. I could feel his warm breath.

"You."

"Do you mean like this?" He stroked my pussy with his tongue.

"Professor Hunter," I moaned.

He put his knees on the tile floor and lifted my thighs over his shoulders. While I was admiring his strength, he slid two fingers inside of me.

I gasped.

"Or maybe you'd prefer that I fuck you with my fingers?" His dirty words made me want him even more.

"Yes!"

He moved his lips to my clit and sucked on it hard. I was pinned against the shower wall, completely immobile. He pumped his hand faster, moving his fingers in and out of me. His tongue continued to stroke my clit, driving me crazy.

"Yes!" I screamed again.

He pushed my thighs even farther apart. The position allowed his fingers to go even deeper. He was licking and swirling his tongue over my clit. I could feel my body begin to shudder in his arms. He placed his lips around my clit again and sucked hard.

"Professor Hunter!"

He continued to thrust his fingers in and out of me as I orgasmed. When I was completely spent, he lowered my feet back to the floor. He grabbed the bottle from the ledge and quickly washed himself in front of me. I just stood there, weakly, staring at him. I felt like I could just let my body slide down the sleek tile wall and fall asleep in the steam. But I wanted him.

He turned around to leave.

"Don't go." I reached out and let my hands slide down his wet abs. I grabbed his erection and moved my hand up and down his shaft.

He didn't say a word but I knew exactly what he wanted. I got down on my knees and stared into his eyes as I let my tongue stroke up and down his length. The muscles in his stomach tensed. I brought my lips to his tip and kissed it. I opened my mouth and licked my lips.

His Adam's apple rose and fell as he watched me. I took his thick, muscular cock in my mouth and slowly slid up and down. I tightened my lips as I heard him groan. I wanted to take him deeper. I took a deep breath and let his tip enter the back of my throat.

"Fuck."

He liked that. I tightened my lips again and went up and down his shaft as fast as I could. Then I forced him deeper into my throat. His cock twitched slightly and he pulled out of my mouth. *Oh my God, is he going to cum on me?* He pumped his fist up and down his length and a hot stream landed on my breasts. It was so sexy watching him lose control. His abs tensed. He looked so sexy standing there above me. Professor Hunter aimed another shot a little higher and it hit my chin. *Shit, don't hit my eyes!* I tilted my head back slightly and squeezed my breasts. His cock pulsed once more and the hot liquid landed once again on my chest. That was so hot. Making him come made me want him all over again. His cum dripped down my chest and stomach and onto my thighs.

"You look so sexy, Penny." He rinsed off under the water as he looked down at me. "I know you don't like when I leave you naked and alone, but I'm going to go make dinner while you finish up if that's alright."

"Okay." I stared at his firm ass as he exited the shower. *So sexy.*

I slowly got to my feet. I put soap on my breasts and washed away the sticky semen, and then grabbed his bottle of shampoo and washed my hair. I took a deep breath as I rinsed off. This was the best day of my life. I didn't want it to end. I closed my eyes and let the water hit my face. I wished it was more of his hot cum rather than hot water.

There was a towel folded on the ground for me when I stepped out. It was the softest, fluffiest towel that had ever touched my skin. Professor Hunter lived like he was in a luxurious five star hotel. After drying off I pulled his shirt over my head. Originally I had planned to wear my jean shorts with his t-shirt, but his shirt was too long. I looked in the mirror. It just covered my butt. I turned to the side. *I think he'll like this.*

I went over to the vanity and opened one of the drawers. I didn't want to snoop but I badly needed a comb. After the swim in the ocean and the breeze from the convertible it was a mess of knots. There was barely anything in the drawer, and everything seemed perfectly in place. I found his comb in the back of it and tried to get the knots out of my hair. I smoothed my hair into a ponytail and found some moisturizer to put through it so it wouldn't get frizzy. Self-consciously, I looked in the mirror at my reflection. I had never not worn makeup around him. Actually, I had never not worn makeup around any boy. I pinched my cheeks to give them a rosy hue. That was the best I could do.

Trying not to think of it, I pushed my dirty clothes and towel into a corner and headed out of the bathroom.

CHAPTER 34

Monday

"You look breathtaking, Penny. I don't understand how everything I own looks better on you."

I could feel my face blush. When I reached him, he grabbed my hand and twirled me around. He was wearing a pair of jeans and a shirt just like the one I was wearing. I couldn't help but realize how normal this was. And comfortable.

I laughed. "It smells amazing. What are we having?" I sat down on a stool at the island in his kitchen.

"One of the only things I know how to make. Vodka chicken."

"That sounds fantastic. So, if this is the only thing you know how to make, do you usually order out?" I let my chin rest in my hands. The granite countertop was cold on my elbows.

"Rarely."

I laughed. "What, do you have a personal chef or something?"

"Yeah." He opened the oven and peered inside. "Almost ready."

"Why do you never volunteer information? It's like I have to force it out of you."

He shrugged his shoulders. "I'm sorry. I'm not used to people asking me questions that aren't going to be used for articles or something. I've gotten good at giving very vague answers. If you'd like to ask me a few questions, I'll be happy to try and answer them for you."

He grabbed two plates, two sets of silverware, and two glasses. He already seemed to be avoiding a question and I hadn't even asked him anything yet.

"I can do that." I slid off the stool and grabbed the dishes from his hands. "Here, or in the dining room?"

"The dining room is good."

I finished setting the table as he came over. "And now for the last part of your ideal date." He uncorked a bottle of champagne and poured me a glass. "I think that covers everything. So how did I do? Was today worth skipping class for?"

"I'd do anything to spend more time with you. Today was absolutely magical." I held up my glass. "And here's to getting to know each other better tonight."

He laughed and clinked his glass against mine. I took a sip of the champagne. I had never even tasted champagne before, but I liked it.

"So," I said and sat down. "How long have you lived in this apartment?"

He sat down across from me. "Ever since I started working at the university."

I looked around again. "So why aren't there any decorations? There isn't a single picture anywhere."

"I wasn't sure how long I'd be staying for."

"Why?" I could tell he was starting to get uncomfortable. He shifted in his chair.

"Like I told you before, I needed a change. But I wasn't sure if the change would be permanent."

"Do you still think you'll go back to New York?" I didn't want to lose him. Whatever this was between us, I didn't want to picture it ending. We had only just started dating.

The timer on the oven went off.

"There's nothing left for me in New York." His expression grew dark. He got up and went back into the kitchen. He grabbed the casserole dish with a pair of potholders and brought it back to the table. Why did he look mad at me? He told me I could ask him a few questions. He put a scoop of the dish on my plate. It was penne noodles, chicken, and vodka sauce.

I didn't pick up my fork. "So, the move is permanent now?" I held my breath as I waited for his answer.

He gave me a smile. "I believe so."

Yes! "What made you change your mind?"

"You."

I looked down at my plate. He was probably just joking, but I felt my face blush regardless. I laughed awkwardly and took a bite of the vodka chicken. "This is delicious."

"Thank you."

I looked up and he was staring at me.

"Do you have any more questions for me, Penny?"

"Only a million more."

He laughed.

"Tell me about your family."

He finished chewing a bite of food. "Well, I have an older sister and a younger brother."

"Tell me about them."

"My sister lives in New York." Professor Hunter finished off his glass of champagne and poured himself another.

"And what does she do?"

"She's a writer."

"Has she written anything that I may have heard of?"

"Probably not."

I wasn't sure whether I should be offended or not. I decided not to dwell on it. He was probably just uncomfortable answering all these questions. "And what about your brother?"

"The last time I heard from him, he was in Costa Rica."

"Wow. What does he do there?"

"Nothing as far as I know. He's been taking time off to travel."

"Well that's fun." Professor Hunter looked so uncomfortable. He must not have been close with his brother. I decided to change the subject. "And your parents?"

"What about them?" His voice was so tense. He clearly did not want to talk about his family. But I wanted to know more.

"Well, where are they?"

"I'm not close with my parents."

"That's a shame."

He laughed. "No, it's not." He shifted in his chair. "And what about your family, Penny?"

I was about to ask why he was fighting with his parents, but he had avoided my next question with a question of his own. "I'm an only child. Growing up, I was really close with my parents. But not as much since I started college."

"And why is that?"

Now I was the one who felt uncomfortable. "I don't know. I feel like some of the best things about college are just things you don't really talk about with your parents."

"You mean like me?"

"Yeah," I laughed. "I mean, I can't exactly tell them about you. I don't even like to imagine how upset they'd be with me."

"So you're ashamed that you're fucking your Comm professor?"

It wasn't just the words that he used, but the way that he said it that made me uncomfortable. "That's not really the way that I think about it. I'm definitely not ashamed. I really like you, Professor Hunter."

His expression stayed the same. What the hell was his problem?

"If that's the way that you think of me, then I guess you've gotten all that you want from me." I felt hurt. He made me think it was more. I wished I wasn't wearing just his t-shirt. I folded my arms across my chest and looked down at the table.

"I knew I wanted you since I first ran into you in that coffee shop. But I wasn't going to pursue you because you're a student. When you showed up in my class it complicated things, though. Every time I saw you, every answer you gave for the daily assignments, and every time we spoke made it impossible for me to get you out of my head. I knew I wanted you. I thought if I let myself give into the temptation I could move on."

I felt so cheap. He just wanted me for my body. He was just like Austin. No, he was worse. I stood up. I had to get away from him. I didn't want him to see me cry.

"Penny, sit down."

I didn't move.

"Sit down, or I'll make you sit down."

I gulped. His words had such a power over me. What the hell was happening to me? I sat back down in my chair and looked at him.

"I don't understand why you're upset. We've already talked about all of this. Everything is different now. I couldn't move on. I don't want to move on. You're all that I think about." He rubbed his face in his hands. "Geez, you have this way of crawling under my skin."

"Why, because I want to know more about you? That's what people that are dating do! I don't know why you always get upset when we try to talk."

"Because I don't want you to know what kind of man I am."

"I think that you're exactly the kind of man that I want." I swallowed hard. I grabbed my glass and took another sip of champagne. "Can you please just try to answer a few more questions without exploding?"

"I'm sorry." He took a deep breath.

"Are your parents wealthy?" I didn't want to antagonize him, but I needed him to answer my questions.

He sighed. "Yes. But everything I have is because of the choices I've made. I don't want a cent from them."

I could tell he was trying hard to stay calm, but there was such anger in his voice.

"Penny, do you enjoy pushing all my buttons?"

"You're always so in control. It's a little fun to see you squirm."

He raised his left eyebrow at me.

"I just feel like you're hiding something from me. And I don't understand why. I told you that I trusted you. Don't you trust me?" My stomach churned when I said it. He shouldn't trust me. I was lying to him about my age. I was being a hypocrite.

He didn't answer right away. I could feel his eyes boring into my soul. *Does he know I'm hiding something too?*

"I do trust you," he finally said.

"So what happened with your parents? Why are you so mad at them?"

"It's complicated."

"Well, you're a professor. You should be good at explaining things. Make me understand."

He sighed. "My whole life they put so much pressure on me. To the point where I felt like I didn't get to make any of my own choices. It took me far too long to realize. And when I finally did, my life was no longer mine at all. I felt like I was drowning. Becoming a professor was the first thing that I decided for myself in a long time."

I could see how vulnerable he was. The strength and control he possessed were gone for a second. He looked up at me.

"So screw them," I said.

He laughed. "Penny, being here, with you...I finally feel like I can breathe again."

"I feel the same way. You make me feel alive."

"Come with me." He got up, put his hand out for me, and pulled me to my feet. I followed him to his bedroom.

My heart was racing. He pulled his shirt off, then his jeans, then his boxers.

"Professor Hunter. I'm a little sore."

"Penny, you'd be surprised to find out how many times you can orgasm in a day. Your body can take it. And I want to show you that this is more than just fucking for me too. So I promise to be gentle."

More than fucking? What is he going to do to me? I really did trust him. I lifted my shirt off over my head so that I was standing naked in his pristine bedroom. Now I was the one feeling vulnerable.

He lifted me into his arms and placed me down on his bed. He kissed the inside of my ankle and traced kisses up the inside of my leg. I felt him lightly nip my inner thigh and then he moved to my other ankle and repeated the process. When he nipped my inner thigh this time, I groaned. My whole body tingled with desire. It didn't matter that I was sore. I wanted him. I needed him inside of me, filling me, claiming my body. I could feel that my clit was swollen when he slowly circled his tongue around it. But it didn't matter. I had never wanted him more. My hips rose to meet him.

But he quickly moved his head and kissed the palm of my left hand. He trailed kisses up my arm, slowly across my shoulder and clavicle, and then down my other arm. When his lips kissed my other palm it felt like every inch of my body was aroused. He had awoken something inside of me that I didn't even know existed. He kissed between my breasts and slowly went down my stomach. *Yes.* That was it.

His lips gently sucked on my clit while his hands massaged my inner thighs. When his fingers finally touched me I knew I was ready for him. But he still entered me slowly, lovingly. My heartbeat quickened even more. His fingers felt so good. He leaned over top of me and kissed my forehead, my nose, and then my mouth. His fingers pressed against my walls, massaging me in the most intimate way. I could feel his erection stiffen as he kissed me deeply. When he pulled away I could see my want reflected in his own eyes. I swallowed hard. My lips parted. I was panting.

He moved one hand under my ass and lifted my hips slightly as he slowly filled me with his length.

"Oh!"

He bit his lip as he looked down at me. I liked when he was rough with me. I loved when he fucked me. And this was somehow completely different, yet the same. He pushed firmly against me, going deeper than he had ever been before. *Yes!* Was it possible that this was even better than fucking? I felt so connected to him. My hands explored the muscles on his back.

He kissed me as he began to thrust in and out of me. My fingertips dug into his flesh. His abs pressed against me as he went in deeper still. "You're so gorgeous," he whispered into my ear. "Every inch of you." He bit my earlobe and I felt myself clench around his hard cock.

"Yes!" I moaned. He kissed me passionately, riding out my orgasm. When my orgasm subsided, he rubbed his nose against mine. A smile curled on his lips.

"I'm not done with you yet. I'll never be done with you." His voice was doused with desire.

He rolled over and pulled me with him so that I was now on top. He grabbed my ass and guided his cock in and out of me. I could see him watching my breasts bounce with every movement. He moved his hands to my waist, slowly slid them up the sides of my torso, and grabbed my breasts in his hands. I continued to move my hips, letting him slide in and out of me, as he firmly squeezed my breasts. He rubbed my swollen nipples and then looked into my eyes as one of his hands slid down my stomach. His fingers began to massage my clit.

"Professor Hunter." I let my head drop back. I was going to come again.

His hands grabbed the sides of my face and pulled me down into him, kissing me. We rolled over again and I was pinned to the soft mattress. He thrust himself a little faster in and out of me. I wrapped my legs around the back of him and grabbed his ass. I pulled him into me. As his hot cum entered me, he closed his eyes and groaned. It was the most wonderful feeling in the world. His hard cock throbbing inside of me was all I could take. My own orgasm washed over me as his heat burst through me again.

He slowly opened his eyes and looked into mine as he pulled out of me. Smolder.

CHAPTER 35

Monday

There was a strange pressure building inside of my chest. It felt like I was about to cry. Why was I falling apart here? I had everything I wanted in this man. But what he had just done to me. The way he had made me feel. Now everything felt more real.

I quickly sat up and pulled my legs in, hugging them close. The tightness in my chest was growing. It felt like I was drowning. I took a deep breath to try to calm myself. *What is wrong with me?*

Professor Hunter sat up and cupped my chin in his hand. "Penny, what's wrong?" His brow was furrowed.

"Nothing." I blinked to try and remove the tears that were trying to fall. I hugged my legs tighter.

He rubbed the side of my chin with his thumb and didn't say a word. He looked truly concerned.

"It's just. For some reason, this whole time, it's seemed like I made this all up. Like it's this fantasy and you're not real. And I'm afraid that I'm going to wake up from this amazing dream and you're going to be gone. That you're just going to disappear."

"I've told you that I'm not going anywhere. There's no reason to be upset about that. Please don't cry." He wiped away one of the tears that had fallen down my cheek.

"But what we just did. I know you said you were going to be gentle. But I expected it to be like the other times. This whole day just seemed different. More intimate. I don't know. I didn't expect to feel so...so..."

"No one's ever made love to you."

I felt embarrassed. He didn't even ask it like it was a question. He just knew. *Why had I opened my mouth?* "Well, I thought so. But no, not like...not like that." I was so pathetic.

"I didn't mean to make you uncomfortable." He rubbed another tear off my cheek. "How many partners have you been with?"

Sexual partners? What the hell is this conversation? "One." I felt so inadequate. If I wasn't uncomfortable before, I definitely was now.

He wrapped his arms around me and pulled me down on top of him. I expected him to say something, but he just held me against his chest. I listened to his steady heartbeat.

I had a feeling that I didn't want to know the answer to my next question, but I couldn't resist asking anyway. "And how many partners have you been with?"

He sighed. "A little more than that."

"How many more?"

"Penny, I don't want you to think poorly of me."

"More than five?"

He sighed again.

"More than ten?"

"I spent a large portion of my college years fairly drunk."

"More than fifteen?"

"We should probably stop playing this game."

"Professor Hunter, you're a slut!"

He laughed. "You seem to enjoy all my experience."

I cringed. I didn't like to picture him with other women.

"And what about your one, Penny?"

"What about him?" I didn't want to talk about Austin. Not at all, ever. But especially not here in Professor Hunter's bed. I slid off of him onto my side and rested my head in my hand.

"One is rather intimate. Is he someone I should be worried about?"

I laughed. "No."

"So you no longer speak to him?"

Did he somehow know that I had seen him this semester? "No. I doubt that I'll ever talk to him again. He's an immature asshole."

"And why is that?"

"Why do you want to know?" I didn't want to be talking about this.

"Because I don't want to make the same mistakes with you that he did."

I sighed. I wanted this conversation to be over. "There isn't much to tell. We dated last semester. He didn't speak to me all summer. He made me feel worthless."

"So you broke up with him?"

"You can't really break up with someone who you never officially went out with."

He took my hand in his. "Penny Taylor, I promise not to make you feel worthless. And I'll try not to act like an asshole." He smiled. His fingers intertwined with mine.

"I don't know, Professor Hunter. From what I've found out about you, it seems like I'm just going to end up as another notch on your bedpost."

He laughed. "That's not who I am anymore."

"I thought it was impossible for people to change?"

"I came here for a change. And I think I'm better off because of it." He pulled me toward him so that my head was resting on his chest again. I let my leg cross over him.

I felt so safe in his arms. I knew why I had gotten so upset tonight. Because I wasn't just fucking my professor. I was in deep. I loved him. *I'm in love with my Comm professor.* I breathed in his sweet scent. This moment could last forever and it wouldn't be long enough.

***

I reached out my hand, expecting to feel his chiseled abs, but all I felt was soft, silky sheets. I opened my eyes. The bed was empty. The sound of the shower must have woken me. I rolled over and looked at the alarm clock on the nightstand. It was 7 a.m. I needed to get back to my dorm room so I could change before my first class. I slowly slid out of bed, lifted my arms above my head, and yawned.

The shirt I had borrowed from him was nowhere in sight. I walked into his closet and turned on the light. I ran my fingers along the row of his dress shirts. If I didn't have to get to class, I'd put one of those on and tempt him to seduce me. I smiled to myself. He had made love to me last night. This was real. He wasn't going to disappear. His intoxicating smell was all around me. I pulled open the drawer that I had borrowed a shirt from last night. There were a few different colors. I grabbed a blue one off the bottom. As I pulled it over my head I heard a clink on the ground.

When I looked down I didn't see anything. I got down on my hands and knees and looked under the bureau. Something shiny glinted from the corner. I grabbed the item and pulled it out from under the dresser. It was a gold ring. *It can't be.* There were words inscribed along the inner band. I took a deep breath as I drew the ring closer to my face in order to read the inscription.

"James & Isabella. 4-30-13."

No. It felt like my heart stopped beating. The tears began to well in my eyes. *He's married?* I gulped. *He's married?!* I was having a hard time processing the words. *How could he do this to me?* I put my face in my hands and shook my head. *How could he do this to her?* The water turned off in the other room. *Shit.* I quickly wiped my eyes and got up off the floor. I had to get out of there. I threw the ring back in the drawer and ran out of Professor Hunter's bedroom.

PART 3

CHAPTER 36

Tuesday

I was blinded by my tears. *How could I be so naive?* He was the predator and I was the prey. And I had willingly fallen into his trap. His perfect physique and his suggestive words had worn down all my inhibitions. I tripped over my own feet and fell onto his kitchen floor. Every inch of me wanted to stay down. I felt so weak. The weight of what I had done was heavy on my shoulders. I was a mistress.

"Fuck," I murmured out loud. I wiped my eyes again and stood up. I had to get out of there. I didn't want to hear his explanations. The guilt would always weigh on me. It didn't matter that I hadn't known it at the time. Either way, I had slept with a married man. I had tried to ask him questions, but he had skirted around the answers flawlessly. He was a manipulative asshole. I ran over to the elevator and looked for the button. I pressed the glowing circle.

"Shit, come on!" I hit the button with my fist. The elevator dinged and the doors slid open. I stepped onto it. I pressed the first button I saw inside the elevator. My heart was racing. The doors slowly closed. *Thank God.*

I pressed my back against the opposite side of the elevator and slowly slid until my butt hit the ground. I hadn't just slept with an older man. I hadn't just slept with my professor. I had slept with a married man. What had I become? That wasn't me. None of that was me. I put my face into my hands and let myself cry. It felt like my stomach was in my chest. Because the truth was, I hadn't just slept with him. I loved him.

The elevator dinged and I fell backwards. I had forgotten that there was a door on this side. *Shit!* I pulled the t-shirt down so that I didn't reveal myself. I was looking up into a man's crotch.

"Miss, are you okay?" His hands were on my shoulders, pulling me to my feet.

"I'm fine, I'm fine." My face was more crimson than it had ever been. I wiped my tears off my cheeks. I was standing half naked in the lobby of Professor Hunter's prestigious apartment building. The man who had helped me to my feet was staring at my legs. He was wearing shorts and a sweaty t-shirt. He must have just worked out. Probably at a gym somewhere in the building. I pulled the sides of my shirt down again. *This isn't happening.*

"Are you sure you're okay?" It looked like he wanted to laugh.

"Yes. Thank you." I stepped back onto the elevator. *Please don't get on.*

The man stepped onto the elevator beside me.

Damn it!

"I'm guessing you weren't trying to go to the lobby," he said. He had stopped staring at me and was now looking at the elevator doors. "Where were you trying to go?"

"The parking garage. Third floor."

The man pressed a button on the elevator. His lips were pursed together and there were a few small lines around his eyes as he tried not to let his laughter escape. "Bad morning?"

"You have no idea." I looked away from him. This was so embarrassing. The ultimate walk of shame. I had never been more mortified in my life.

"I suppose it will only get better from here then."

"God, I hope so." I squeezed through the doors as they were still opening and ran as fast as I could. The cement floor of the parking garage was freezing against my bare feet. I wrapped my arms around myself and ran toward Professor Hunter's convertible. Luckily my bag was still on the passenger seat of the car. I pulled my sunglasses out and put them on my face. If I was lucky, no one would notice me on my way back to my dorm room. My beach towel was wadded in a ball at the bottom of the bag and it was cold and damp. I sighed. I grabbed my bag and hoisted it over my shoulder.

I looked around the parking garage for a set of stairs and ran toward them. Professor Hunter would have realized I was missing by now. Would he try to come after me? Would he even realize something was wrong? I ran down the stairs and stepped outside of the parking garage. There was a chill in the air this morning. It was as if autumn had appeared overnight.

If I went toward Main Street, I'd easily be able to find my way back to my dorm. But I didn't want to be seen in just a men's t-shirt. My teeth chattered as I crossed the road. I walked as casually as possible down a side street. People lived here. Respectable families were probably just waking up for their normal days. *Please don't see me.* I quickened my pace and turned down another street.

My phone buzzed. I grabbed it out of my bag and looked down at Professor Hunter's text:

"I would have driven you home. Persuading you to miss two classes would have been way too irresponsible."

Persuading me to have sex with you when you're married was irresponsible! That pretentious bastard! I shoved my phone back into my bag.

A car drove by and beeped at me.

Are you kidding me? Screw this. I began running. I didn't care if anyone saw me. I just wanted to be safely in my dorm. Behind one of the houses ahead of me, I could see the small parking lot by my dorm. I looked around but didn't see anyone around. I ran through someone's yard. The ground was slightly muddy and I tried to ignore the squishing noise that my feet were making and the mud splattering on my legs.

I peered around the back of the house to see if anyone was there. The coast was clear, but there were large bushes all along the perimeter of their backyard. *Damn it!* I moved a few branches with my hands and squeezed through as best I could. I tried not to cry out as the small thorns pricked against my bare skin. When I got untangled from the foliage, I was left with a torn shirt, tons of tiny scratches on my arms and legs, and splotches of mud on my calves and shins. But my dorm was right there. And everything was silent. Thankfully college students were always reliable at not waking up until they had to. I ran through the parking lot and up the stairs of Sussex. I quickly pulled out my wallet and pressed the access card against the sign.

The familiar buzz of the doors unlocking almost made me cry. I opened the door and ran into the building, up the stairs, and to my room.

Panting, I unlocked the door and tiptoed into my room. Melissa's light snoring greeted my ears. *Oh, thank God.* Finally something had gone my way. I grabbed my shower caddy and went to the bathroom. I needed to get the smell of Professor Hunter off of me.

I locked the shower door, pulled off Professor Hunter's destroyed t-shirt, and closed the curtain. The water stung the cuts on my arms and legs. The bottom of my feet were sore and scratched too. But soon I didn't feel the pain, just the shame of what I had done. The pressure I had felt building in my chest last night was back. *Why did I let myself fall in love with such a creep?* I grabbed my soap and began to scrub my skin harder than I ever had. *Get off of me. Get off of me!* I began crying again. I lifted my face under the showerhead and let the water wash away my tears.

I dried off, wrapped my towel around myself, and stepped out of the shower. *Just don't think about him.* I brushed my teeth and combed my hair. Back in my room, I put on a pair of jeans, a t-shirt, and a light jacket. My phone buzzed. I hesitated before pulling it out of the canvas beach bag. I swiped my finger across the screen and saw another text from Professor Hunter.

"Did you get back to your dorm okay? You left your clothes here..."

He could tell something was off. Good. I didn't have anything to say to him. He could figure it out on his own. *Fuck him.*

CHAPTER 37

Tuesday

My anger hadn't dissipated. If anything, having all day to think about it made me even angrier. I continued to stare at the roses on my desk. The cocky liar roses. I should have seen some kind of sign, but there hadn't been any. Professor Hunter had been so sweet. I took a deep breath. *Screw him.* I got up and lifted the vase off my desk. It was tempting to throw them in the trash, but they were so pretty. Instead, I put them into my closet and closed the door.

"Okay." Melissa held up the two bags and scrutinized the handwriting. "I think that says vegetable lo mein. This one must be yours." She handed me one of the bags and sat down on her bed.

I opened up the bag and pulled out the chopsticks and cute little cardboard container. Chinese takeout was my comfort food. And right now I needed it more than ever.

"So, are you going to tell me why you wanted Chinese food tonight?"

"What do you mean?" I ripped the paper off the chopsticks and snapped them apart. I could barely use chopsticks, but I refused to eat Chinese food without them. It was half the fun. I could feel Melissa's gaze on me.

"Penny, you only ever want Chinese takeout when you're upset."

"That's not true." I wished I was alone right now.

Melissa laughed. "Right. So, you're saying that nothing is wrong?"

"Yeah, everything's peachy."

"Okay, so two things real quick. First, no one uses the phrase peachy unless they are in fact not peachy. Plus, your roses are gone."

"People say peachy all the time. That's a thing. And my roses are still here, I just moved them."

Melissa looked around the room and then at the trash. "Where?"

"In the closet."

Melissa laughed. "And why are your roses in the closet?"

Because I hate Professor Hunter! "Allergies."

"Penny, you are not allergic to roses."

"I think I might be."

"Why?"

"I have the sniffles."

"You're being weird." Melissa took a bite of her food. "So you're really not going to tell me what's wrong?"

"No."

"So there is something wrong then?"

Crap! I didn't want to answer her question. Instead, I fumbled with my chopsticks and somehow got some lo mein into my mouth. My phone buzzed but I didn't look at it. It was probably Professor Hunter and I didn't want to know what he had to say.

"Did you and James have a fight?"

I tilted the cardboard container so that I could shovel some of the food into my mouth.

"I mean, you hid the roses. You're not all smiles anymore, even though you just spent all day and night with him yesterday. And you're ignoring his texts. So what did he do?"

She was good. "He didn't do anything. It's more what he didn't do." He forgot to tell me he was married. He left off the fact that he was a cheating pig.

Melissa ate quietly for a moment. She was definitely scrutinizing me. "And is that making you feel better?"

I had tilted the container again. I knew I was being barbaric, but my patience with the chopsticks had waned awhile ago. "Yes," I said with my mouth still full.

Melissa laughed. "You know, if he doesn't even realize that you're fighting, he won't be able to fix whatever it was that he didn't do."

"I know."

"So maybe you should talk to him?"

"Whose side are you on anyway?"

"Yours, of course. But I also know how stubborn you can be. And maybe you shouldn't let go of a good thing just because it suddenly got tough."

It wasn't just hard. It was horrible, immoral, disgusting. I just wanted the conversation to end, so I nodded my head. "Maybe you're right."

Melissa smiled. She loved being right.

"How's Josh?"

"He's good." She bit her lip. I could tell she was holding something back.

"What?" I asked.

"He invited me to the Sigma Pi formal." She couldn't hold back her smile.

"That's awesome."

"Mhm. Penny, I really like him."

"I know. And I'm really happy for you guys." I was able to say it sincerely despite my dreadful mood.

CHAPTER 38

Wednesday

Professor Hunter lifted his shirt over his head and stared down at me. His tanned abs made desire explode through my body, all the tension between us gone. He leaned over me, his strong arms on either side of me. I wanted him. Why wasn't he kissing me? I ran my hand through his hair.

"Penny." He rubbed my cheek with the side of his hand. "I'm not yours to touch," he said seductively. "I told you it had to be a one-time thing."

***

I woke up panting. Professor Hunter could even arouse me in my dreams. My heart was racing. He had warned me. Kind of. He had wanted it to be a one-time thing. He had told me he thought if he gave into temptation he could forget about me. He didn't just want to forget about me, he needed to. I pictured the suitcase in his office. He was probably traveling back and forth to visit his wife. *Shit.* And he had told me he didn't want me to know what kind of man he was. There were so many signs. And I had thrown myself at him without thinking twice about any of them. I had acted like a slut. I pulled my phone off my desk and opened up the message I had ignored last night.

"Penny, I had a wonderful day with you. And a wonderful night. If there's something that I've done to upset you, I'll fix it. Just tell me what it is."

I typed out, "I'll talk to you after class," and pressed send. Melissa was right, we needed to talk. Mostly I needed to apologize for tempting him to cheat on his wife. He shouldn't have done it, but I was to blame too. I needed to tell him it was over before it got any worse. I rolled out of bed and began getting ready.

As I pulled the textbooks out of my bag, my fingers brushed against soft petals. Tyler. I picked up the flattened rose from the bottom of my backpack. Maybe Professor Hunter was right. There wasn't such a thing as a friendship rose. I opened up my closet and looked at the beautiful roses that Professor Hunter had sent me. The one in my hand was wilted and sad looking in comparison. I closed the door, poured some water in a cup, and put Tyler's rose in it on my desk. Despite its appearance, that rose was without a question the sweetest. Once I ended things with Professor Hunter, maybe I could finally give Tyler a fair chance.

But this was going to be hard. I put on waterproof mascara just in case. Even though I was mad at Professor Hunter, I still loved him. It was going to be awhile before I could shake those feelings. I had thought that Austin had broken my heart. But that didn't even compare to this. I actually felt a pain in my chest. And my stomach hurt. My Chinese food fix hadn't helped at all.

I pulled my backpack over my shoulder and left my dorm room. The air was chilly again today. A few leaves were even turning yellow and red. It was time for a fresh start. This whole time I had thought Professor Hunter was just a dream. Now he needed to become one. I strolled into Smith and up the stairs to Professor Hunter's classroom. No, the Comm classroom. I needed to change my way of thinking about things.

I made my way to my usual seat. My heart was already pounding. I smiled as Tyler walked in. He came over to me and sat down.

"Want to grab lunch with me today?" he asked.

"Definitely."

"How about Grottos again? That was delicious."

"That sounds perfect."

"I actually have some news to share with you."

"Yeah? What's up?"

Professor Hunter walked into the room and I stopped breathing.

"I'll tell you at lunch," Tyler said.

Professor Hunter's hair was unruly and he was wearing his glasses. It didn't look like he had slept at all. He looked at me and I could see the pain he was feeling. I felt the same way he did. Not talking to him had been impossibly hard. For a second all I wanted to do was kiss him. I broke eye contact and looked down at my desk. I needed to be stronger than that.

Professor Hunter cleared his throat. "Passion," he said. "Passion is what drives a good speech. Passion drives everything. And it's probably one of the reasons why you chose your majors."

I heard the squeak of the chalk on the board and looked up. I had to will myself to not undress him with my eyes.

"Without passion, there really is no meaning in life." He turned around and locked eyes with me again.

Is he trying to justify his actions? I had lived this long without passion and I was fine. I took a deep breath. But was I really? The way I felt around Professor Hunter was so different. It was like I was alive for the first time.

"Today I'd like us all to talk about something that we're passionate about. Ray, kick us off."

Ray stood up. "I'm passionate about any good booty." The class laughed and he began to sit down.

"Ray, don't you dare sit down." I had never heard Professor Hunter sound so angry before. Except for when he talked that way to me in private.

Ray laughed awkwardly and continued to stand there.

"Passion is not humorous. Unless your passion is humor. Don't make a joke of my assignments, Raymond."

"I'm not, man."

"That's Professor Hunter to you. Get the hell out of my class," he growled.

Ray leaned down and grabbed his backpack. He left the room without turning around. The whole class was silent.

Professor Hunter cleared his throat. "*I* am passionate about teaching. That would be an acceptable answer." He called the next name and the girl rose to her feet. It looked like she was shaking.

I tuned out her answer. What the hell was happening? Had Professor Hunter completely lost his mind? I had never seen a professor freak out on a student like that before. He had a hot temper. I remembered what Melissa had said about how he got fired from his last teaching job. It probably was true.

"Penny Taylor," Professor Hunter said. The way my name rolled off his tongue made all my muscles clench.

I rose to my feet and locked eyes with him. "I'm passionate about honesty." I quickly sat back down. *That's right, Professor Hunter, I know your secret!*

He raised his left eyebrow. Did he really not know what I was referring to? How dense was he? After the last student shared what they were passionate about, Professor Hunter dismissed the class.

"See you at Grotto's," Tyler said and walked off.

When the class had finally emptied, I got to my feet and walked toward his desk. My heart was pounding. I needed to be strong. He was a pig.

"Penny." Professor Hunter put his hand on my arm. I didn't want to melt under his touch. Would his effect on me ever go away?

"I'm sorry, Professor Hunter. We need to end this before we make it any worse." I took a step back from him, removing his hand from me.

"End this? Have your feelings for me changed?"

"Professor Hunter, everything's changed."

"You're right, I like you more than ever." He smiled at me, but the smile didn't go to his eyes. He looked upset.

I shook my head. "I know."

"Then what's the problem?"

"Professor Hunter, I know." I took a deep breath. "I know your secret."

I could see his body tense. I expected him to start talking right away, but he didn't begin explaining his side. He just stared at me, waiting for me to explain. Which gave me a terrible unsettling feeling. He didn't know what I was even referring to. He had more than one horrible secret. I probably hadn't even scratched the surface.

"The fact that you don't even know what I'm referring to is disgusting," I said. I could feel the tears beginning to well in my eyes.

He stepped toward me and put his hand on my arm again. "Penny, let's go to my office to talk about this."

"I'm not going anywhere with you." I took another step away from him.

"Whatever you think you know, you couldn't possibly understand. Just give me a chance to explain."

Why do I have an urge to console him right now? The hurt in his eyes was weighing on me. "No, I think I do understand. And I'm sorry that I let anything happen between us."

"Don't say that, Penny." He was getting mad. I didn't want to fight with him. And if cheating on his wife wasn't his only secret then I didn't want to be anywhere near him.

"You were right to hide what kind of man you are from me. You're not at all who I thought you were. Don't text me, Professor Hunter." I turned briskly and walked out of the room.

"Penny!"

As soon as I left the room I let the tears stream down my cheeks. I couldn't believe that he wouldn't even admit it. And what other horrible secrets was he hiding? I kept walking so that he couldn't come after me.

CHAPTER 39

Wednesday

"Hey, Penny," Tyler said. He was all smiles.

I took a deep breath and smiled back at him. It felt so good to smile. We walked into the restaurant together and the hostess showed us to a booth. I sat down across from Tyler. He was looking at me curiously.

"Are you okay, Penny?"

"What? Yeah, I'm fine." I looked down at the table and tucked a loose strand of hair behind my ear. I was suddenly nervous to be around him. "So have you figured out what you're going to talk about in your next speech?"

"You know what, I think I have. But you'll have to wait and hear about it in class."

I laughed. "Why? Is it something that's going to embarrass me again?"

"You're so conceited. My speech has nothing to do with you. Geez, I do that one time and set a precedent." He laughed. "At the same time though, you get pretty easily embarrassed, so it's hard to tell."

I rolled my eyes at him. "So I really can't know? I don't get a special advanced screening of your speech?"

"No, it's a secret."

I bit my lip. *Secrets.*

Our waiter came over and Tyler ordered a cheese pizza for us. When he left, Tyler was staring at me again.

"Melissa's super excited about the Sigma Pi formal," I said as casually as I could muster. "It sounds like a lot of fun."

"Oh, did Josh ask her?"

"Yes." I waited a minute. I thought he might ask me, but he stayed silent.

"You look different," he finally said.

"How so?" *Sad maybe? Upset? Emotionally drained?*

"Tan," Tyler said and smiled. "What, did you go to the beach or something?"

I burst out crying. I wasn't sure if it was the reminder of my date with Professor Hunter, being rejected by Tyler, or just being with someone I felt so comfortable with. But I sat there crying in the middle of the restaurant.

"Penny?"

A moment later I felt his arms around me. He pulled me to his chest and rubbed my back. Why was I crying about Professor Hunter? Screw him! I took a few deep breaths to stop my tears from falling.

"I'm sorry, Penny," Tyler whispered. "You don't look tan at all, I swear."

I couldn't help but laugh. I felt so comfortable in Tyler's arms. Everything I had wanted had actually been right in front of me the whole time. I tilted my head back slightly. He was looking down at me, concern etched across his face. I didn't want him to be concerned for me. I wanted him to want me. I leaned in and placed a kiss on his lips. He hesitated for a second and then kissed me back. All that waiting. All that pent-up passion. He pushed my back against the side of the booth and leaned into me. I felt a warm heat course through my body as his kisses became more fierce. He did still like me. This felt so right. I grabbed the collar of his shirt and pulled him even closer to me.

But almost as quickly as it started, Tyler pulled away. "Shit, Penny." He stood up and rubbed his hand through his hair.

"I'm sorry, Tyler. I was wrong before. I don't want to be just friends."

"Why now?" He was looking everywhere but at me.

Why was he so upset? Isn't this what he wanted? "Because I'm slow."

He laughed, but it sounded forced. "Penny, I did what you wanted. I just started seeing someone."

I stared up at him. "Oh God." I cursed under my breath. "Tyler, I'm so sorry. I didn't know. I'm sorry. I'm going to go." I got to my feet.

"Penny, we haven't even eaten yet."

"I'm not hungry. I'm sorry, Tyler. Please just pretend this never happened." I pulled my backpack over my shoulder and fled the restaurant.

***

I had made two men cheat in the course of one week. I flopped down onto my bed and screamed into my pillow. *What the hell is wrong with me?!* I sat up and pulled my laptop onto my bed. I had been putting it off ever since I had found Professor Hunter's wedding ring. But I needed to know the truth. I turned on my computer and clicked on the internet icon. He wasn't on Facebook, but certainly I could find him online.

I typed "James Hunter" into Google. I held my breath as I clicked on the images button. And there he was, smiling back at me from my screen. No, there *they* were. I clicked on an image with him and a woman. She was gorgeous. She had straight, shoulder length brunette hair that was perfectly smooth. Her eyes were un-proportionately big on her face, like a Disney princess. Her skin was tan and I had never seen someone so skinny with such big breasts. Maybe they were fake. I looked at the caption. James and Isabella Hunter at the 50th New York Film Festival. Professor Hunter's arm was wrapped around her waist and he was smiling at the camera. Isabella was looking off to the side, laughing at something. They looked so happy. Were they still this happy?

Not anymore. Because of me. I went back to the web tab and typed in "James and Isabella Hunter." An article came up describing their philanthropy. Another picture of them smiling was plastered to the top of the article. They were somewhere in Africa, surrounded by scantily clad children. In another article they were volunteering together at an animal shelter in Brooklyn.

I searched through dozens more articles with the two of them. I stumbled upon a picture from the end of last year, from something called The Tech Awards Gala. Professor Hunter had apparently won some award for technology benefiting humanity. It had to have been around the time that he had moved here. Professor Hunter was smiling, but his smile didn't reach his eyes. It was the same way he had looked at me earlier today. Like he was haunted by some secret. Isabella was smiling for the camera, but she didn't really look happy.

What was I doing? I had no place analyzing their relationship. It doesn't matter now. It was over. *It's over.* It was time to stop stalking them. It was out of my hands. I clicked out of the browser and opened up my email. There was only one message waiting in my inbox and it was from Professor Hunter. *I shouldn't even look at it.* I bit my lip. Looking at it wouldn't hurt. I just needed to make sure I didn't respond. I needed to ice him out. I opened up the email.

Subject: Our discussion isn't over
Penny,

I wish you wouldn't always feel so compelled to argue with me. I told you that I have done some things in my past that I regret. I am not withholding information from you to be spiteful. I'm doing it to protect you. If you will allow me to come talk to you, I can explain.
-James

Seriously? Trying to protect me? That jackass. My anger flared up, stronger than ever. But there was hurt there too. It felt like my chest was being crushed with a ton of bricks.

"So I heard about what happened with Tyler. Did you want to talk about it?" Melissa asked.

I hadn't even heard her come into the room. I was too busy fuming over Professor Hunter's email. I was still mortified about what had happened with Tyler. "No."

"Are you sure?"

"Melissa, why didn't you tell me he was dating some-one?"

Melissa laughed. "You told me you two were just friends so I figured he already talked to you about it. And since you two are just friends, I figured it didn't matter to you either way. Plus you were upset about James."

"But you let me kiss him!"

"Whoa! You cannot blame this one on me, Penny."

"I'm sorry, I know. Melissa, it was so embarrassing." I put my face in my hands.

"I know." She jumped onto my bed and put her arm around me.

"How do you even know about it? Was he making fun of me?" I could feel myself blushing. A whole frat was probably laughing right now at my expense.

"No, Penny, not at all. He came back to the frat house all upset and Josh went to talk to him. I just happened to eavesdrop on the conversation."

I laughed. "So what did you find out?"

"That you assaulted him at Grottos."

"That's not true!"

Melissa laughed. "I know. I'm just kidding. He said that he had invited you to lunch to tell you he had taken your advice and had started dating some girl. But then you had a meltdown and when he went to comfort you, you started making out with him."

"He kissed me back. This isn't all on me." I had to de-fend myself. Tyler wanted that kiss as much as I did.

"Of course he did. He's crazy about you."

"Well it's over now. I'm completely mortified."

"But you ran out on him before he could talk to you about it. He just asked a girl to the Sigma Pi formal. They aren't serious yet. Or exclusive."

"But still, I don't want to be the other woman. And I never meant to put Tyler in an awkward situation."

"You're completely overreacting, Penny. It's not like he's married or something. It's not a big deal at all."

I felt like I was going to throw up. Professor Hunter was married. And that was a big deal. It was a huge deal. Everything was so messed up.

Melissa hugged me. "Really, Penny, don't even worry about it. It will all blow over. Unless you don't want it to. If you really like Tyler, I don't think it's too late to tell him. Besides, dating someone closer to your own age would be a lot easier."

"I'm just so confused." I put my head back in my hands.

Melissa rubbed my back. "Have you still not talked to James yet?

"I tried. It's hard. I'm just so mad at him."

"Well no matter what you decide, you need to figure out where you stand with James if you want to start dating Tyler."

"I know." I took a deep breath. "I'll try talking to him again."

CHAPTER 40

Friday

"Hey, Penny," Tyler said as he sat down next to me.

My face was already crimson. I didn't want to have this conversation. "Hey," I said, but continued to look down at my desk.

"What, was the kiss that bad?" Tyler asked.

"Tyler." I put my face in my hands. My stomach was in knots.

"Penny, look at me."

I moved my hands and looked up at him. He was wearing jeans and a blue t-shirt. The blue from his shirt made his eyes pop. Why was I so attracted to guys that were unavailable? "Tyler, I'm so sorry. I didn't know that you had a girlfriend. I'm so, so sorry."

Tyler laughed. "I don't have a girlfriend. I only just started seeing her."

"Are you going to ask her to be your girlfriend?"

"I don't know. That depends on a lot of things. I do like her. And I thought that it was what you wanted. You're very confusing, Penny."

So Melissa was right. They weren't serious yet. "Is it Claire?"

"Claire?"

"The girl who you talked to in the dining hall on steak sandwich day. You know...the well-endowed blonde girl."

Tyler laughed again. "No, not Claire. Her name is Natalie."

I was so confused about everything, but I knew that I was jealous. "You kissed me back."

Tyler smiled. "I can't seem to resist you. Even though you've turned me down about a million times."

"So you aren't mad that I kissed you?"

"Mad?" Tyler laughed. "I'd only been waiting a whole month for a second kiss."

I started laughing, but quickly stopped when Professor Hunter walked in. He was his usual sexy self, but he had dark circles under his eyes. He looked exhausted. There was stubble on his face. The tie around his neck was a little loose, which gave him a slightly disheveled look. He was in pain. The same pain that I was. But how could I feel sorry for him when he had caused our problems? For some reason all I wanted was to go up to the front of the classroom and hug him, though. I wanted to comfort him. *What is wrong with me?*

I grabbed my paper and pen and shoved them into my backpack. I couldn't stand to see Professor Hunter this way. And I didn't want to do something that I was going to regret.

"Tyler, I'm actually not feeling very well. Can you take notes for me?"

"Penny?" he hissed, but I was already pushing through the door.

***

I was furious at myself for missing Professor Hunter. I drummed my fingers on my desk. Maybe Melissa was right and I should try talking to him again. It was possible that there was something I didn't understand. Hearing his side of the story, if anything, might give me closure. *No.* He was the one that should be apologizing. But he didn't even know what he needed to apologize for. He had too many secrets.

My phone buzzed. It was probably Professor Hunter. Was he finally ready to tell me he was married? I picked up my phone and slid my finger across the screen. It was a text from Tyler.

"Hey, I have the notes from class. Come let me in."

I smiled to myself. Here was a guy who had stopped kissing me in order to fully disclose the fact that he was seeing someone else, even though they weren't exclusive. And Professor Hunter didn't even have the balls to tell me he was married. Fuck him. I jumped off my bed and went to go let Tyler in.

Tyler was standing there with a smile on his face. He was so cute. "Hey, Penny."

"Hi, Tyler." I pushed the door open farther so he could walk in. We went up the stairs to my floor.

"Are you feeling better?" Tyler asked as we walked down the hallway.

"Yeah, I'm fine. You always seem to come to my rescue."

Tyler shrugged. "That's what friends do. Just for the record, it's also what people who are more than friends do."

"More than friends, huh? Is that where you think we are?"

Tyler opened up my door and closed it behind us. As soon as the door shut, he put his hand on the small of my back and pulled me into him. His face was only a few inches from mine. "You tell me."

My heart was racing. His breath smelled minty. He was handsome, funny, and honest. *This is what I need.* I stood on my tiptoes and kissed him. He immediately kissed me back, more passionately than he had at Grottos. I reached up and grabbed his hair, pulling him closer, kissing him deeply. He took a step forward and pushed my back against my bureau, pinning me in place. His hands moved to my waist. I could feel his erection pressed against me. He wasn't just what I needed, he was what I wanted.

I lifted one of my legs and wrapped it around him. He quickly grabbed my ass and lifted me up so I could wrap my other leg behind him. He pressed himself harder against me.

I moaned softly. He pressed his erection against me again. "Tyler," I panted and wrapped my arms securely around his neck.

He grabbed my ass tighter and carried me over to my bed. He placed me down on the edge of it and spread my thighs even wider as he leaned into me. I grabbed the bottom of his shirt and pulled it up his torso, revealing his abs. I swallowed hard. He quickly pulled his shirt the rest of the way off and tossed it on the ground. I let my hands slide down his muscles to the waistline of his jeans. I unbuttoned and unzipped them. He grabbed my hands. My heart was racing.

"Are you sure this is what you want? I don't want you to knee me in my junk again." He smiled down at me.

"Yes. I want you." My mind was confused, but my body wasn't.

He leaned over and kissed me again. His hands pushed my shirt up and over my head. He unhooked my bra and slowly pulled it down my arms. "Penny," he groaned. He leaned in and kissed me again, letting his hands wander to my breasts. I tilted my hips up to him and he pressed his erection against me again.

"You have no idea how long I've been waiting for this," he whispered in my ear.

"Me too." I grabbed the sides of his jeans and started to pull them down.

"Have you talked to James yet?" Melissa said as she opened the door. She placed her keys on her bureau without looking over at us.

Crap!

"Who is James?" Tyler asked.

Melissa's head snapped toward us. "Oh my God!" She was staring at Tyler's abs. I had already begun pulling my shirt back on, but Tyler had only zipped and buttoned his pants. I tucked my bra underneath my comforter.

"I can come back later," Melissa said, but didn't turn around.

"Please," I said, my face turning bright red.

"Wait," Tyler said. "Who is James?"

Oh my God.

I shook my head back and forth at Melissa and she just stared back at us. "He doesn't know about James," I mouthed to her as best as I could.

"James is...my dad," Melissa said slowly.

"You call your dad James?" Tyler asked.

"Always have." Melissa shrugged her shoulders. "He's just very businesslike. But that doesn't mean he's not a good father, because he is. He's great."

Tyler stared back at her. "So why is Penny talking to your dad?"

"Well," Melissa paused but only for a moment. "He's planning a joint birthday party for us and he needs Penny's invitation list."

Tyler looked at me. It didn't look like he believed a word that Melissa had said. And he shouldn't have. Lies on top of lies. "So, have I made the list?"

"Yes," I said quickly. *Oh please stop talking, Melissa.*

"Yeah, it's going to be a Halloween themed party, since both our birthdays are in October," Melissa added. "It's going to be a blast."

Tyler sat down on the bed beside me.

"So, does this mean you two have finally admitted to liking one another?" Melissa asked.

I looked up at Tyler and smiled. Despite Melissa's intrusion, I did feel like Tyler and I were in a good place.

Tyler winked at me and turned back to Melissa. "Actually, no. I thought Penny made all her male friends take their shirts off upon entering her dorm room. Is that not a thing?"

"Ugh," Melissa said. "I'm going to leave you two alone."

"Unfortunately," Tyler said and looked down at his watch. "I need to get going." He hopped off the bed and grabbed his shirt from the floor. After he pulled it back over his head, he leaned over and whispered in my ear, "to be continued, Penny." He grabbed my face in his hands and kissed me.

If my face could possibly turn any redder, it did.

"Bye, Melissa," Tyler said and walked out the door.

"Oh my God," Melissa said before Tyler had even closed the door. She sat down next to me on my bed. "Out of bed with James and into bed with Tyler, huh?"

"Melissa, we didn't have sex."

"Yeah right."

I needed to change the topic before it got any more awkward. "Thanks for covering for me about James."

"Well, have you talked to him? You really do need to clear the air before you move forward with Tyler. It's only fair to both of them."

"I know, I know. I'm going to."

"When?"

I sighed. I didn't want to think about Professor Hunter. "I'll do it this weekend."

"So how about Tyler's six pack?"

I laughed. "He is sexy, isn't he?"

"I couldn't stop staring. Sorry, awkward."

CHAPTER 41

Saturday

Professor Hunter had sent me a few more texts asking to meet with me. But I couldn't see him. I had never been so angry with someone in my life. I opened up my email and clicked on the one from Professor Hunter. Maybe I could end this through email. I reread what he had written.

Subject: Our discussion isn't over
Penny,
    I wish you wouldn't always feel so compelled to argue with me. I told you that I have done some things in my past that I regret. I am not withholding information from you to be spiteful. I'm doing it to protect you. If you will allow me to come talk to you, I can explain.
-James

    I forgot how angry his email had made me. He was so full of himself. I quickly wrote back to him.

Subject: Trying to Protect Me?
Professor Hunter,
    I thought that I was naive, but I believe that description fits you better. I don't think that I'm the woman in your life that you should be protecting.

-Penny

There. I felt better already. I pressed send. It was cowardly to hide behind my computer, but I didn't have the guts to do it in person. It didn't take long before my computer dinged, signaling that I had a new email.

Subject: You're the Only Woman in My Life
Penny,

I'm not sure what you think you know about me. But I can tell you that I'm falling for you. There is no woman in my life that is more important to me. It's you. I'm coming over now.
-James

Why was I smiling right now? I bit my lip. Yes, his words were sweet, but he was lying. He was treating me like a child. I wasn't the only woman in his life. I was the *other* woman! I quickly typed out my response.

Subject: Don't You Dare
Professor Hunter,

Don't waste your time. Even if you come here, I'm not coming out to talk to you.
-Penny

He couldn't come here. I didn't want to see him. This had to be done through email. It was the only way that I'd be strong enough to confront him. My computer dinged again.

Subject: I Do Dare

Penny,

Stop being so stubborn. I'm leaving now. I'll see you in ten minutes.

-James

Crap. I had quickly lost control of our email conversation. Was there anything I could say so that he wouldn't come? It didn't seem like it. I took a deep breath. Could I do this? I just needed to not look at him and his stupid beautiful face. My attraction for him had blinded me before. I needed to make sure that wouldn't happen again. If I could focus on his adultery, I could be strong. He was an awful person.

I glanced in the mirror, fixed my hair, and wiped away some oil on my face with a tissue. I changed into a nice pair of yoga pants and a tank top. *Why am I trying to look nice for an adulterer?* I closed my dorm room door behind me and went out the back of my building to where he usually came to pick me up. His car was already there. My heartbeat was already accelerating and I hadn't even seen him. I walked down the steps and approached the car slowly, trying to remain calm. Professor Hunter opened the passenger's side door from the inside.

"Get in the car."

"But I don't want to go anywhere," I stammered. The idea of being so close to him in the car made me feel uncomfortable. I didn't trust myself around him. His hair was smoothed and he was clean-shaven, unlike in class earlier. He was wearing a t-shirt, a jacket, and jeans and I could smell his intoxicating scent through the open door.

Professor Hunter glared at me. "I'm not taking you anywhere. I just want to be able to talk to you in private."

I looked around. It was a chilly night and most of the students were either out partying or snuggled up in their dorms. "There's no one around."

"Penny, get in the car."

I didn't want our conversation to start this way. I sighed and sat down in the passenger's seat. He drove the car to the small parking lot by my dorm, pulled into one of the last spots, and cut the ignition. He stared out the windshield.

I thought he would start talking, but he stayed silent. My heart was beating so loud that I thought he might be able to hear it in the silent car. He was gripping the wheel of the car tightly and his knuckles were turning white. I glanced down at his ring finger. There weren't any tan lines or anything. I thought that's what I was supposed to look for. Was it possible that I was wrong about everything?

He finally turned to me. "I thought you weren't going to come out and see me."

There was something definitely wrong with me. All I wanted to do was start making out with him. I crossed my arms over my chest and looked out my window. "I figured I owed it to you to hear your side."

"You're cute when you're upset."

He was the infuriating one, not me. I was already fuming. We weren't supposed to be talking about us. We were supposed to be talking about him and his wife. "Why didn't you tell me?" I asked. I clenched my jaw.

"Tell you what?"

He was still going to play dumb? This was fucking ridiculous. "How could you possibly not know what I'm referring to? What is wrong with you?"

Professor Hunter took a deep breath. "You looked me up online, didn't you?" His brow was furrowed. Why was he pissed at me? What else was there online about him besides his hidden wife?

"No! Well, yes. But that has nothing to do with anything. I found your ring, Professor Hunter." I could feel the tears welling in my eyes.

He nodded his head, absorbing the information. But there was a slight smile on his face. Why the hell did he look relieved? What else was he hiding from me? He was such an ass.

"So you have nothing to say to that?" I asked.

"It's not what you think." He put his hand through his hair.

Stop doing sexy things! "And what is it that you think I'm thinking?"

He raised his left eyebrow. *Damn it! Don't look at me like that!* All the muscles below my waist seemed to clench. This car was stifling. The smell of him was everywhere, wearing me down.

"You're probably thinking that I'm a lying cheater that you want nothing to do with."

I swallowed hard. "Am I wrong?"

"Yes."

"Enlighten me." I couldn't believe I was having this conversation, with my professor no less. This situation was unbearable. I could feel myself starting to sweat.

"First of all, I never lied to you. I withheld information that I deemed unimportant to our relationship..."

"Unimportant? You're such an asshole," I said, cutting him off. I grabbed the door handle.

"Penny." He put his hand on my shoulder. His touch made me tingle.

"And you did lie to me. At the country club when you said you didn't relish sharing me, you made me believe that I wasn't sharing you either. You even denied having a girl-friend. If I had known you were married..." my voice trailed off as I started to cry.

"Penny, please don't cry." Professor Hunter reached over and wiped my tears from my cheek.

"Don't touch me." I pushed his hand away. "How could you do this to me? Why didn't you just tell me then? I trusted you!"

"Because Isabella and I are over."

"What? You're divorced?" I sunk into the passenger's seat. *Thank God.* I wasn't a mistress. I felt the weight fly off my shoulders. "You still could have told me."

He sighed. "It's just a matter of finalizing the paper-work. I would have told you once it was official. I just didn't want to upset you for no reason."

"So you're technically still married right now?"

"Technically, yes, but I've already signed the divorce papers. It hasn't been a smooth process. But I have no connection to Isabella at all. We're done. We've been done for a long time."

I stared at him, waiting for him to elaborate. Why was he so horrible at talking to me? "Well, what happened?"

He pressed his lips together. "We didn't love each other."

"Then why did you get married in the first place?"

"It's a long story."

I turned toward him and pulled my legs up onto the seat. "I have some time to spare."

Professor Hunter looked uncomfortable. He leaned toward me slightly and put his hand on the center console. "Do you really want to talk about this, Penny? All you need to know is that it was a mistake and it's over."

"Please. I need to know." I put my hand on top of his. I wanted him to open up to me. I didn't want there to be any more secrets between us.

Professor Hunter squeezed my hand. "Okay." He sighed. "Isabella's parents are good friends with my parents. Ever since we were little, our parents always pushed us together. But I just never clicked with her. She was always so cold.

"In high school, I started dating a girl named Rachel. Whenever Rachel came over to my house, my parents were completely dismissive. It was clear that they didn't think she was good enough to be part of our family. They always made her feel so unwelcome. When I finally confronted them about it, they told me that if I didn't break up with Rachel they wouldn't pay for me to go to college. And I'm not proud of what I did. My life with them was all that I knew. I didn't want to have to be on my own. I didn't know how to live without money. I was young and stupid."

Professor Hunter was looking down at my hand. He rubbed my palm with his thumb. The pain on his face almost made me start crying again. He must have loved

Rachel. But I didn't feel jealous, I just felt sad for him. I wanted to climb over into his seat and hug him.

"I broke up with Rachel the next day. And my parents began to make it clear that I was expected to eventually marry Isabella. Isabella was the only one they would ever approve of. They said that it was in my best interest to marry someone that wasn't after my money. I was so unhappy. When I told you that I was drunk most of college, I was serious. I completely lost it. I spiraled to the bottom. But my parents just kept telling me it was what was best. So eventually I just accepted the fact that I had to marry Isabella. Instead of worrying about it, I threw all my time and energy into the tech company I wanted to start. And when it blew up, I asked Isabella to marry me, because that was the next step I was supposed to take. Before I even realized what was happening, the wedding was planned, and everyone had been invited. I knew I didn't love her, but I walked down the aisle anyway. And I made promises to her. I vowed to keep those promises. And I did. I tried so hard to make it work.

"But she didn't love me either. She enjoyed dressing up and playing the part of my wife. Isabella loved the lifestyle, but she didn't love me. She was cold when we were alone. We barely talked. I knew she slept around. I tried to ignore it. I wanted for us to work out because our parents wanted us to be together. Neither one of us were happy. But she was still my wife, so I kept trying to make it work. I was always loyal to her. I tried to make her happy. When I decided to sell my company she freaked out. She couldn't believe that I'd rather spend my days doing something meaningful. And she definitely didn't support my decision.

It's funny, because my parents told me we should be together because she wasn't after my money. But really, the only reason that Isabella married me was because I had money."

I bit my lip. So that's why he wasn't close to his parents. They had controlled his whole life. Professor Hunter had told me his story while staring down at my hand. I squeezed his hand and he turned to me. There was so much pain on his face. Failing in his marriage had clearly devastated him. Maybe not living up to his parents' expectations had devastated him more, though.

"I'm sorry," I said. I cared about him. I didn't want to see him upset. He had this way of drawing me in.

"No, I am. I should have told you. Being here teaching, being with you, this is what I've been missing. I don't want this to mess up what we have."

I looked into his eyes. He was so sincere. He rubbed my palm with his thumb. His light touch sent shivers down my spine.

"I've always been told what to do. I've never had to make choices. But I chose you. And when I walked into my bedroom and you were gone it hurt like hell. My whole life has been painful, living in a way that I didn't want to live. But nothing was as painful as you leaving and not talking to me. Seeing you in class was torture."

"I couldn't see you either. That's why I left class today. I could see that you were feeling all the pain that I was feeling. I've never been so heartbroken."

He leaned over and took my chin in his hand. "Don't do that to me again. I'll tell you whatever you want to know. No more secrets."

"Okay." My heart was beating fast. He was going to answer all my questions. I needed to make sure that him liking me wasn't part of the reason why he was getting divorced. "When did you file for divorce?"

"Last year I walked in on Isabella having sex with someone else in our bed. I filed for divorce the next day."

"And came here?"

"Yes."

He was back to his short answers. I remembered Melissa telling me that Professor Hunter had been fired from his last job. She had made a joke about how he had probably punched the dean in the face or something. "There's a rumor that you got fired from your last job."

Professor Hunter grimaced. "It's not a rumor; it's true."

"What did you do? Have sex with a student?" I asked the question as casually as possible and laughed awkwardly.

"What? No, Penny. I haven't made a habit of sleeping with students. You're the exception." He shifted uncomfortably in his seat.

So he hadn't gotten fired because of that. What had he done, then? He hadn't answered my question. "So, what did you do?"

"The dean of the college was the one that I walked in on having sex with Isabella. It didn't end well."

Melissa was right?! "Did you have a fist fight or something?"

"Penny, he was in my bed. It's one thing to suspect it; it's another to see it."

"You have anger problems, don't you?"

He rubbed his hand down his face and then back up. Everything he did was so sexy.

"I don't think I'd put it that way," he said.

"So what would you call it?" I tucked a loose strand of hair behind my ear.

"Passion maybe." He leaned over and kissed me. Any leftover anger I had disappeared when his lips touched mine. I grabbed the collar of his jacket and pulled him closer to me. I wanted to make him forget his pain.

He stopped kissing me for a moment and stared at me with his piercing brown eyes. "God I missed you," he whispered.

"I missed you too."

He leaned over me and pushed a button. My seat began to slowly recline. He started to move over the center console and his ass hit the horn.

I started laughing as he straddled me. He silenced me with a kiss. His hand slid from my cheek, down my neck, and onto my breast. He squeezed it hard before letting his hand wander down to the waistline of my yoga pants.

"Professor Hunter?"

"You said there was no one around."

"Shouldn't we go back to your place?"

"You tortured me for almost a week, Penny. I'm not waiting another second. Switch places with me."

I ungracefully slid to the side and got on top of him, bumping into the door and dashboard as he laughed at me.

"Ow," I muttered.

He placed a kiss on my lips as he slid my yoga pants and thong down my thighs. Every inch of me felt alive with temptation. Professor Hunter really wasn't a bad man.

He was still who I had fallen in love with. And I wanted him. I wanted him so badly. I slid off my shoes and kicked off my pants as he pushed his jeans and boxers to the floor of the car. His massive erection had already sprung to life.

I leaned over and kissed him. Without hesitation, he grabbed my hips and pulled me down onto his length. The sensation of him filling me made me gasp. I pressed my hand against the passenger window.

"Don't put me through that again, Penny." He kissed my neck as he moved my hips faster and faster.

"Never." His hands slid to my ass and he slammed his cock into me. I moaned as his fingers dug into my skin. I loved the way he knew exactly what to do to make me completely surrender my body to him. He pulled me closer to him.

"Promise me."

"I promise," I said breathlessly.

The seat belt buckle hit my knee and I quickly pushed it aside. The angle in the car was awkward but the sensation of him inside me was all that mattered.

"You're mine," he growled.

I felt a pang of guilt about Tyler, but the thought quickly disappeared as Professor Hunter thrust himself deep inside me again.

"Yes! I'm yours!" I moaned.

The windows were soon completely fogged up besides for my handprint. Professor Hunter continued to guide my hips, going faster and faster.

"Come for me, Penny." He lifted his hips slightly, pressing his erection into a spot that I didn't even know existed. *Oh God!* The sensation made my whole body shake.

"Professor Hunter!" I clenched myself around him as his hot cum shot through me. He pulsed inside of me, again and again.

I collapsed on top of him. He kissed the top of my head and wrapped his arms around me.

CHAPTER 42

Sunday

I reread my speech again and took a deep breath. My stomach was in knots, and not just because of the speech. Professor Hunter had finally opened up to me, and I was the one that was still hiding the truth from him. He probably wouldn't want anything to do with me once he found out I was only 19. And then there was Tyler. How could I have feelings for two men at once? My room felt hot. I put my hair into a ponytail and started to read my speech again.

"That's quite the hickey, Penny," Melissa said.

"What?" I ran over to the mirror. "Shit." I tilted my head and looked at the small bruise on my neck. I quickly pulled my hair tie out and let my hair fall over the dark spot.

"So you hung out with Tyler again last night, huh?"

I began to blush. "No, last night I was talking to Pro...choo!" I tried to cover up my mistake with a fake sneeze. I added a light cough. There were too many secrets, and too many things to remember. "I must be getting a cold or something. No, last night I was following your advice and talking to James."

"Penny, you've gone from future cat lady to quite the slut."

I put my hand over my hickey. "Melissa!"

"I'm just messing with you. But really, do they both know about each other now? You're allowed to date more than one person at a time, but you should probably be upfront about it. James really must be sexy as hell because Tyler is hot...like really hot."

I sat back down on my bed. "I don't think I know how to date two people at once. And I don't think I want to. What should I do?"

"Make a pro-con list?" Melissa grabbed a sheet of paper. "Okay, pros for James?"

"Well, he really is sexy. And he's sweet. He's also very mature. And I have so much fun when I'm with him. He's so spontaneous."

"Penny, you're forgetting that James is loaded. Money is definitely a pro, even if you don't think so."

I winced. "That's really not important to me.

Melissa rolled her eyes. "Too late, it's on the list. Now Tyler."

"Tyler is really sweet too and sexy. But he's also a great friend. He's thoughtful and he's definitely patient. He's a really nice guy."

"Okay, cons for James?"

"James can be pretty controlling." *Or is that a pro?* I felt myself blushing. "He kind of has a bad temper and he is quite a bit older. He can be pretty mysterious at times too." *And he's my professor, I have to keep our relationship a secret, and I have to lie constantly.*

"Isn't him being mysterious a good thing? I feel like that probably makes him even sexier."

I shrugged. "I don't like that he's held things back from me." *But he just told me his secrets. We're in a good place.*

"Cons for Tyler?"

"Well, he's graduating soon. So I don't really know what his plans are after school."

"And?"

"I don't know. Tyler is really nice. There aren't any other cons I can think of."

Melissa held up the list. "James definitely has more cons than Tyler."

I bit my lip. Of course James had more cons than Tyler.

"Well I think you know how you feel now."

"What?"

"Penny, you look like you're in pain."

I shook my head. "No, it's just...all those different points aren't even with each other. Some things are more important than others."

Melissa put the paper down. "I think I know what this is about. It's the sex, isn't it?"

"No!" I bit my lip again. "I don't know. It's just that James...he makes me feel...ugh," I put my face in my hands.

"Okay, so the sex is amazing. And what about Tyler?"

"We haven't done that."

"You're joking."

"No."

"So maybe that's your answer. You need to have sex with Tyler and then you can properly decide."

"I can't do that to James."

"You were about to on Friday when I walked in on you guys."

"But that was before I talked to James."

"Well, the answer seems pretty obvious then. It's James. Clearly it's always been James."

***

I sat at my desk hoping that the speech before mine would never end. Because as soon as it did, I was up. I glanced down at the outfit I had worn to try to impress Professor Hunter. *Or is it Tyler?* Either way, it was too much. My tank top combined with my pushup bra showed entirely too much cleavage, and my skirt was too tight and too short. I don't know how high the heels were, but they were definitely too high for me to comfortably walk in. *Why did I choose this outfit?*

"Penny Taylor," said Professor Hunter.

Here we go. I grabbed my notes and shakily approached the podium. By some miracle, I didn't break my ankle in my heels.

I looked out at the class. Tyler was smiling at me. Seeing him gave me a boost of confidence. He looked sexier than ever.

I glanced down at my paper. My speech sucked. I took a deep breath. I had a better idea. Tyler staring at me with his sexy smile was just the confidence boost I needed. "I could lie about the reason why I chose to major in marketing. I could say it was to get a decent job when I graduate or that someone recommended it to me. But that's not true. I picked it for one reason only. Because sex sells. And everyone loves sex."

Professor Hunter shifted uncomfortably in his seat as he watched me. I liked seeing him squirm.

"Using sex in advertising does require some skill, though. The first step is knowing your target audience. In the case of this speech, my audience is Professor Hunter and a class of about 60% guys. So I figure that this would be received favorably." I untucked my tank top and pulled it over my head.

I paused for a moment to make eye contact with the class. Tyler and the majority of the guys in the class looked excited, Professor Hunter was scribbling something furiously, and a lot of the girls were rolling their eyes.

"One common pitfall of sex in advertising is that an ad might only target one gender, but really, both guys and girls are probably going to view it, so it's important to cater to both. Can I please have a volunteer?"

Tyler's hand shot into the air, along with a few other guys in the room.

"How about the handsome gentleman in the back row. Come up here and give me a hand."

Professor Hunter looked less than thrilled as Tyler made his way to the front of the class. He was wearing jeans and a polo. He looked sexy as hell.

"Like I was saying, it's important to cater to both sexes." I grabbed the bottom of Tyler's polo and pulled it over his head. His abs were even more fantastic than I remembered. "Isn't this more appealing, girls?" I asked, and the girls in the audience definitely seemed to agree. Professor Hunter, on the other hand, did not. His eyebrows were lowered more than ever before. I wanted him to know what it felt like to have to share me. And I wanted Tyler's hard cock inside of me. I was aching for him and only him.

"Another consideration when using sex in advertising is to decide how explicit to make it." I grabbed Tyler's hand and brought it to my lips. I lightly bit the tip of his index finger.

Tyler gulped.

I slowly slid his finger in and out of my mouth. There was fire in his eyes. He was going to fuck me harder than I had ever been fucked.

Professor Hunter cleared his throat. "I think this speech is running a bit long, Miss Taylor."

"Length is important. Sometimes, you just need to give your audience exactly what they want." I unbuttoned and unzipped Tyler's pants. He pushed his jeans and boxers to the floor and stepped out of them and his shoes. Despite everyone watching, Tyler had a huge erection. *Huge.* It was even better than I had imagined. He was completely naked, waiting for me, wanting me. I had never seen anything sexier in my life.

I turned to the class. All the girls were staring at Tyler. But they couldn't have him. He was all mine.

"Take your clothes off!" one of the guys in the class yelled.

I took a deep breath. *Are you sure you want to do this, Penny?* A quick glance down at Tyler's throbbing cock helped me make up my mind. *Yes.*

"Miss Taylor, you shouldn't be doing this," Professor Hunter said, interrupting my train of thought.

"What, like I shouldn't have googled you?"

Professor Hunter looked furious. *Good.*

"Thanks for the distraction, because that reminds me, distractions are a big problem for advertisers. So, sometimes delayed gratification is not ideal in advertising. You need to nail your point home." I reached back and unhooked my bra. Then I let the straps slide down my arms, revealing my breasts to everyone in the class. I flung it in the direction of Professor Hunter before sliding my skirt and thong down my legs.

My heart was beating out of my chest. Before today, only two guys had seen me naked. Now an entire class was watching me. *No going back now.*

I looked over at Tyler and bit my lip. He got the message. He trailed his hands over my breasts and down the front of me. His finger sunk inside of me.

"You're so wet baby," he whispered in my ear. "You've been wanting me for so long."

I dipped my head back, letting him tease me with his experienced hands.

"That's enough!" Professor Hunter stood up and slammed his fist against the desk.

"I do appreciate your input, Professor Hunter. In fact, I've learned that audience input is very important for marketing. That's why they have focus groups. So let's have a focus group right now. By a show of hands, who wants Tyler to fuck my brains out?"

Professor Hunter's hands were balled in fists, and both stayed firmly on his desk. The rest of the class had a different opinion. Every guy in the class raised their hand, and even a few girls did.

"It looks like you're in the minority, Professor Hunter." I turned to Tyler. His eyes were ablaze. Just the look he was giving me left me wanting. "Fuck me, Tyler." As soon as the words left my mouth, Tyler lifted me in his arms and I wrapped my legs around him.

"I'll show you what it feels like to have a real man inside of you." He pushed my back against the chalkboard and slammed his thick, hard cock inside of me.

"Yes!"

He slid his length in and out of me. "Is this what you want, Penny? Is this what you've wanted this whole time?"

"Yes, Tyler. I've always wanted you. I've never stopped thinking about you." I grabbed a fistful of his hair and brought his face to mine. I kissed him hard, letting my tongue collide with his. He continued to slam his cock into me, faster and faster.

I ran my hands down his biceps. His muscles tensed under my fingers.

"Faster!" I screamed. I couldn't get enough of him. I wanted more.

He pumped faster for a few more seconds and then pulled out.

"Tyler," I panted. "I need you. Please. God I need you."

"I know you do." He turned to the class. "Where should I fuck her next?" Tyler asked the other students.

"At the podium," a few people said in unison.

"Put your hands on the podium, you little slut," he demanded.

I walked back over to the podium, and followed Tyler's instructions. I arched my back and looked over my shoulder at him.

"By the time I'm done with you, you're going to forget anyone else has ever been inside of you. I'm going to claim your pussy. You're going to scream my name in the middle of the night. You're never going to get enough of me."

"Please," I begged. I ached for him. I wanted his cock to fill me again.

"Sex does sell. It's the only thing that sells." He grabbed my hips and thrust himself deep inside of me.

"Yes!" I screamed.

He went faster and faster.

"Oh, Tyler!" I couldn't take anymore. Nothing had ever felt this good. The podium screeched forward from the impact of his pounding. The pleasure was so intense.

"Scream my name louder, baby. Let the whole class know who owns you. I want everyone to know that you're mine."

"Tyler!" I screamed at the top of my lungs.

CHAPTER 43

Monday

I woke up panting, an intense orgasm washing over me. My body was trembling. *What the fuck was that?* My sheets were slightly damp from sweat. Had I seriously just orgasmed from a dream? I reached down and felt my wetness. I moaned slightly at my own touch. *What the hell is wrong with me?* I sat up in my bed.

It was just a dream, right? *Oh my God.* I looked at my phone. It was still Monday morning. Speeches didn't start for an hour. My heart was pounding. I took a deep breath and tried to slow my pulse. Melissa had just gotten in my head about having sex with Tyler. That was all. But that dream was so intense. And hot. Maybe I had gotten in my own head about having sex with Tyler. I quickly got out of bed, grabbed my shower caddy, and walked to the bathroom.

This was ridiculous, I had already made my decision. Melissa was right, it was Professor Hunter and it always had been Professor Hunter. I lathered my hair and rinsed it under the warm water. *What, like I shouldn't have googled you?* My words from my dream came back to me. I knew what was going on. I had that dream because something was still bothering me about Professor Hunter and my conversation. He thought I was upset because I had looked him up online. What else would I have found out about him if I had searched longer? I quickly finished showering, wrapped my towel around myself, and almost ran back to my room.

I didn't have much time before class, but I could do some light snooping. I typed "James and Isabella Hunter divorce" into the search bar. The article at the top of the search results was from just a few weeks ago. It was titled, "The Fairytale Couple Calling it Quits?" I sighed with relief. Professor Hunter was telling the truth about getting divorced. But it was an interview with Isabella and I wanted to see her thoughts on what was going on, so I clicked on the article anyway.

The beginning was about how Professor Hunter had gotten a teaching opportunity that he couldn't pass up. That was a good cover-up for him leaving her. I read some more. I gulped and reread Isabella's quote: "I will be moving to join him soon. He already has a place picked out for us. He's even waiting for me to decorate it. We've really never been happier. Any rumors that you've heard about our split have been completely fabricated."

Completely fabricated. I swallowed hard. *Never been happier.* I thought about Professor Hunter's empty apartment. There wasn't even one picture hanging on the wall. *He's waiting for her to decorate.* And then there was the suitcase in Professor Hunter's office. I had decided it must have been for traveling back and forth to talk to his divorce attorney and sign documents. But had he really been traveling back and forth a lot to see her? He had even done it once during the week and had to cancel class. How could I have been so blind? Would I never learn? I had let him manipulate me again. Why did I have to fall in love with such an asshole?

Because he's sexy and dangerous. I shook my head. I didn't need danger to be happy. Professor Hunter certainly hadn't made me happy recently. Just sad, upset, frustrated, and guilty. Tyler was a good choice. Tyler would never lie to me. And he wasn't my professor. And he wasn't eight years older. And he certainly wasn't married.

There wasn't anything left for me to search. I didn't care about what else Professor Hunter was hiding. A wife that he was pretending to divorce was enough. And I was done. Last week had been emotionally draining. Professor Hunter and I were just too different.

I closed my laptop and opened up my closet. The roses were turning black and lots of the petals had fallen to the floor. That was it. Our relationship lasted about as long as a dozen roses. I pulled on a pair of skinny jeans and high heeled boots, hooked on my favorite pushup bra and put on a tight black, v-neck shirt. I grabbed a lightweight jacket and an infinity scarf. After applying a small amount of foundation, mascara, and eyeshadow, I glanced in the mirror. I tilted my head a little and saw the hickey that Professor Hunter had given me. It was like he had branded me. I added a little concealer to the hickey to cover it up. After scrutinizing it in the mirror, I was ready to go.

I walked to class way faster than usual. My nerves must have made me jittery. I sat down at my desk, crossed my legs, and tapped my foot as I waited for Tyler. Melissa was right. I needed to be honest. Tyler deserved that. I needed to tell him that I was seeing someone else, but that I was going to end things. And that I wanted to be with just him. Tyler was seeing someone else too though. I wasn't sure what his reaction was going to be, but it was a conversation we needed to have.

Tyler walked into the room with a huge smile on his face. He was wearing jeans and a polo, just like he had in my dream. I shook my head. He wore that most days. That wasn't unusual. *Get a grip.* When he got to his desk he leaned down and kissed me.

I hadn't expected that. I hesitantly kissed him back. If Professor Hunter walked in and saw us I'd be mortified. He'd freak out. I told him I wasn't seeing Tyler. Soon my dream returned to me and my heart started beating fast. It felt like we had really had sex right in this room. I felt my face blushing.

He pulled away. "Good morning, Penny." He sat down in his chair. "You look really pretty today."

"Thanks, Tyler."

"You have no idea how many times I've walked into this room and wished I could kiss you like that."

I smiled. I had really only ever thought about Professor Hunter in this room. Except for my dream where Tyler had fucked me right on the chalkboard. I gulped. Right at the podium where I'd be giving my speech in a few minutes.

"Hey, are you okay?"

"Yeah. There's just something that I need to tell you. Do you want to get dinner tonight or something?

"Sounds good to me."

"Oh, Tyler, you never gave me the notes from Friday. Anything helpful for our speeches today?"

Tyler laughed. "Um, not really. I actually didn't even take notes in this class. I just wanted an excuse to come see you. Professor Hunter was talking about fighting or something on Friday. Like how in your speech you need to make the audience listen. Almost like it's a battle you need to win. It was really weird. You know how he is. All of his advice is super unhelpful and strange."

Interesting. Was that because Professor Hunter was fighting for me? I felt sad for a moment but shook the feeling away. He should be fighting for his marriage. My anger was growing again.

"Are you ready to finally find out why I chose economics and finance? I think you'll like my speech."

"Does that mean you're finally going to answer my question of what you want to do when you graduate?"

"Indeed."

Professor Hunter walked in, and I couldn't even help but turn my attention to him. It wasn't just the danger, he was the sexiest man I have ever laid my eyes on. *Why does he have to be so unbelievably sexy?* He was wearing a crisp suit that hugged his body perfectly. He locked eyes with me and smiled. But his expression immediately changed. He could probably sense how angry I was. His eyebrows lowered and he suddenly looked brooding.

That's right! I found out that you were lying to me again, you asshole!

Professor Hunter cleared his throat. "Okay, time for speeches. I'm excited to learn why all of you chose your majors." He pulled the podium to the middle of the room and made his way to the seat in front of Tyler. Professor Hunter's scent reached my nose, but it just fueled the flame growing inside of me. I had never been angrier in my entire life.

"Adam Zabek, you're up," Professor Hunter said once he had pulled out his papers to grade the speeches with.

Adam and a few other people went and then it was my turn.

"Penny Taylor." My name seemed foreign in Professor Hunter's voice. I was used to him saying Penny in a seductive, sweet way.

"Good luck, Penny," Tyler said with a smile.

Professor Hunter seemed to tense at Tyler's words. Good. I wanted Professor Hunter to be as upset as I was. It would serve him right if I really did fuck Tyler in front of the class.

"Thanks," I said and stood up. I walked past Professor Hunter and slowly to the front of the room, making sure not to trip on anything.

I knew you were supposed to envision the audience naked, but in my dream they had all seen me naked. Certainly my speech today would be less embarrassing than that. But it hadn't really been embarrassing. It had been insanely sexy. I held the sides of the podium. Everyone was staring at me, it was like they knew what I had dreamt. Tyler was even smiling at me and Professor Hunter looked angry. I looked down at my speech. *No.* No, I had something else to say. The same courage from my dream suddenly washed over me.

I locked eyes with Professor Hunter. The anger continued to swell to the surface. Something seemed to snap inside of me. *Fuck him and his stupid, beautiful face.* Someone cleared their throat. *Shit. How long had I been standing up here?*

"I am currently majoring in marketing. And for some reason I'm having a really hard time remembering why I chose it." I picked up my paper in my hand and waved it around. "I have a whole list of reasons on here why marketing is a great major, but I'm not sure how much of that I can believe anymore. Because sometimes you think you know something, but actually you have no idea what it's really like. Marketing is like that. It's a complete lie. I mean, we're all taught that marketing is sexy, right?" I blushed remembering my dream. "But it's really not. Marketing is ugly on the inside. Hideous, really."

I looked at Professor Hunter. He was fuming. It looked like he wanted to yell at me. Good. *Screw him.* I wasn't even close to being finished. My anger was bubbling over and I couldn't stop it now.

"Marketing lures you into getting something that you don't really need or want. A product can't cheat on you. A product can't lie to you. But a marketer can. And a marketer doesn't blink an eye when they lie and cheat. They hook you in and sell you awful products that you don't even want. You know what? I'm actually thinking about changing my major because of this assignment. Because I can't for the life of me think of a reason to continue pursuing marketing. Because marketing is a fucking joke."

"That's enough!" Professor Hunter slammed his fist on his desk.

"Marketing can go to hell." I grabbed my paper and ran out of the room.

"Penny!" I heard Tyler yell as the door closed behind me.

What the hell did I just do?

CHAPTER 44

Monday

The rain started to fall as I stood outside my dorm. I didn't have my sensor pass to get into the building. *How could I leave class without getting all my stuff?* I shook my head. That wasn't the question I needed to answer. More like, how could I give a speech filled with strange metaphors about Professor Hunter and marketing? My anger had just boiled over. It had almost been as bad as my dream. *The whole class must think I'm completely insane. Geez, am I insane?* Everything was a complete disaster. I wasn't even sure what I had said in my speech, but I was pretty sure it was time to drop the class. Was it past the deadline yet? There was no way I could ever face anyone in that class ever again. I had acted so immature. I wanted to know what Professor Hunter was thinking. I took a deep breath. *What is Tyler thinking?*

The light rain felt good against my flushed face. I closed my eyes and tilted my head toward the sky as I leaned against the brick wall. No one was coming in or out right now because it was during class. I was going to have to wait for awhile. It wasn't too late to go back and grab my bag, but I couldn't make myself do it. My speech was supposed to be why I chose the major that I did. I had ended it with "marketing can go to hell." I would never live this down.

Finally someone came out of my dorm building. The girl gave me a weird look, probably concerned that I was a crazy homeless person trying to break into the building. But I was able to quickly grab the door handle before I got locked out again. I ran into my dorm and up the stairs. Melissa didn't have class right now, so our room would be unlocked, but she'd be in our room. Could I face her? All I wanted to do was bury myself under the covers of my bed.

I slowly opened the door. Melissa was on her feet and running over to me right away.

"Tyler just texted me. What's going on?"

I was sick of the lying and the secrets. I burst out crying.

Melissa gave me a big hug. "Penny, what happened? Tyler said you ran out of class during your speech?"

"It was worse than that." I pulled away from her. Melissa closed the door.

"Sit down, tell me everything."

And I wanted to. I so badly wanted to tell her about dating my professor and then finding out that he was married. And why couldn't I? I trusted Melissa. She was my best friend. I sat down on my bed and she sat down next to me. She rubbed her hand on my back.

Why couldn't I seem to tell her? Professor Hunter had broken my trust, I could break his too. I put my face in my hands. No, I couldn't. Despite everything I still loved him.

"I just lost it, Melissa. I don't even know what I said during my speech. But it definitely had nothing to do with the topic."

"I thought you wrote your speech yesterday? You didn't even seem nervous."

"I wasn't nervous. I just got so mad and snapped."

"But why?"

Melissa's phone buzzed. She gave me another hug and hopped off the bed. "Look, Tyler's here. He brought you your stuff that you left in class. I'm going to head out and give you two some privacy."

I wiped my tears away and looked up at her.

"We can talk later, okay? Penny, it can't possibly be as bad as you seem to think." She grabbed her backpack. "I'll see you later. And I'll pick up Chinese takeout after my classes are over."

"Thanks, Melissa," I sniffed. I grabbed a tissue from my desk and blew my nose.

She smiled and left the room. I blew my nose again. What was I going to say to Tyler? I grabbed another tissue and blotted my eyes.

After a few minutes I heard a knock on the door.

"Come in," I said without moving from my bed.

Tyler walked in, carrying my backpack. He didn't look like his usual happy self. "That was quite the speech, Penny."

I groaned. "I don't know what happened, I completely lost it."

He walked over to me. I thought he might hug me or try to kiss me, but he just dropped my backpack on my chair and stood there and looked at me instead.

Finally he spoke. "I didn't have Melissa's number. I used your phone to text her so that I could let her know I had gotten your bag. I didn't want you to worry." He pulled it out of his pocket, put it on my desk, and slid it toward me. His eyes were locked on mine. *God, does he know about Professor Hunter? Why hadn't I changed his name to James in my phone?*

"Do you want to tell me who your speech was about? Or should I try and guess?"

I gulped. "My ex."

"Now, is that the same ex as it was when we first met?" He shoved his hands in his pockets. He looked so pissed. And he should be. It was awful for me to sneak around with Professor Hunter behind Tyler's back.

He definitely knew. "Tyler, that's what I wanted to talk to you about at dinner tonight. It's true, I had started seeing someone else. But it didn't work out. We're done. I'm going to end it. I was going to tell you."

"And why do I find that hard to believe?"

"It's true. It's over." I could feel the tears welling in my eyes. "Tyler you have to believe me."

"You told me you weren't ready to see anyone because you were still getting over your ex. So I guess what you meant by that is that you just didn't want to date me?"

"Tyler, that's not what it was at all."

"Remember when we were watching The Princess Bride together and I asked you why Buttercup was always so mean to Westley?"

"Yes."

"You said that it was because she didn't realize that she loved him yet."

"I know." I bit my lip.

Tyler laughed. "You know, I convinced myself that was what was happening between us. That one day you'd just wake up and realize that I was perfect for you."

"Tyler, I really like you."

"But it's never just us. You never liked me enough to date just me. I'm always competing with someone."

"No, there's no one to compete with. Tyler, it's just you."

"Penny," he laughed. He was shaking his head back and forth. He looked down at his sneakers. "It wasn't just one kiss, was it?"

"What?" My heart was racing.

"With that professor. Your answer to the most scandalous thing you've ever done."

"You read my texts?"

"Penny I would never invade your privacy. I didn't read your texts. But when I went to text Melissa, Professor Hunter tried to called you."

I swallowed hard. "No, it wasn't just one kiss."

"You were dating Professor Hunter this whole time?"

"Yes, I was, but I'm not now. I'm sorry I couldn't tell you. He didn't want me to tell anyone. We'd both get in trouble."

He nodded his head. "Look, I just wanted to make sure you got your stuff. I'm not here to give you a lecture about how it's wrong to date your professor. I'm just gonna go. I'll see you in class, Penny."

"Tyler, please don't go. You don't understand. I met him before I even knew he was a professor. Everything was just so complicated. I should have told you that I was seeing someone, though. I'm sorry."

"Penny, you're not the person that I thought you were." He opened up the door and walked out.

CHAPTER 45

Monday

I pulled my knees into my chest. Tears ran down my cheeks. Tyler hated me. His rejection stung worse than I ever imagined. I didn't just like him, he was also one of my closest friends. And I had ruined everything. I was mad at Professor Hunter for not being honest with me, and I had done the same thing to Tyler.

I deserved to be hated. I wasn't the person that I thought I was either. I had fallen in love with a married man. And I had strung Tyler along for far too long. Who had I become? I lay down in my bed and pulled my comforter over myself. I felt so cold. Before I knew it, my pillow was damp. I cried until I couldn't cry anymore. I had gotten what I deserved. I had broken the rules.

My phone buzzed but I ignored it. I just wanted to be alone. I didn't think it was possible, but I started crying again. I got off my bed and went to my closet. I pulled the dead roses out of the vase and threw all of them in the small trash can, then slammed my closet door. I grabbed the single rose that Tyler had given me from my desk and threw it down on top of the others.

I opened up the fridge. A pint of Ben & Jerry's Chunky Monkey was waiting for me. It was soft from being in the small, weak freezer portion of our mini-fridge, but that wasn't going to deter me. I grabbed a spoon and sat back down on my bed. *Delicious.* Who needed men when there was ice cream in the world? I ate half of it before I started to cry again.

A knock sounded on the door.

I tried to stay as quiet as possible, but continued to eat my ice cream. Hopefully whoever was out there would just think no one was here. People on my floor could be so annoying.

"Penny?"

I stopped mid-bite. Professor Hunter? How the hell did he get in my dorm?

"Penny, it's me. Can I please come in?"

I set down the pint of ice cream on my desk. He couldn't be here. People would see him. I quickly wiped my tears away and opened the door. He was still wearing his suit from class. His hair was unruly from the rain.

"Oh, Penny." He grabbed my face in his hands and wiped my tear stained cheeks with his thumbs.

"What are you doing here?"

"I needed to see you."

"Don't you have a class?"

"I cancelled my classes for the rest of the day."

"But, Professor Hunter..."

"The most important thing right now is that we talk." He stepped back and closed the door. "I think it's safe to say that something is bothering you."

He looked so out of place in my dorm room, with his dark gray suit and dress shoes. I suddenly felt self-conscious. There were clothes strewn on the floor and my pint of ice cream was sitting on my desk melting. And his roses were in the trash. I moved slightly to the right, to block his view of the trashcan.

"How did you know which room was mine?"

"Your name is on the door."

"So you walked around the whole building looking at all the doors for my name? Are you trying to get caught?"

"Everyone's in class. And you're avoiding talking to me. If you don't tell me what's wrong, it's impossible for me to fix."

"I don't want you to fix anything." I couldn't think straight when he was staring at me like that. His smoldering gaze made my thoughts swish together. I turned away from him.

"Penny." He walked into the center of the room and turned me toward him. "Just tell me what's wrong. I mean, I gathered from your speech that I'm a lying cheat who's ugly on the inside. I'd like to know why you think that. Because I thought that we were in a good place. Unless you were talking about someone else." His face looked grave. He was thinking about Tyler. I gulped.

"On Saturday you asked me if I had looked you up online and you were really mad. So I was thinking maybe there was more to find out about you."

"So, you googled me?" His look was impassive. He wasn't giving anything away today.

"I just wanted to make sure you were telling the truth."

"I would never lie to you, Penny." He grabbed both sides of my face again. He always seemed so sincere, but he never truly was. I looked at his mouth. I wanted to kiss him, but I needed to be strong. I shook away from his grip.

"I found an interview with Isabella that makes it seem like you were lying. And it was only from a few weeks ago."

"You can't believe everything you read in tabloids."

"This one seemed pretty convincing."

"So what did it say exactly?"

"That you two have never been happier. And that the rumors of your split were completely fabricated."

Professor Hunter sighed. "I told you that it hasn't been a smooth process. She won't sign the papers. She's being incorrigible."

Our beach trip flashed in my mind. He had taken a phone call and I had overheard him saying "just sign the damn papers." He had been talking to her. How had I not seen all the signs?

"She said in the interview that you were waiting for her to decorate your apartment."

He looked down at me. "She's lying."

"Then how did she know your apartment hadn't been decorated?"

He crossed his arms over his chest. "Because she's been there before."

"What? Why?" I was jealous. Of his wife. *What is wrong with me?*

"She came a few months after I moved here to talk about our relationship. Or lack of one I guess."

"I don't know if I can trust you."

"And I don't know if I can trust you."

"Why? I haven't done anything wrong." But that wasn't true. If anyone had been paying attention to my speech, I had basically told our whole class that Professor Hunter was an asshole. I hadn't told him that I was only 19. And I had almost started a relationship with Tyler, despite promising Professor Hunter that I wouldn't see him.

"I saw Tyler Stevens coming out of your building when I pulled up."

"He just came to drop off my stuff that I left in class."

Professor Hunter raised his left eyebrow. He knew I was lying. He could read me as well as Melissa could.

"After I found your wedding ring, I told myself we were over. I was in so much pain. I had never felt so broken before." My tears started to well just thinking about the ache in my chest. "So I started to think about my relationship with Tyler. I thought maybe it could be more than a friendship. He's always wanted it to be more. It just seemed like the right time."

Professor Hunter took a deep breath and leaned against my bed. He looked distraught. "You're dating him?"

"No. I thought I wanted to. But I was still confused about you. I've been a mess if you can't tell. I still don't know how I feel. Things seemed easy with Tyler. You just have so much baggage. I think I was just trying to get over you."

"By getting under someone else?" He was gripping my comforter in his fists.

He had been cheated on by his wife. And now me. I was a cheater. He wasn't the bad guy, I was. "It didn't go that far, Professor Hunter. And it never will. Tyler found out about you and he wants nothing to do with me."

Professor Hunter's body tensed. "What do you mean?"

I looked into his eyes. He was going to think I was so stupid. "Tyler looked at my phone. He saw that I had missed calls from you."

"You had me in your phone as Professor Hunter?" He looked incredulous.

"I'm sorry." I wanted to cry again. "I don't think he'll tell anyone."

Professor Hunter pulled me into his chest. I could hear his heart beating, slow and steady. Now he knew about Tyler. It was time for him to leave my dorm thinking I was an awful person too.

"Can I walk you out?" I asked.

He pushed my shoulders back slightly and looked down at me. "You want me to leave?" There was so much pain on his face.

"No."

"Then I don't want to go."

"But I broke your trust. I had told you Tyler and I were just friends."

"And you were just friends when you told me that. I broke your trust by not telling you about my marriage. Even though I never said I wasn't married."

"So neither of us lied, but we both hurt each other."

Professor Hunter nodded his head.

"Then I guess we're even?"

A sly smile crept across Professor Hunter's face. "Penny, you're hard to control. And I'm used to being in control."

I gulped. I knew he was. The way he touched me, the way he could make my body react to him; he was always in complete control. His hands were still on my shoulders. I didn't understand why he was still here, but I was glad that he was. Even though I had been angry with him, I still loved him.

"So what do we do now?" I asked. It felt like we were in a stalemate. We had both hurt each other and neither one of us knew if we could trust the other.

"Penny, what do you want to do?"

"I don't know."

"You're the one that needs to make a decision. I still want you. I don't care about what happened between you and Tyler. All I care about is what we have."

"I've never felt the way I feel about you with anyone before. You make me feel like I'm living for the first time. But I'm sick of secrets. I don't want to hide that I'm dating you anymore. All the secrets make everything so much harder."

"Who do you feel like you're keeping secrets from?"

"Melissa."

"So tell Melissa that I'm your boyfriend."

I gulped. *Boyfriend?* My heart was beating fast. I had never heard anything more glorious in my life. "Is that really what you want?"

"Yes, I want you to be my girlfriend, Penny. I told you before that I didn't relish the idea of sharing you. I don't want you to be with anyone else *ever again*. Just me." He leaned down and kissed me hard. When he pulled away, he looked around my room.

"So this is where you live?" Professor Hunter pulled off his suit jacket and draped it over the back of my desk chair. He had a mystified look on his face.

"It's a dorm room. What did you expect?"

He shrugged his shoulders. "I haven't been in one for awhile. It's a lot smaller than mine was." He turned to the montage of pictures on my bulletin board. "You're quite popular." He smiled at me.

I laughed. "No, not really."

"Why do you always put yourself down like that?" He reached for my hand. "Don't you see how wonderful you are?"

"No one else sees me the way that you do."

"All I see is you."

I gulped.

He looked over my shoulder. "Do you always make a habit of sleeping with clothing that you've stolen from people?" He pulled his sweater out from underneath my comforter.

My face flushed. "Just you."

"Just me." He traced his finger along my jaw line.

I wanted him to kiss me.

"This past week has been exhausting," he said.

"Then maybe we should take a nap."

Professor Hunter's lips curled into a smile. "As you wish." He slowly pulled his tie loose and unbuttoned his dress shirt. He laid both on top of his suit jacket. I would never stop admiring his sculpted torso. He unhinged his belt and pulled it free. He sat down in my chair and leaned over, unlacing his dress shoes.

I bit my lip as I watched him. Unlacing shoelaces shouldn't have been sexy, but everything he did somehow seemed sexual. He kicked off his shoes and socks and stepped out of his dress pants. Professor Hunter was standing in my dorm room in just his boxers. He folded his pants and draped them on the back of my chair.

"Are you going to join me?" he asked with a smile.

I had been staring. I unzipped and unbuttoned my pants, slid them down my legs, and pulled off my black t-shirt. I was left in just my panties and bra.

He picked up the pint of ice cream from my desk and took a spoonful as his eyes gazed over my body. "Delicious," he said seductively.

I wasn't sure if he was talking about the ice cream or me.

"Get in bed." He put the lid on the ice cream and put it back into the fridge.

I pulled the sheets back, hopped into my bed, and slid all the way over so that he could join me. He climbed in beside me. The twin bed was barely long enough for him and definitely too small for both of us together. He put his head down on the pillow beside me and looked into my eyes.

We stared at each other in silence for a few minutes. Him lying beside me felt so normal and so comforting. The pain in my chest had completely subsided.

"What are you thinking?" he whispered.

"That I'm not that tired." I moved closer and wrapped my legs around him.

"I thought you wanted to nap." He put his hand through my hair, pushing it away from my face. His hands on me made my whole body alert.

"Not anymore."

"Thank God." He pulled me to him and placed a kiss on my lips.

CHAPTER 46

Monday

I groggily opened my eyes. Professor Hunter and I were still intertwined on my bed. I took a deep breath, ensconced by his heavenly scent, then slowly unwound myself from him until his face was a few inches from mine. He looked so peaceful as he slept. I hadn't realized how much pain I was causing him. I ran my fingers down the side of his beautiful face, but he didn't even stir. He had made love to me slowly and gently, but so passionately. His feelings for me hadn't changed at all. And neither had mine. The way he had stared into my eyes as he had made love to me made me feel closer to him than ever.

His words from earlier made me smile. He didn't want me to be with anyone else ever again. I was his. He hadn't said it, but I knew that he loved me. And I loved him. This was real, more real than anything I had ever experienced. I ran my fingers down his neck and traced his clavicle.

He blinked and slowly opened his eyes. "Hey," he said and smiled at me.

"Hey, yourself."

"Were you watching me sleep?"

"Mhm. Not in a creepy way, though."

He laughed. "I didn't think it was creepy until you said that it wasn't. Now I'm not so sure." He reached over and tucked a strand of hair behind my ear.

"Did you sleep well?"

"Your bed is extremely uncomfortable."

"You get used to it."

He raised his left eyebrow skeptically. "But I do find it easy to fall asleep next to you. You're the only person that seems to be able to make me relax." His hand slipped down my back and he grabbed my ass.

I laughed. "Melissa is going to be back soon."

"Did you want me to stay and introduce myself?"

"I don't really want you to leave, but I think it's better if I tell Melissa alone."

"Are you kicking me out?" He had a playful grin on his face.

"It's nothing personal."

He placed a kiss on the tip of my nose and got up. I loved seeing him standing naked in my dorm room. After bumping into him in the coffee shop, I never would have thought I'd ever see him again, let alone date him. He pulled on his boxers and pants. When he put on his shirt, I got up and slowly buttoned it for him. He smiled as he watched me. After buttoning one of the last buttons, I pulled his collar and brought his lips to mine.

"You're making it hard for me to leave," he said after a soft kiss.

I laughed and let go of his collar. I quickly dressed as Professor Hunter laced his shoes. Once his tie was tied, he looked around my room again. He eyed the roses in the trash.

"Not a fan of roses?"

"Oh I am. It was just that a domineering professor gave them to me. Or else I would have loved them."

Professor Hunter laughed. "Before I leave, let me see your phone."

My cell phone was still sitting on my desk. I grabbed it and handed it to him. He typed in something and handed it back to me. I looked down and saw that he had changed his contact name to James.

"I thought I wasn't supposed to call you James in private?"

"Apparently your phone isn't private."

I bit my lip. So he was mad. He rubbed his thumb along my lower lip and gave me a small smile.

"My girlfriends usually call me James."

"That makes it sound like you have more than one girlfriend right now. Am I one of several?"

"Dozens."

I nudged his shoulder with my hand.

"No, just you, Penny." He grabbed his suit jacket and draped it over his shoulder. "Let me know how your conversation with Melissa goes."

"I will." I wrapped my arms around his neck and kissed him again. "I'll text you later, James."

CHAPTER 47

Monday

Melissa came in the door with two bags. She kicked the door closed with her foot and put her backpack on the ground.

"Hey, Melissa."

"Hey! Wow, you look a lot better, Penny. Did you take a nap or something?"

"Yeah," I sighed. "And I do feel a lot better."

"Okay, this one is yours." She tossed me one of the bags as she sat down beside me on my bed.

"Thanks for picking up dinner." I opened up the container and snapped my chopsticks apart.

"So how did your conversation with Tyler go?"

Tyler. I felt sick to my stomach thinking about him. I had treated him so horribly. I twirled a noodle around my chopsticks. "Not great."

"Did you tell him about James?"

"He found out on his own. James tried to call me while Tyler had my phone."

"Oh. Well, he's dating someone else too. He couldn't have been that upset."

"But it wasn't just that I was dating someone else. It was that I had lied about it to him. I kept using getting over Austin as an excuse to not date Tyler, when really I was seeing James the whole time. I should have told him right away." *Just like I should have told you.* Maybe I should have let Professor Hunter stay to explain things.

"What did Tyler say to you?"

"I hurt him, Melissa. He hates me."

"I'm sorry, Penny."

Things with Professor Hunter were great, but I had lost one of my closest friends in the process. Even though I had told Tyler I only wanted to be friends, I had lied to him about the reason why. And then I almost jumped into bed with Tyler as soon as there was a glitch in my relationship with Professor Hunter. *What is wrong with me?*

As if hearing my question to myself, Melissa said, "Okay I have to ask. What is going on with you? Dating two guys at once is really not like you."

"No, it's not at all. I guess I was going back and forth in my head just because I was mad at James. I've never had such an instant connection with anyone before. It's really hard to explain."

"When we went through the pro con list between James and Tyler, Tyler clearly won. But I could tell that you wanted to be with James. I get it. Either there's that connection or there isn't."

I nodded.

"There's one thing I'm still confused about, though. Why didn't you just tell Tyler you were seeing someone else right away? Were you worried you were going to hurt his feelings?"

On paper, Tyler had won. *Why hadn't I just told him I was seeing someone, without saying it was Professor Hunter?* Because I told Melissa that I was dating someone else. It was because I knew I could see myself with Tyler too. I really could. I had been keeping him as a backup plan. I was an awful person.

"I never really believed James could possibly like someone like me. I thought our relationship was doomed from the start. I think I wanted Tyler to like me. Because I knew he would be great to date too. Please don't think less of me. Tyler was my backup plan."

Melissa laughed. "Everyone has a backup, Penny. I don't think anyone has ever made Tyler a backup before though, because he is damn sexy." She paused. "Sorry."

I looked down at my food. "Do you think he'll ever want to be my friend again?"

"Penny, I don't really think men and women can be friends. I already told the two of you this when you were both pretending to be friends. Someone always wants more, and in this case you both wanted more. Unless Tyler is gay. If he's gay, you guys can be friends."

"He's definitely not gay."

"Then you were never just friends and never can be just friends. Besides, if you ever wanted to get serious with James, he would probably get jealous if you were friends with another guy."

Professor Hunter was jealous. He had asked me on our first date not to see Tyler anymore. Melissa was so good at stuff like this. I should have been talking to her about everything from the start.

"Okay, so what happened with your speech today then? You said you were mad?"

It was time to tell her now. I swallowed hard. "Remember when I slept over James' apartment last week?"

Melissa nodded.

"When I woke up I wanted to change into clean clothes." I tried not to blush. I had actually been naked and needed something to wear. "So I borrowed a shirt from one of his drawers and I found his wedding ring."

Melissa stared at me. I thought she was waiting for me to say just kidding or something. When I didn't, she said, "What an asshole. Oh my God! And I convinced you to try and work things out with him? Why didn't you tell me, Penny?!"

"I was embarrassed. I was so mortified. I felt like it was partially my fault and I felt so guilty. But your advice was actually good. Because when I talked to him on Saturday I found out that he had left his wife. He filed for divorce last year."

"So they're divorced? Well that's a relief, you little home-wrecker." Melissa smiled.

My stomach knotted. "The divorce isn't official yet. Apparently she won't sign the papers."

Melissa scrunched her mouth to the side. I could tell that she still thought Professor Hunter was sleazy. She definitely didn't approve. But she didn't know how sincere he was when he talked to me. He didn't love his soon to be ex-wife.

"Are you sure he's telling you the truth?" she asked.

"Well, that brings me to this morning. It really seemed like he was, but I wanted to look it up to make sure. And I found an interview with his wife saying that everything was fine between them. So I freaked out."

"You need to learn how to control your temper, Penny. I get being upset, but ruining your Comm speech because of it? You probably failed."

"It would have been easy to get over before my speech if I didn't have to see him while I was giving it."

"I thought you said he wasn't in your class?"

"He isn't exactly." I took a deep breath. "He teaches it. James is the guy from the coffee shop. He's Professor Hunter."

Melissa laughed. "Right, like you'd date a professor."

I stared back at her.

Melissa's jaw dropped. "You're shitting me, Penny?"

"Ever since meeting him in the coffee shop I couldn't stop thinking about him. And seeing him in class three times a week made it impossible to get over him."

Melissa just stared at me.

"I wanted to tell you right away, but if anyone found out, we might get in trouble. And he came over today after my meltdown in class. He promised me that he was telling the truth about his wife. And I believe him. If you could have seen how upset he was that I was mad at him... He would never hurt me." I knew I was rambling but Melissa was still just staring at me. "He asked me to be his girlfriend. And I said yes. I know it probably sounds crazy, but I want to be with him. Melissa, please say something."

"Well it makes sense now."

"What?"

"Dating James is against the rules. Tyler was a safe choice, but you wanted a bad boy."

"That's not true." *Was it true?* I found Professor Hunter irresistible. Was I drawn to him because he wasn't good for me?

"Your boyfriend is a married professor. And you're a student. So, yes, I think you could classify him as a bad boy. Penny, bad boys are exciting, but they are always the wrong choice. Haven't you ever seen a romantic comedy?"

"Melissa, you don't even know him. He makes me so happy. He's wonderful." And sexy and dangerous. *Oh my God, I've fallen for a bad boy.*

"He makes you miserable, Penny! You've been a mess this whole past week. I've never seen you this upset and crazy before."

"Because I love him! And I was heartbroken when I thought it was over."

"I'm sorry, I am. I don't want to be judging you, but..."

"Then don't. Just be happy for me."

Melissa scrunched her face to the side again. "I'm sorry. I am happy for you. So you really love him, huh?"

"Yes." I smiled.

"I need to meet him."

"Okay, you can definitely meet him now. He almost stayed today but I told him I needed to talk to you first."

"Thanks. I would not have appreciated being blindsided with this. I can't believe you're dating your professor!"

"And you can't tell anyone, Melissa."

"That's going to be hard."

"Trust me, I know how hard it is."

"I can't even tell Josh?"

"Hopefully he doesn't already know. I haven't asked Tyler not to tell anyone yet. But if Josh doesn't know, please don't tell him."

"Wait, Tyler knows that James is Professor Hunter? He doesn't just think you're dating someone?"

"No, he knows."

"You have to text him. Like now. He's probably bad mouthing you to the whole frat."

"I don't think he'd do that."

"Text him, Penny."

I grabbed my phone off my desk and quickly typed out a message to Tyler. "Tyler, I'm really sorry about everything. If you could please not tell anyone about Professor Hunter though, I'd really appreciate it. I'm hoping that we can still be friends." I pressed send. Tyler thought I was no longer with Professor Hunter. If he knew I was with Professor Hunter again, he definitely wouldn't ever speak to me again. I put my phone back down on the desk. I just wanted to be happy about Professor Hunter asking me to be his girlfriend. Dealing with everything else made it hard for me to be excited, though.

CHAPTER 48

Wednesday

I sat down in my usual seat and took a deep breath. After my meltdown during my speech I knew people would be making fun of me. I was blushing already and no one else was here yet. It had taken every ounce of my willpower to come to class today. The deadline for dropping the class had passed. Besides, now I wanted to stare at Professor Hunter again.

As my classmates started to stroll in, I kept my eyes on my desk. There were a few snickers, but no one actually said anything to me. The chair next to me squeaked against the linoleum. I looked over as Tyler sat down.

"Hi," I said, trying to muster as much cheer to my voice as possible.

"Hey, Penny," he said without looking at me.

"Tyler?"

"Penny, I really don't feel like talking right now."

"Okay," I said softly and looked back down at my desk. "But I am sorry."

"You're sorry?" Tyler scoffed. "Right, I'm sure that you're real sorry that you're fucking our professor."

"Tyler!" I hissed.

"I can't do this." Tyler stood up and moved to the empty seat in front of him. I bit my lip. I had never wanted to hurt him. Our friendship meant so much to me, but he had never wanted to be my friend. There was nothing I could do to fix it.

When Professor Hunter walked into the room, Tyler's back stiffened. I closed my eyes. It was too painful to see Tyler this way. I so badly wanted for him to be happy.

"So, the first day of speeches was interesting," Professor Hunter said.

Several students laughed. Professor Hunter gave me a reassuring smile.

"I'm hoping that today will be a little more toned down. But I guess we shall see. First up, Heather Matthews."

Professor Hunter made his way to the back of the room. Tyler looked in the opposite direction as he walked by. Professor Hunter gave me a smile as he sat down in the seat next to me that was usually occupied by Tyler. I put my left elbow on my desk and rested my chin in my hand. I didn't care what anyone had to say during their speeches, all I wanted to do was stare at Professor Hunter.

He pulled out a stack of papers and began writing as Heather started talking. Professor Hunter folded the sheet of paper he was writing on and slid it onto my desk. He turned his attention back to the speech.

I slowly unfolded it and looked down at the message:

I wish we were alone right now.

I grabbed a pen out of my backpack and quickly wrote a response:

TEMPTATION

And what would you be doing to me if we were alone?

I slid the paper back onto his desk. I tapped my foot and bit the end of my pen, anxiously waiting for his response. When the person speaking finished, he quickly scribbled me a note and placed it on my desk.

Come to my office during lunch and find out. And stop biting your pen. That's not what belongs in your mouth.

I lowered my pen. I looked over at him and he flashed his panty dropping smile at me. Everything below my waistline clenched. I gulped and quickly turned away. There was no way that this afternoon could come soon enough. My heartbeat was already accelerating in anticipation. I folded the paper and slipped it into my pocket. The thought of the naughty words so close to my skin made me even more excited.

When class finally ended I was surprised to see that Tyler didn't move. He waited patiently as the class emptied out. Then he rose from his seat and turned around.

"Mr. Stevens," Professor Hunter said.

"What you're doing is wrong," Tyler said. There was venom in his voice. I had never expected him to confront Professor Hunter. I gulped.

"Not everything is so black and white," Professor Hunter said calmly.

"In this case, it is."

"I beg to differ."

It looked like Tyler wanted to say something else, but instead he just glared at Professor Hunter. "This isn't going to end well," Tyler finally said.

"Are you threatening me?"

Tyler laughed. "No, I would never threaten my professor. I'm fully aware of where the line is, unlike some of us." Tyler shook his head, walked past us, and exited through the back door.

Professor Hunter was silent for a moment. "Penny, is that something I should be worried about?"

"I don't know. I asked him not to tell anyone."

"Then there's no use dwelling on it." He leaned in and gave me a swift kiss on the lips.

"Do you still want me to come to your office for lunch?"

"Of course." He held out his hand. I grabbed it and he pulled me up.

"Is 12:30 okay?"

"Sounds good. I'll pick us up something." He looked over his shoulder to make sure the room was still empty and then kissed me again. But this time it was hard, fierce, and possessive. When he drew back I felt slightly dizzy. He kissed my hand. "Until later."

CHAPTER 49

Wednesday

My Stat professor droned on in what he thought was English. But I didn't understand a word of it. I had missed class on Monday and I was more confused than ever. By the time class ended, I had several pages of notes that made zero sense. I sighed and put them into my backpack. I was probably going to need to hire a tutor.

I pulled my backpack over my shoulder and headed out of class. The sunlight hitting my face made me smile. Right now wasn't the time to think about school. I had a lunch date with Professor Hunter.

I made my way across campus and toward the business and economics building. Professor Hunter had never invited me to his office before. I had always just showed up. The last time I had been there was the first time we had had sex. Just thinking about it made me excited. He had completely possessed me.

I opened the door to Lerner and made my way upstairs. Professor Hunter's office was on the third floor. My heart was racing when I reached his door. I knocked and stepped back. When he opened the door he looked both ways, grabbed my arm, and pulled me inside his office. As soon as he closed the door, he pressed my back against it.

"Penny."

"Professor Hunter."

He leaned forward and touched his nose against mine. "I thought you were going to start calling me James?"

"It's hard to break a habit. And besides, we are in your office."

He smiled and pulled away. "We should probably eat." He released me and my back slid down the door.

"Oh." I was breathless. I wasn't thinking about food. Professor Hunter walked over and sat down behind his desk. There were two wrapped sandwiches and bottles of something on his desk.

"I picked up sandwiches from Capriotti's. I wasn't sure what you'd like, so I just got two of my favorite."

"And what is your favorite?"

"Turkey, lettuce, provolone cheese, and mayo." He looked at me hopefully.

"That sounds delicious." I sat down across from him, grabbed one of the sandwiches, and unwrapped the paper. "It's actually exactly what I would have ordered." I took a bite. "So good."

He laughed. "We have more in common than I thought."

"Apparently so." I slowly chewed my sandwich. There was a question gnawing at me. "Can I ask you something?"

"Of course." There was a small line across his forehead. He was still uncomfortable talking to me about personal things.

I wanted to ask him how much longer his divorce was going to take, but I didn't want to upset him. Instead I tried to keep things up-tempo and said, "I failed my speech, didn't I?"

"You'll have to wait until tomorrow to find out just like everyone else. No favoritism, remember?"

"I thought you were joking. So I really don't get special treatment?"

Professor Hunter shook his head.

"None at all? I really think there should be certain perks to dating a professor."

"Well, that depends on what you have in mind. I think maybe there could be. I'm sure you could persuade me if you really wanted to."

I put my half eaten sandwich down on the paper. "This is good. But I'm actually hungry for something else."

Professor Hunter lowered his eyebrows slightly. He knew exactly what I was referring to, and I could tell he wanted it. I stood up and walked around his desk, trailing my finger along the wood.

"I've had dreams about what you did to me on this desk." I leaned against it and gripped the edge in my hands.

His Adam's apple rose and fell. "It would be better to relive it." He lightly brushed the inside of my thigh with his fingertips.

I gulped. "That's not exactly what I had in mind." I lifted my foot and pushed it against his chair until his chair had rolled back from his desk. I knelt down in front of him and pushed his knees apart. *This is going to be fun.* I ran my hands up his thighs and slowly unbuttoned his jeans. He was looking down at me under his thick eyebrows. I wanted to make him moan. He was letting me take control and it was invigorating.

"You're going to want to scream. But don't make a sound." I repeated the words back to him that had made me want him so badly.

"Penny." His voice sounded strained.

I unzipped his pants and he lifted his hips ever so slightly. He wanted my mouth around him, claiming every inch of him. I opened the flap on his boxers and pulled out his rock hard cock. I locked eyes with him as I brought my lips to his tip. I slowly took him in my mouth and tightened my lips around him.

Professor Hunter moaned softly.

I swirled my tongue around his shaft as I sucked him all the way down. The way he was staring down at me under his thick eyebrows made me ache between my legs. He gripped my hair in his fist and shoved his cock deeper, hitting the back of my throat. Now I was the one moaning, and the vibrations of my mouth seemed to make him even harder.

A knock sounded on the door.

"Shit," Professor Hunter said under his breath. He quickly zipped up his pants. Without thinking, I climbed underneath his desk. "No, Penny, don't..."

"Hello, James." The office door squeaked as someone walked in. He had a deep, husky voice that I didn't recognize.

Professor Hunter cleared his throat. "Ben, I was just in the middle of lunch." I heard the shuffle of paper on Professor Hunter's desk. He was probably pulling my sandwich toward him. If Ben had any sense, he'd know there was someone here. Two sandwiches and two drinks meant two people. I bit my lip.

"Well don't let me bother you." I heard the click of the man's shoes as he walked over to Professor Hunter's desk and sat down in the chair I had been sitting in. "Hungry today, James?"

Professor Hunter laughed.

Then I got an idea. It was fun and dangerous and exactly what I wanted to do. I ran my hand up his thigh and grabbed his zipper in my fingertips. I didn't care that someone was here. He didn't seem to think anything was amiss, and I didn't want to wait to have Professor Hunter's cock back in my mouth.

"No," Professor Hunter said firmly. He held my hand away from him. But I didn't listen. With my left hand I slowly unzipped his pants and pulled out his cock. He was still hard; he wanted me. I put my mouth around him again and took him as deep as I could.

"Really? Two sandwiches is normal for you?"

"No," he groaned. "I mean, yes." I heard him take a bite of his sandwich and moan lightly. "Yes, I'm quite hungry today."

"What kind of sandwich is it?"

"Turkey, from Capriotti's." Professor Hunter shifted forward in his chair slightly, pushing me down deeper.

"It looks good."

The possibility of getting caught made me crave him even more. His taste, his touch, his cock deep inside my aching pussy. *Oh God.* I slid my lips up and down Professor Hunter's shaft, licking and sucking every inch of him.

"It's fucking fantastic." Professor Hunter's voice sounded tight. I wanted him to unwind and find his release in my mouth.

"I'll have to try one," Ben said.

"Yes!" Professor Hunter cleared his throat. "You have to. They're irresistible."

Ben was quiet for a second. "I will then. I've heard lots of good things about Capriotti's. But I don't want to disturb your lunch, James. I just had a quick favor to ask."

I wanted Professor Hunter to explode in my mouth. I went up and down, faster and faster.

"Oh," Professor Hunter said. I almost giggled. He had meant to say it as a question, but it came out as more of an exclamation. "What's the favor?" he asked a little more calmly. I could tell he was close.

"It's for my class. I was just wondering if you could come and talk to them about some of the catalysts that made your company explode. So they can see how marketing makes all the difference."

I took Professor Hunter's cock all the way to the back of my throat and felt him pulse between my lips.

Professor Hunter slammed his hand against his desk. With his other hand, he grabbed a fistful of my hair and pushed his thick cock even deeper into my throat. "Fuck," he groaned.

A second later, his hot cum filled my mouth. I drank him down greedily.

"Are you okay, James?"

"Yes. I'm just excited to talk to your class." Professor Hunter sounded like he was out of breath. "I'll do it. Just email me the details."

"Thank you, I really appreciate it." Ben's chair squeaked as he stood up. "I think I might go get one of those sandwiches right now."

"I can't recommend it enough." Professor Hunter sighed.

"Have a good afternoon, James."

"You too, Ben."

I heard Ben's feet shuffle across the floor and then the door close behind him. Professor Hunter stood up, put his hand out for me, and pulled me to my feet.

"Your mouth is a miracle, Penny. But I will get you back for that," he growled.

"And when will that be?"

"When you least expect it." He leaned in and kissed me, pressing my ass against the edge of the desk. "I forgot how much doing naughty things in public gets you off. You're probably dripping wet, wanting me more than you ever have before."

I already wanted him, but his naughty words sent a shiver down my spine. I didn't just want him, I needed him and only him, deep inside of me, making me scream.

"I am. I want you so badly."

A smile curled on Professor Hunter's lips. He pulled my leggings down and pushed my thong to the side. "Just like I thought." His finger pressed against me, teasing me. "You're so wet for me, Penny." He brushed the tip of his nose against mine.

My heart was racing. I tilted my head back and he answered my call, ravaging me with a kiss that made my head spin. He bit my lip and plunged a finger inside of me.

I gasped.

He slid his finger in and out of me in a torturous rhythm. "I didn't realize that my cock in your mouth turned you on so much."

"Everything about you turns me on."

He slid another finger inside of me.

I moaned softly. He began to pulse his fingers faster, deeper. I could feel myself clenching around him, climbing higher and higher, like only he could do to me. He pressed his thumb against my clit. I gripped the edge of his desk. He curved his finger slightly, hitting that spot that I never knew existed before meeting him.

"Yes!" I screamed and shattered around his fingers. My release washed over me as he pulled his fingers out and slid them into his mouth. I gulped, watching him. Everything he did was so sexy. I wasn't done with him yet. I moved my eyes down his torso to his pants. His erection was bulging against the zipper, eager to come out.

"I only have a few minutes before my next class," Professor Hunter said.

"Then you better fuck me fast."

He raised his left eyebrow. "Penny, I know I can make you come in sixty seconds." There was a challenging look in his eyes. "Turn around and place your hands on the desk."

I quickly followed his instructions. I had never wanted something so badly in my life.

He hooked his thumbs around my waistband and slid his hands down my ass and thighs, pushing my panties and leggings to my knees. He pushed me forward so that my torso was on top of his desk and my ass was jutting in the air, waiting for him.

He ran his fingers down my spine. "This is going to be fast and rough, just the way you like it." I heard the zipper on his pants. The waiting was killing me. I needed him to fill me. As if answering my silent pleading, he slapped my ass hard and thrust his huge cock inside of me. The sting of his hand and his cock spreading me wide made me gasp.

He slid his length in and out of me slowly, making the pain turn into immeasurable pleasure within seconds. I gripped the other side of his desk and pushed back into him, wanting more.

He slammed into me and began pumping relentlessly, fucking me harder than he ever had before. My hip bones dug into the side of his desk, but all I could feel was him inside of me. His cock made me forget about everything.

He leaned forward and brushed my cheek with his knuckles as he gyrated his hips. "You only have thirty seconds left, Penny. If you don't come, then you'll just have to wait."

"I'm so close," I moaned. He couldn't leave me like this, aching and wanting. He pulled my hair, making me arch my back. He gripped my hair tight and used it as leverage as he thrust faster. The sensation made me clench around him.

"That's right," he growled. "Come for me, Penny."

And as if he had given me a simple instruction, I found my release. My toes curled as he continued to thrust in and out of me, riding my high. He gripped both sides of my waist and a moment later I felt his hot liquid fill me.

He groaned softly and pulled out of me, leaving an empty feeling between my thighs. I heard him zip his pants and I rose from his desk and turned around.

He knelt down in front of me and kissed each of my hip bones. There were red lines on my flesh from the pressure of being fucked hard against his desk. I swallowed hard and watched him as he pulled my thong and pants back up. He placed another kiss on each of my hip bones.

"I'll be by your place at eight."

"What?" I couldn't think clearly. I had no idea what he was talking about. But I wasn't going to protest, I wanted to see him as much as possible.

"To meet Melissa, remember?" He stood and placed his hand gently on my cheek. "That's tonight, right? I'll bring dessert."

"Oh."

"Brownies or something, Penny." He traced my lips with his thumb. "Not me this time."

I smiled. "Sorry, I'm having a hard time thinking straight."

Professor Hunter smiled back at me. "I don't think I'll ever get enough of you," he whispered.

I looked longingly into his eyes. "I know that I'll never get enough of you." I loved him. There was no doubt in my mind. I loved him so much.

CHAPTER 50

Wednesday

Last time Professor Hunter had been here I hadn't known he was coming. So I wanted to make sure my dorm room looked better this time. I grabbed the last piece of clothing on the ground and tossed it in my hamper.

"Geez, hasn't he been here before?" Melissa was watching me.

"Yeah, but I don't want him to think I'm messy."

"But you are messy."

I put the bottle of Windex down on my bureau. "I guess you're right."

"Is there anything else I should know?"

"About Pro...I mean, James?"

"Ew, do you call him Professor Hunter?"

"No," I lied. I could feel my face turning crimson.

"You're so weird."

"Melissa, please don't embarrass me."

"I promise that I'm not on a mission to embarrass you. But I do have some questions for him. If I happen to mortify you along the way..."

"Melissa."

"I'll be on my best behavior." She lifted her hands in the air, pretending to surrender.

I didn't believe her for a second. My phone buzzed and my stomach rose to my chest. I grabbed it and read his text. "He's here."

"So go let him in." Melissa crossed her legs on her bed.

I gave her one last pleading look and went to go let Professor Hunter in. I opened the back door to our building. He was standing there in a leather jacket, jeans, and a t-shirt. He truly looked like a college student, the most handsome college student in existence. It had started to rain, which made his hair glisten. He stepped inside and kissed me.

"Penny," he whispered.

"James," I said breathlessly. My knees felt like jelly.

"Is she excited to meet me?"

"I think so."

"You don't seem very confident." He had a playful grin on his face.

"It's just that she can be kind of intense. Please just remember how much I like you."

"I'm sure it won't be that bad. I brought brownies." He held up a pan covered with aluminum foil. Brownies were second only to condoms on my list of favorite things that come in foil.

"I'd rather have you." I was feeling bold, a feeling I knew would disappear as soon as we walked into my dorm room.

"Maybe later. Right now, I promised to meet your friend." He pulled back and put his hand out for me. I let him lead the way up the stairs to my room. I took a deep breath as I opened the door.

"So you're the elusive Professor Hunter?" Melissa asked.

I closed the door behind us, hoping that no one on our floor had heard her.

Professor Hunter gave Melissa a charming smile. "Please, call me James. And you must be Melissa." Professor Hunter put out his hand for Melissa to shake.

Melissa hesitated a moment too long and then shook his hand. She was being awful on purpose. Letting them meet was looking like a terrible idea already.

"I brought brownies." Professor Hunter lifted the pan in the air.

"Yum! Did you bake them yourself?" Melissa asked.

Professor Hunter paused. "No. I doubt they'd be edible if I had."

"You don't cook?"

"Not very often." Professor Hunter scratched the back of his neck. He looked so uncomfortable. I wound my arm around his.

"He has a personal chef," I offered. *Could this be any more awkward?* Melissa was going to spend the whole night rapid firing questions at him.

"Very fancy," Melissa said. She crossed her arms in front of her chest. "It's strange, I never pictured a professor in our dorm room."

"I never pictured myself in a student's room either. It just happened."

Melissa smiled. "So, tell me about yourself."

"Well, I grew up in New York. I lived there my whole life until I moved here last year. I'm sorry, what is it that you want to know exactly? Something specific?"

"Where did you go to school?"

"Can I sit down?" He gave me a smile. He was handling himself well, despite Melissa's onslaught.

"Yes," I said. But I was curious to know where he went to school too. I had never asked him about that before. I pulled out my desk chair for him. Professor Hunter took off his jacket, put it on the back of the chair, and sat down. I jumped onto my bed and sat Indian style.

"I went to Harvard." *Harvard, wow.*

"Your parents are wealthy then?" Melissa asked.

"My parents are wealthy, but I had a scholarship to Harvard."

"Impressive."

"Thank you."

"But even so, you're very handsome and your parents are wealthy. Most things in your life must have been handed to you."

A flash of anger crossed Professor Hunter's face. He took a deep breath. "In some regards, yes. Many things that were handed to me I didn't want though. I owe my success to myself, not my family. Do you have another question for me?"

"Well there's one main one. Why is it that you want to date students?" Melissa wasn't backing down.

"I don't want to date students." He emphasized the plural. "You seem to have gotten the wrong idea about me. I just want to date Penny."

"So you have never dated any students besides Penny?"

"No, I have not."

"Can you really even date someone if you're married?"

Professor Hunter looked at me. He was surprised that Melissa knew that. Was he mad at me for telling her? I couldn't tell from his expression. Maybe he looked a little hurt. I didn't realize telling Melissa would betray his confidence. My stomach churned uneasily. He turned back to Melissa. "I'm getting divorced."

"But you're technically still married."

"Melissa, my soon to be ex-wife has been cheating on me for almost as long as we were together. As far as I'm concerned, we are no longer married."

Melissa was quiet for a moment. "I'm sorry about your wife. But you are still married. How much longer will your divorce take?"

I was silently thanking Melissa. She was asking him questions that I didn't have the confidence to. And for some reason, Professor Hunter was answering her questions without hesitation.

"I honestly don't know. I thought she would have signed the papers by now. I've given her everything she wants."

"It seems wrong to pursue a relationship in that situation."

"I have to disagree. There hasn't been anything that's felt so right in my life."

"It may feel right, but there are consequences. Won't you get fired if someone finds out about you and Penny?"

"Not necessarily."

Watching Melissa and him talk was like watching a ping pong tournament.

"But aren't you thinking about Penny too? If this gets out, no one will believe the grades you've given her. No one will see her as just another student. Even other professors will question her grades. I know that she's just with you, but people may think she's been with other professors too. Her whole college career will be in jeopardy. You may be fine with getting fired, but she still has to go to school here."

I hadn't really thought of that. *Will I really be seen differently?*

"I think that Penny can make her own choices." He looked over at me. "I've thought about all the possibilities. And I'm willing to risk it as long as she is."

"I am." I smiled at Professor Hunter. I was all in. The future didn't matter right now. For the first time I wasn't worried about what might happen. I was enjoying right now. But I'd be lying if I didn't see a future between us. I couldn't imagine my life without him.

"And you aren't at all concerned about your age difference?" Melissa continued.

Shit. I had been so caught up in everything that I had somehow forgotten about my own secret. Would Professor Hunter even want to be with me after I told him the truth? I bit my lip.

"No, it doesn't concern me." He paused. "How about we have those brownies?" Professor Hunter suggested.

"Why, because chocolate makes all women's problems go away?" Melissa scoffed.

"I'm just hungry." Professor Hunter shifted in his chair. "What are you majoring in anyway, criminal justice?"

"I'll get plates." I hopped off the bed and found some paper plates from the closet. I pulled the tinfoil off the pan.

Melissa stared at him. "No, political science."

"Do you want to be a lawyer?"

"This isn't really about me, James, it's about you."

"I was under the impression that we were supposed to get to know each other tonight."

"Yes, I want to be a lawyer. Now back to you. I find it hard to believe that you can't find someone to date that's your own age." Melissa was being relentless.

"The only person I want to date is Penny. I don't know what else I can say to make you believe me."

Melissa sighed. "Okay."

"Okay?"

"I believe you. I'm sorry about all the questions. I'm just looking out for Penny. Dating a professor just isn't like her."

I froze as I was cutting the brownies. *Please don't say I'm a future cat lady!*

"I would hope not," Professor Hunter said.

"That's a little hypocritical."

"Then I guess I'm a hypocrite." He smiled at me.

My body relaxed. It always did when his gaze was on me. I finished cutting the brownies and handed them out.

"These are really good," Melissa said sweetly. I relaxed even more. Maybe her onslaught was finally done.

"I'll pass on your compliments." Professor Hunter put his half eaten brownie down on the plate. "So, if Penny isn't the type of girl who dates a professor, what type of girl is she exactly?"

Melissa laughed. "The type of girl who likes to stay in on a Saturday night. She doesn't break the rules. I mean, I thought she was joking when she told me she was dating you."

"I break the rules sometimes." It was weird just sitting there watching them talk about me.

"No you don't. You're ridiculously straight laced. I basically have to drag you out of the dorm on weekends."

Professor Hunter laughed. He put down his plate, stood up, and sat down on the bed next to me. The tension in the room seemed to completely evaporate once he put his arm around me. He wasn't a professor in our room anymore; he was my boyfriend. I was the luckiest girl in the world.

Melissa smiled at us. "Going from taking no risks to dating a professor is a huge leap. I didn't really understand it. But seeing you two together..." Melissa shrugged. "I get it."

"Well I'm glad we have your approval. Your opinion seems to be very important to Penny, and therefore important to me."

"And I promise not to tell anyone. Your secret is safe with me."

"Thank you, Melissa."

"And let me officially invite you to our birthday party. I'm sure Penny has already told you about it."

"Actually, she hasn't invited me yet." Professor Hunter smiled at me. "Or mentioned it at all."

Melissa laughed. "Well, normally I guess you couldn't come. But since it's going to be close to Halloween we're having a costume party. So as long as you wear a good costume, I think it'll be okay."

Professor Hunter flashed me a smile. "I wouldn't miss it."

My stomach was in knots. I needed to tell him that I was only 19. Now I was afraid that I had waited too long. The lie seemed worse and worse the longer I waited.

"Can I come over to your place for a bit?" I asked Professor Hunter. I would tell him tonight, no matter what.

He rubbed my back. "Of course."

"I'm sorry, I just have one more thing to say before you go."

"Melissa," I pleaded.

"No, it's okay," Professor Hunter interjected. "What is it?"

"You better not hurt her."

"I won't."

"Well, you already have. So your word is hard to believe. I've never seen Penny act the way she did this past week. And you two may have forgotten about that, but I haven't."

"That was just a misunderstanding."

"Maybe if you're more upfront about your baggage, things like that won't happen."

"I won't hurt her," Professor Hunter repeated. For the first time he looked truly angry. I held my breath.

"That's all I can ask." Melissa finished her brownie. "You two are cute together."

Professor Hunter looked down at me. "It's getting late. If you wanted to come over for awhile, we better get going." He got off my bed and put on his jacket.

I slid off the bed and put our plates in the trash.

"Penny, can I talk to you for a second?" Melissa asked.

"I'll pull the car around," James said. He extended his hand to Melissa. "It was...interesting to meet you, Melissa."

"Good choice of words. I'm sorry if I made you uncomfortable." Melissa shook his hand.

"Looking out for your friends is a good quality to have. I hope to see you again soon. You're going to make a good lawyer."

It looked like his words made Melissa blush. So his charm did extend to everyone. Professor Hunter walked out the door, leaving the two of us alone.

As soon as the door closed I turned to Melissa. "You promised you'd be on your best behavior. What the hell was that?"

"I'm sorry, Penny. I didn't mean to lie. I just had so many questions for him."

I sighed. "So, what did you think?"

"He's very handsome. *So* handsome. And he seems nice."

"Stop being vague. Tell me what you really think."

"Penny, I don't know what it is exactly, but I don't trust him."

"He answered all your millions of questions. What else could you possibly need to know?"

"It just seems like he's hiding something. I don't know how to explain it. Penny, I want you to be happy."

"I am."

"Just be careful, okay?" She reached over and squeezed my hand. Her concern made me slightly uneasy. Maybe he was hiding something else.

CHAPTER 51

Wednesday

Professor Hunter was waiting for me when I walked out of my dorm. He was leaning against the car with his arms crossed. It was still drizzling, but he didn't seem to notice. He looked angry. But when I reached him, he smiled and opened up the door for me. I climbed in and he shut the door behind me. I buckled my seatbelt as I watched him walk around the car to the driver's side. He got in and we immediately sped off. His silence was unnerving.

"I'm sorry about all of Melissa's questions."

"It's okay."

He looked straight ahead at the road. He was gripping the wheel so tightly that his knuckles were turning white.

"It doesn't seem like it's okay."

"When I told you to tell her about me, I thought you were just going to say that I was your professor."

"I thought I was allowed to tell her everything? She would have asked questions if I didn't tell her what our fight was about."

"You should have asked me if it was okay."

"I'm sorry."

"I like to keep my personal life private, Penny."

"I know. Even from me." I folded my arms across my chest and looked out the window. We were pulling up to his apartment building. I was already suspicious that he was hiding things from me. And now Melissa's words haunted me too. The car circled the garage and Professor Hunter parked it with ease between his assortment of other cars. He cut the ignition and got out of the car. I pushed my door open without waiting for him.

He grabbed my hand and walked quickly toward the elevator, pulling me with him. Why did I find him so sexy when he was angry and demanding? He slid his access card in the reader and the doors opened. He pulled me inside.

"I said that I was sorry. I should have asked you."

"It's not just that."

"Then what is it?"

"Your friend hates me. She didn't even give me a chance. I think that maybe it's because she has someone else in mind for you."

"She doesn't."

"So, she dislikes Tyler too?"

"This has nothing to do with Tyler. She's just looking out for me."

"I don't think that's true."

"Stop!" I lightly pushed his chest.

He grabbed my hand. His eyes were ablaze as he stared down at me. He pushed my back against the elevator wall and lifted my hands above my head. Desire exploded through my body. His kiss was possessive and intense, leaving my whole body wanting. Every inch of me felt alive. His erection pressed against my thigh, growing with every second. When the door dinged open, he pulled away.

"Oh God."

He smiled at me. I blushed. I hadn't meant to say that out loud.

Professor Hunter tossed his jacket on the floor and pulled off his t-shirt. "You have a way of crawling under my skin."

"I don't mean to."

"Yes, you do."

"Professor Hunter, I need to talk to you."

"I don't want to talk." He walked over to me and pushed my shirt up the sides of my torso. There was only one thing on his mind. And I wanted it too.

But I needed to be strong. If I didn't tell him now, it would just get worse and worse. "But I have something important to tell you."

He pulled my shirt the rest of the way off. "It can wait." His lips were on mine and the rest of my resolve dissolved with his kiss. It had the same intensity as our kiss in the elevator.

He pushed me down onto the pristine couch and got on top of me. His tongue swirled around mine as I moved my hand down his six pack. I traced his happy trail with my fingertips and grabbed his erection through his jeans. He moaned into my mouth.

I fumbled with the button and zipper on his jeans and wrapped my hand around his length. His breathing hitched as I moved my hand up and down his shaft.

"I know that you're angry with me." He unhinged my bra and gently pulled it down my arms.

"No, it's okay," I panted.

He leaned down and kissed my neck. He moved down, leaving a trail of kisses across my breasts, sucking hard on each nipple. I wanted him so badly. He kissed down my stomach and past my belly button. I lifted my hips and he pulled off my leggings and thong with one swift move. He spread my knees apart and slid his hands up my thighs. I gulped.

"I want you to be angry. That'll make this even better." He brought his lips down to my clit and sucked hard.

"Professor Hunter!" I arched my back.

He sucked it again in response and let his tongue answer my needs. He pushed my thighs farther apart, shoving his tongue deeper inside of me, driving me insane. I pushed my face into one of the pillows and moaned.

"Yes! I need you," I groaned. "Please."

With his free hand he pushed his pants and boxers to the ground. I bit my lip, anticipating him inside of me. But instead of climbing on top of me, he grabbed my hand and pulled me to a seated position, shoving his fingers deep inside of me. I gasped with pleasure.

He shoved his thick cock into my open mouth and grabbed a fistful of my hair. I wanted him inside of me, but I craved the taste of him. I mimicked what his fingers were doing, sliding up and down his shaft faster and faster. I tightened my lips and looked up at him as he closed his eyes in ecstasy. I grabbed his ass and went down as deep as I could, letting him fill the back of my throat.

He groaned and pulled out of my mouth. "I don't want to cum in your mouth. I want your pussy clenched around me, with you screaming my name."

I loved when he talked like that. It was so dirty but it turned me on even more.

He pulled his fingers out of me and I groaned in protest. "Baby, we're not even close to being finished."

He pulled me off the couch and bent me over the armrest. "Spread your legs, Penny." His voice had a low growl to it. He had never sounded so sexy. I followed his instructions and held my breath. I thought he'd thrust himself deep inside of me right away but nothing happened. A chill ran down my spine and my body shook. His fingers brushed against the back of my knees and I arched my back. The anticipation was killing me. His fingers ran up my thighs and over my ass. He slid his hands to my hips and gripped them tightly as he plunged himself inside of me.

"Yes!" I screamed. It was everything I wanted and more. So carnal, so raw.

His cock pounded relentlessly, filling me, stretching me until I couldn't take anymore. Professor Hunter grabbed my shoulders and pulled me to a standing position, tilting his cock and hitting the spot that only he could find. I gasped. The sensation was too much. I was just about to come when he suddenly pulled out.

He pushed me back down onto the couch.

"Roll over," he demanded.

I turned. The want in his eyes matched my own. Everything inside me felt so wound up. I needed him. Only he could unwind me. "Professor Hunter, I'm so close," I panted.

"I know." He got down on top of me and grabbed my ass, lifting my legs into the air. My lower back hovered over the couch cushions.

"Please," I begged.

He raised his left eyebrow.

"Please, Professor Hunter. Fuck me!"

He thrust himself inside me again. He gyrated his hips, hitting every nerve inside of me. His hands moved to my hips and he gripped them firmly as he began to move slowly in and out of me. I tried to move my hips to make him go faster, but he had me locked in place. He rocked back slightly and then pushed himself deeper, all the way inside of me, filling me with every inch of him.

I exploded into a million pieces as his hot liquid shot into me. Professor Hunter collapsed beside me and pulled me tight against his chest. His heart was racing. I tilted my head back and he kissed me softly. I wanted to stay in this moment forever.

CHAPTER 52

Wednesday

As his heartbeat slowed, I knew it was time. There was nothing preventing me from telling him my secret now.

"You called me baby."

"I'm sorry, did you not like that?"

"No I did. You've just always called me Penny. Or Miss Taylor. Everything you say sounds sexy though. You could call me anything."

Professor Hunter smiled. "And you've always called me Professor Hunter."

"I think you like that I keep calling you that."

"You do, huh?"

"It makes everything sexier. Mysterious and forbidden. Wrong but so right."

"Nothing is wrong about you and me." He tucked a strand of hair behind my ear. "Melissa said something after I left, didn't she? I can tell that something is bothering you."

"No, it's not that." *Only partially.*

"Hold that thought." He slowly rose from the couch.

I stared at him longingly.

"What, have you not had enough?"

"I'll never have enough of you."

He smiled and zipped up his jeans. "I'll be right back. I have something for you."

I slowly sat up. I grabbed my panties off the floor. I went to pick up my pants but suddenly had a better idea. I pulled Professor Hunter's shirt on instead and sat back down on the couch.

"God you're sexy." He reemerged from a room that I hadn't been in yet.

I could feel my face flushing.

"This is when you look the most beautiful. When your hair is mussed up, your cheeks are pink, and you're wearing one of my shirts."

He pulled a wrapped box out from behind his back.

"But my birthday isn't for another few weeks."

"It's not for your birthday." He sat down beside me and placed the box in my hands. It was wrapped perfectly with white paper and a silky pink bow.

"What is it?"

"Open it, baby."

I smiled at him. I pulled the bow loose and tore into the paper. I lifted up the lid and slid the tissue paper to the side. It was a new bikini. It was a deep blue, the same color as the ocean. There were more strings than I was used to seeing on a bathing suit, but it looked beautiful. I ran my fingers across the fabric.

"You didn't need to do that."

"I wanted to. Besides, it's my fault that we lost your last one."

I laughed. "We didn't lose it. You somehow convinced me to get naked in public and it got stolen."

"I hate to break it to you, but it didn't take that much convincing." He leaned in and kissed me gently.

"But this is probably the most expensive thing I own now. It's too much." I put the lid back on the box and pushed it back into his hands.

"Penny, it's a gift."

"I know. I'm sorry, I do love it. But I'm not used to getting extravagant gifts like this."

"Well you better get used to it. I want to be able to buy you things. I want to get you everything you've ever wanted."

I shook my head. "I don't want anything. I just want you."

"That's refreshing to know." He cupped my chin in his hand. "I've never met anyone like you." He leaned in and kissed me again.

Professor Hunter pulled back and ran his hand through his hair. "Well, don't get mad at me. I didn't realize that you weren't going to like getting presents. I also picked up a few other things for you for whenever you want to spend the night."

"What?"

He stood up and held his hand out for me. I grabbed it and he pulled me to my feet. He led me past the kitchen and into his bedroom. He flipped the light on in his closet. A row of his shirts was missing, and in their place were tons of clothes. *For me.*

I ran my hand along the jeans, t-shirts, short dresses, skirts, and blouses. I looked down. And shoes? There were a new pair of sneakers, some flats, and a few high heels with varying lengths of stilettos.

Everything still had the tags. "I can't accept all of this. I mean, I can't accept any of this. Please tell me that you can return everything?"

"I can, but I'm not going to."

"Why?"

"Penny, your face lit up when you saw everything. I understand that you aren't used to being showered with gifts. But I want you to have these things, or else I wouldn't have bought them for you. I want you to be comfortable staying here whenever you want."

I felt myself blush. "It's all so nice. But how did you even know my size?"

"I think I know your body pretty well." He put his hand on the small of my back. "And you left your clothes here that one morning."

I cringed remembering when I had run out on him. I had never meant to hurt him. And I was about to again. I needed to tell him the truth.

Professor Hunter opened up one of his drawers. There were at least a dozen pairs of lacy panties with matching bras.

"So these are the kinds of things you like me to wear?" I thought of the cotton thong I was wearing. I suddenly felt self-conscious.

He pulled me into his arms. "I prefer you in nothing at all."

I was losing my resolve again. Whenever he touched me it was like a spark of electricity through my whole body.

"Professor Hunter, this is all too much. I appreciate the gesture, but I don't need any of this."

Professor Hunter wrapped his arms tighter around me. His intoxicating smell was making my head spin.

"I feel like a Disney princess. Which makes you the handsome prince that rescued me. But I didn't even realize that I needed rescuing."

Professor Hunter laughed. "If I'm the prince I certainly hope that you'll be my princess."

I smiled up at him. "It's like I moved in without having to actually move any of my things. I guess that is rather convenient."

"It is."

"So you really want me to keep all this stuff?"

"I'm going to want to spoil you. That's something that you're going to have to accept. I want to give you everything. But I bought these things for you mainly because I want you to consider spending more time here. I thought that having these things here would make that easier."

Is he asking me to move in? Kind of? My heartbeat quickened. I barely even knew him. That was insane.

"Besides, your bed is so uncomfortable," he added.

Oh God, he is asking me to move in. I had waited too long to tell him my secret. It had gotten so serious so fast. "I don't mind my bed. Actually I'm really used to it. It's quite comfortable now."

Professor Hunter's face fell. "I'm not trying to pressure you, Penny. I know I have some things I need to deal with. And I promise that I am dealing with them. I'm just hoping that you'll consider spending more time here. I'm happiest when you're next to me." He traced his thumb along my lower lip.

"You mean like a few nights a week?"

"If that's what you want."

"What do you want?"

"If it was up to me, I'd have you here all the time." He leaned down to kiss me, but I pulled away.

"I need to talk to you."

"We are talking. And I can't think of a better conversation to have."

"No, I mean I need to tell you something." I grabbed his arms and unwound myself from him. I walked out of his closet and sat down on his bed. It was so soft. I hadn't realized how tired I was. Part of me just wanted to lay down and have him hold me all night. I wanted to be with him all the time too. But he didn't know me. And I had a feeling that I didn't know him either.

He sat down beside me. "I'll return everything. I didn't mean to make you uncomfortable."

"It's not that. I love the idea of spending more time with you. I just need to tell you something."

"Okay."

I felt like I was in a dream. After being so mad at him last week, it seemed surreal that my secret was what could potentially ruin us. But maybe he was still holding something back too.

"What's wrong, Penny?" He squeezed my hand.

"I don't want there to be any more secrets between us," I said.

He gazed into my eyes. I thought he might offer one of his, but he stayed silent. He looked unsettled. I didn't want to do this; I didn't want for this to end. I moved so that I was sitting on his lap, facing him. I put my hands on the sides of his face and he moved his so that they were on the small of my back.

"You're so handsome. I still don't know what you see in me."

"I see everything that I've always wanted." He kissed my cheek where a tear had fallen.

"I need to tell you something. And you have to promise that you won't get mad."

"Just tell me." He kissed my other cheek where I had shed another tear.

I leaned in and kissed him. I wanted to remember what it felt like for him to want me, for him to trust me. He moved his hand to the back of my neck and pulled me into him. Everything seemed so simple when we kissed. It was just right. It was perfect. I moved my head back. He was looking at me with the familiar lust in his eyes. If I wanted, I could have him again right now. And I really wanted to. I placed one last swift kiss on his eager lips.

"You have to promise," I said again.

"Okay. I promise that I won't get mad."

"My birthday is on October 15th."

"That's good to know. I'll make sure to clear my schedule."

"No, that's not what's bothering me." I grabbed his hands from my back, moved them to his lap, and held them firmly. I was never going to let go of his hands. If I let go, he might slip away from me. "I lied to you."

Professor Hunter's brow creased, but he didn't say a word.

"I've been lying to you ever since you walked me home from that party. I didn't mean to. At first I just didn't want to get in trouble. But now it's so much more. I don't want to hurt you. I don't want this to be over."

"Penny, I told you that I'm not going anywhere. Just tell me." He squeezed my hands.

I took a deep breath. "I'm not a senior."

I could see his body tense. It looked like I had slapped him across the face. He didn't look mad though, just surprised.

"I'm a sophomore. But my birthday is October 15th. I'll be 20 in just a couple weeks."

His handsome features looked strained. "You're only 19?" He pulled his hands away from mine. He was already slipping away.

"I'm practically 20."

He ran both his hands through his hair. "Oh God, I've been serving you alcohol. I could have been arrested."

"I know, I'm sorry."

"You're only 19?" His voice sounded pained. He put his hands on his cheeks and rubbed his scruff. "Penny."

"I know that I should have told you."

"You made me feel awful for not telling you about Isabella. And the whole time you were lying to me?"

"I know, I'm so sorry."

"I told you how hard it is for me to trust people. This is why. Because no one is trustworthy. I thought you were different."

"Professor Hunter, please. That's my only secret. You know everything about me now. You can trust me. It's still me. It's just two years difference. Two years is nothing."

"It's not the age. It's that you lied to me."

"If I had told you that first night, you could have reported me to the dean. I would have been kicked out of school."

"I never would have done that."

"But it's your job."

"I don't care about my job! I care about you. I had a crush on you. It took every ounce of control I had to not lift up that short, sparkly skirt you were wearing and have my way with you right there in the middle of campus."

"I didn't know that. All I knew was that I was drinking underage and I had a crush on my professor. I was so out of my comfort zone. I didn't know what to do."

"Well you should have told me."

"I know, and I'm sorry."

I reached for his face, but he pushed my hand away. "I thought you were different. I let myself fall for you, even though I knew better."

My stomach churned. "I've fallen for you too."

He ran his hand through his hair. "The things I've done to you. If I had known you were a teenager I wouldn't have..."

"Don't say that. Don't take away what we have. I love you." I was choking on my words. "Professor Hunter, I love you. I love you so much."

Professor Hunter looked distraught. "Penny, you don't know what love is." He pushed me off his lap.

"You promised you wouldn't get mad."

"Damn it, Penny! You made me believe that this was real. I let myself dream about a future with you. We only had to wait two semesters. I wanted to be with you. But six? Six semesters?"

I couldn't stop my tears. "Stop using the past tense."

"What do you expect, Penny? You waited a whole month to tell me. Why didn't you just tell me when we first started dating?"

"That's exactly why. Because we had only just started dating. And I'm obsessed with you. I knew you'd be mad. I knew that you'd leave me. I wanted to have you as long as possible."

"That's not an excuse. If you had believed what we had was real, telling me your age wouldn't have mattered."

"So what we have isn't real then?"

Professor Hunter stood up and rubbed his hands across his face again. "What finally gave you the nerve to tell me the truth?"

"Because it was the only thing holding me back from happiness."

"That's a selfish reason."

"I know. But I never meant to hurt you."

"Well you did."

"I'm so sorry."

Professor Hunter went to his closet and pulled a shirt on. "I'm going out."

"Where? Professor Hunter, it's late. Please stay. We can try to work this out. Don't walk away from what we have."

"I'll be at a bar so that you can't follow me. Or do you have a fake I.D. too?"

"No, I don't."

"Good." He walked out of the room. I stumbled off the bed and ran after him. He was already standing by the elevator. He hit the button and the doors opened.

"Please don't go." I walked over to him. I wanted him to hug me and tell me everything was okay and that he loved me too.

He stepped onto the elevator. "I believe that you know how to let yourself out." The doors slid shut and he was gone. I pressed my hand against the cold metal.

My whole body felt numb. I thought telling him would be a relief. A part of me thought he would forgive me. He had asked me to move in with him. And now he had kicked me out. Not just from his apartment, but from his life.

CHAPTER 53

Tuesday

I sat down in the coffee shop and stared at the door. This was where I had first met Professor Hunter. The memory usually made me smile, but today it made me feel sick to my stomach. A month ago I had sat here, hoping to run into Austin. The hurt of him blowing me off was no comparison to how I felt now. It felt like I was drowning. Everything seemed bleak. I had no appetite. I couldn't sleep. My hands shook slightly as I lifted my coffee cup. I took a sip, but it had no taste.

After Professor Hunter had walked out on me, I had wandered down to Main Street, searching for him in the rain. Every time I called him it went straight to voicemail. I traced my fingertip along the bottom of my lip, trying to remember what his hands on me felt like. I wanted to cry. I didn't care that I was in a crowded coffee shop, I had never felt so alone in my life.

Professor Hunter had cancelled class on Friday. And on Monday he looked completely fine. He hadn't glanced at me once. If he had, he would have seen the silent tears fall down my cheeks. I had made a mistake and I was sorry. But he wouldn't forgive me. I needed him to forgive me. And I was hoping to run into him outside of class. Maybe he would talk to me here.

I pulled out the piece of paper from my pocket and unfolded it. I looked down at the sheet with my grade written on it in Professor Hunter's sexy scrawl. He had handed out the grades on Monday, but the paper was already slightly worn from being folded and unfolded so many times. I ran my index finger along his words.

Student: Penny Taylor

Topic: Marketing

Miss Taylor,

You don't know how much it pains me to see you hurt. Just give me a chance to explain. I can't lose you.

As for your speech, I am in awe of you. Your passion is inspiring. Even though you strayed off topic, the whole class could learn a lot from you. And the fact that your passion is for me makes everything more real for me. I feel the same way about you. Minus the anger.

But it is usually best not to cry and curse during presentations, Miss Taylor.

Grade: A-

P.S. Now I know how it feels. I just need some time.

I wiped away the tears as I reread his P.S. It was in a different color ink, so it must have been written after he had learned that I wasn't a senior. He needed time. But time was killing me. My phone buzzed. I had to get to class. I folded the paper and shoved it back into my pocket. I grabbed my umbrella in one hand and my coffee cup in the other and walked out into the rain.

Penny and Professor Hunter's sexy story continues in:

Addiction

THE HUNTED SERIES – BOOK 2

Temptation has quickly turned into addiction. Penny fell
hard for her mysterious professor, but secrets have torn
them apart. After all, scandalous affairs are meant to go
down in flames.

Now that he's not speaking to her, she feels numb. And
what hurts the most is that he appears to be completely
fine. As she struggles to accept that their relationship is
really over, her best friend's crude advice is in the back of
her mind- the best way to get over someone is to get under
someone else.

Will she be able to move on, or is her addiction to her
alluring professor only just beginning?

ABOUT THE AUTHOR

Ivy Smoak is the international bestselling author of *The Hunted Series*. Her books have sold over 1 million copies worldwide, and her latest release, *Empire High Untouchables*, hit #10 in the entire Kindle store.

When she's not writing, you can find Ivy binge watching too many TV shows, taking long walks, playing outside, and generally refusing to act like an adult. She lives with her husband in Delaware.

Facebook: IvySmoakAuthor
Instagram: @IvySmoakAuthor
Goodreads: IvySmoak